Pressing Flowers

by KATIE BLANCHARD

For my sister, Christa,
and her one-in-a-million heart.

PROLOGUE

It is ultimately the silence that wakes me when the quiet isn't what I'm supposed to hear. A massive ache in my gut is telling me something isn't right, and a quick swipe to the left of me confirms it.

Ben isn't home. My husband has been gone for three hours. I must have fallen asleep after he left. I've been drained with Penelope sick.

Go lay down. I'm going to take a ride with Amelia.

Now, he isn't answering his phone. I leave Penelope with my mother-in-law and let my car steer onto the road. I know which roads he takes, his favorite route to just drive when he wants to think. I will simply retrace his steps. He must be out of cell phone service with a flat tire, not uncommon in this country town.

The radio is low, but I leave it on. The silence would be too much, the gnawing feeling in my chest is screaming too loud. I try Ben's cell phone again. No answer. Come on, Ben, pick up. Pick up, please. Again. Nothing. And that's when it happens.

I drive around the bend in the curvy road and catch sight of flashing lights. I scan the area, desperate for something that will disprove my gut. There's a blue car in the middle of the road. I'm no good with car names or types, but I know it isn't Ben's. Thank God. Police car. Police car. Firetruck. Ambulance. No.

No. No. No.

Mangled in a tree off the side of the road, I see black. Black SUV. License Plate. HMV-9876. Dammit. That does me no good. I don't know his license plate number. I don't even know my own. Who remembers their license plate number? It can't be his. I would know. Something inside of me would click, right? This is probably what delayed him, this accident. The battery on his phone must have died, and he took the long way home, that's what happened. I start my three-point turn, sure to find the route Ben must have taken, when I see it.

An Ozzy Osbourne sticker in the upper left corner of the back window of that black SUV that can't be Ben's. No. My heart drops. The world is standing still at this moment, but everything is moving fast. I throw the car in park, bolt out the door. I notice the EMTs working around a tree fifty yards from the SUV. A cop is running toward me but I reach the driver side before he can catch me, and there he is.

Ben. He's slumped over to the right, and his face isn't visible, but I know him anywhere. I know every part of his body. I've cataloged every inch, and that is his neck, his shoulder, his shirt, his ear, his blood. The chill in the October air cuts through me, and I fear I'll never be warm again.

I'm able to reach in; the window must have been down. On closer inspection, I see it was busted. No. This is awful. I gently shake him. "Ben! Ben!"

"Ma'am, I'm sorry but you can't be here. Please, go back to your vehicle." The cop is firmly pushing me toward my car. He thinks I'm here as an onlooker, just a rubberneck gawker who stumbled upon the scene, but he is wrong. I'm involved. I'm the reason.

"Like hell I will! That's my husband!" I shout. I'm battling him, every muscle in my body is combating his guidance. I stare now, into his eyes, letting him know I mean business. Ben tells me I have the meanest eyes when I'm mad and, I use them on the officer now. I'm met with no resistance behind them, just wide eyes and an open mouth. His hand goes slack against my upper arm, and I use it as my chance to break in the direction of the SUV again, not allowing myself time to comprehend what those tragic eyes mean.

"Ben! Ben!" He isn't moving. He must just be unconscious. He'll be okay. He's just unconscious. "Ben, you're going to be okay." I'm stroking his hair; it's matted with blood, the usual softness gone. In fact, he is covered in blood. Oh, God. I see it inside his ear, in his hair, his neck. Where is it coming from? "Where are you hurt, Ben? Where is the bleeding coming from?" I'm searching him over, trying to find a wound to explain all this blood, and the horrible feeling in my stomach hits me again.

I place my hands on the edge of the driver's window and hoist myself halfway inside. The glass cuts me, and I jump back. The pain hardly registers as the blood pours over my fingertips and drips down to the earth. "Ben!" The officer is back again, pulling me away from the vehicle.

"Come with me, ma'am." The tone of his voice has changed. He is no longer the officer demanding the gawker to go away now; he is softer. I hear the training in his voice; this is the part where he delivers bad news. This is his voice for it.

"NO!!" I shove his arm down. Shouldn't I be arrested by now? This is assaulting a police officer, is it not? I run from him. I run all around the vehicle, catching sight of the damage. The massacre. The front of the car is crumbled in, pushing upwards to the heavens. The side by the tree is bent in, the car shaped like a U. Everything is bent, broken, or scratched badly. What happened here? I run my hand over the side fender just before it meets the tree and find a flower stuck in between the metal. I pluck it from the carnage prison and hold it tightly in my hand. The blood from my cuts soaking the petals. I can't get into the passenger side.

The officer catches up with me and is no longer gentle, he roughly grabs my upper arm and pulls me away. He is successful, dragging me against my will, but the need for answers causes me to fight. I yank him backward, throwing him off balance in a game of tug of war with my body as the rope.

"Ma'am, you need to come with me. Now!"

"Ben?" Half-heartedly I call out, hoping my husband will perk up and respond, tell me what has happened and that he'll be okay. "Will it all be okay?"

"I . . ."He is at a loss for words, but he needn't have them.

ONE

3 and a half years later

I feel the pressure of the comforter on top of my body, and I'm aware of the mattress curving around my weight. Sure enough, I'm awake. Motionless, my eyes closed, I work to keep my mind blank. It's no use. Reality crushes around me like it has every single day for over three years now. Ben is not next to me. But my ears are still desperate, foolish things, straining to hear light snores but detecting nothing. There is nothing to hear. Well, there is something.

My keen hearing picks up on the doorknob turning, then the door giving way to a groan when Penelope has pushed it to a certain limit. Monday through Friday, this is the routine. My "alarm clock" comes in to wake me before she goes to school. Seven years old, nearly eight, my daughter can care for herself in the morning allowing me the sleep I crave. The rest that I need. I pretend I'm still sleeping, not sure why I do it. Maybe people like to pretend they're sleeping in someone's presence to see what happens when their guard is down. An espionage mission, self-assigned, to see what your loved one is really like when you aren't paying attention. It's just like an accidental butt dial; you stay on past the point of realization only to find out what you can hear. We long for the reassurance that we are loved even when we are not around when no one thinks we are listening.

I listen carefully to her pausing. Does she look at me with love, taking in my quiet slumber with a full heart? Or does she know by now? Does she understand it yet, that I'm the one who took away her father? She doesn't pause long, leaving zero answers to the questions I ask.

"Mommy." Her voice is soft, it has been fading in volume the last few days and the time before the bus comes has decreased in conjunction to when she wakes me. She's getting tired. Tired of me. She is the only one who understands my pain, why I need to sleep, but even she can't remain supportive. I long for the reassurance that she loves me when I'm not around.

I do the fake stretch of a waking woman, really play up the whole scene for her. When I flutter my eyes open, she clouds my vision. My daughter is a brown-haired beauty; pouty lip smile, boundless energy radiating from her being, olive skin. Her eyes, however, are a piercing jade that screams of a maturity far beyond her years. Of a failure. I failed her, I sent her father out one night, and he never came home. For that, I can never forgive myself. It is for that reason her eyes hold the depth of pain. I am the reason she is without a father.

"Hey, baby. What time is it?" I even allow my voice to sound groggy, not much of a play on my part considering I live in a constant state of exhaustion. She frets with the bottom of her shirt, so I gaze at my actual alarm clock. I have five minutes until her bus comes, two minutes less than yesterday. I shake the thought from my head and rise to a seated position. I slip into my old tattered slippers and rub my hands down my face. I feel the mounded skin of my palms. The scars of broken glass, a reminder as if I didn't relive the pain of that memory daily. They ache as they come alive, the heap of scar tissue stiffening the natural movement. As we walk out the room, I catch a glimpse of my appearance.

My dark circles sag lower than I'd like to admit other parts of my body do, and the limpness of my brown hair adds to the ragged appearance. There's no point in taking in my clothing; they're the same ones I wore yesterday and the day before. When you work out of your home, there is no point in getting dressed. Besides, I plan on going to sleep on the couch after Penelope's bus comes anyway. Keep with tradition, the daily routine.

I shuffle out to my station on our pale gray sofa. I notice that the cushion is beginning to concave and mold to the shape of my bottom, a hazard of frequency. Penelope is slipping on her jacket and shoes, so I peer out the blinds for her bus. Sure enough, the darn giant Twinkie-mobile is just down the street. Not a lot of time at all today.

"Bus." I grunt out. I let go of the blinds and shift my body toward the spot where I know she will reside in mere moments for the farewell hug. She slings the backpack over her shoulders and comes forward for a hurried kiss and hug.

"Bye, Mom." Just like that, she rushes to the front door and heads out. Bye, Penelope. Have a good day. Isn't that what moms are supposed to say? Do they wish their kids good luck? I don't say anything; I just turn back to the window to watch her leave. I cover my body with the afghan that sits on the couch. Everyone leaves. "I left a waffle in the kitchen for you, and I made you a cup of coffee." Her voice startles me. I didn't know she came back inside. I whip my head around to face her.

"Love you." I rush out before she can disappear again. She stumbles on the doorstep, before gaining her feet again. She looks at me, stunned.

"I love you, too." Then she smiles. Hopeful. Foolish. Beautiful. Then she is gone again.

When the bus brakes in front of the driveway, I watch as Penelope turns around to wave at the house. It's a charade, a clever one we play every day. I throw my hand against the window, my part in the act. It isn't for my benefit; she has already said her goodbyes. I know why we do it, so inquiring minds will stop asking her where her mom is. *Why doesn't your mom wait with you, Penelope?* She answers them now, as she takes her seat. *See, there she is. We wait inside together.* It is entirely possible Penelope likes the fact that I stay hidden, she usually criticizes my attire for the day. On a rare good day, last month, I asked her if she wanted me to wait outside with her. She lost her mind, was absolutely against it. I watched the wheels turn behind her eyes. She had to stop me from mortifying her. I was an embarrassment to my daughter.

I toss the afghan back and put a judging eye on my appearance; stained sweatpants, old t-shirt, oversized cardigan sweater, my hair is in a bun and no makeup. No, couldn't at all be a humiliation. I snort and stand to make my way to the promised coffee waiting for me in the kitchen. I walk the worn path on the floor from the living room rug to the dull hardwood floor of the dining room. After I have my cup of coffee, I'm going to shower and get dressed today. I can at least do that, it is a lie I tell myself, but maybe today it will become the truth.

The dining table is cluttered with this week's clean laundry, only two clear places remain in front of the seats we occupy at dinner time. I think I'll order pizza tonight. We had it Monday, but a Friday feels more pizza-y to me. Every night I either order from the local pizza or Chinese restaurants, or I'll venture out to one of our favorite fast food joints. I hardly ever cook, and even then, it is a frozen meal. I brush past the pile of boxes that need to go down to the curb for trash collection, finally arriving at the threshold of the kitchen.

The wallpaper border in here is peeling, the line of lemons have turned to faded patches of citrus despair. The flooring, a 70's style linoleum, has chipped in most places except for one square. The dreaded square that preserved itself in mint condition underneath an old stand up freezer. When Ben and I removed the freezer after purchasing the house, we were met with this eyesore square. The old floor looked better faded and chipped; the pristine condition was orange swirls that over time had turned a tolerable brown. I flip my middle finger at the patch of ugliness as I turn to the corner of the counter that houses the coffee maker.

The one thing in our kitchen renovation that did get done was the countertop. It is the bow on a turd. A puce colored turd trimmed with lemon wallpaper and brown or orange swirls. I wanted to do many things with this kitchen when we first moved in; it was going to be a dream come true. Gray cabinets, dark wood floors, stainless steel appliances, and any wall color but puce. The dream turned into a nightmare, my living nightmare I cannot escape. Ben is gone. I lost all motivation to turn the house into a home; it's merely a casing to house the bodies left behind from the wreckage.

I fill my coffee cup up. Black. *Like your soul.* My husband's morning joke echoes off the walls in this lonely space. He never missed a morning to mock the way I took my coffee. The joke is on him now. I don't have a soul anymore. He took it with him when he left. When I made him leave. I gaze upon the waffle that Penelope made me. I should eat, but in the morning I lack the appetite, blaming it on my mind replaying that night over and over while I sleep. I raise my mug to my lips and my eyebrow to the waffle in apology. Not today.

I pass by Ben's favorite chair on the way back to the couch. It is now a refuge to the junk mail and magazines still coming in his name. "You should get a start on sorting that stuff out, Ben, or you'll never get to sit there." I pull my laptop from the coffee table, determined to finish my work early today so that I can sleep until school is out. I work for an online news company, specializing in guest articles. My job is to proofread and edit those articles before sending them further down the line to be posted on the site. I have somehow been fortunate enough to find a job that allows me to stay home. I didn't work when Ben was alive. I was mainly just a stay at home mom to Penelope with odd jobs here and there. It worked best for us. Now, I had to bring in some money. His life insurance policy covered the significant things for us, but it isn't an endless supply, and I still needed to pull in revenue.

I flick the television on for background noise; the bonus is that it drowns out the incessant drip of the bathroom faucet. Better get started if I want to nap. I pull up the first email and begin.

My shrill doorbell will cut through your brain like a machete when it goes off, which is what it is doing now. Why? Why is it doing that? If that is the postman thinking he needs to hand deliver whatever package he has, I swear I'm going to hit him over the head with the ugly lamp that Ben's aunt gave us. I glare out the front picture window to spot the offending guest, ready to kill whoever it is intruding on my impending nap.

Mom.

I roll my eyes so hard in the back of my head that I'm sure whiplash has occurred. What does Emma Woods want today? My mother will never get it through her head that I'd rather just ignore her calls than have her show up at my house unannounced for a visit. I look around the house, a habit I'm sure all daughters have when their moms come to visit, checking the state of tidiness. Not even close. All this house is going to get me is a verbal lashing from my mother, who so much as strokes out at the sight of dust.

I push the laptop off my legs, I only made it to the second article in my inbox, and I certainly didn't shower as I told myself I would. "Just a second!" I holler as my mother dares to press the doorbell button once more. It sends a screeching pterodactyl noise through the speaker again. I am dismantling that little demon today. I'm sure the sledgehammer is still in the garage. Thinking about the button shattered into tiny pieces on the concrete patio gives me a slight thrill, I even toy with the idea of committing the act right now in front of my mother. I picture the scene and the absolute terror that would be etched on Emma Woods face forever. Instead of going to the garage for the sledgehammer, I throw open the front door to let in the distraught middle-aged woman who they say gave me life.

"Mom." I greet her with the best civility I can muster. My mother and I have never been on the best of terms, not entirely my fault. I tolerate her for the benefit of Penelope having her grandmother around. They get along famously, and I won't tear that away from my daughter, but that doesn't mean my relationship with my mother has come close to mending itself.

"Really, Miriam, you could at least brush your teeth. Look at you!" She waves down my body in disgust as she bristles past me.

"No, please do come in." She has always been impervious to my sarcasm, but even that remark has gained me the side eye. The rebellious child in me jumps for joy at the thought of getting under her skin, a task not available to the average amateur.

"Miriam, I've come to speak with you on important matters, and I'd prefer you not jest." She has set her scolding tone in place. I wave my hand in defeat, another day then I have nothing but time. She paces back and forth across the floor. I select the couch as the best seat for the show. She does this often, works herself into a great fury over something small, then she comes over and lets herself burst all over my carpet. When my sister, Charlotte, and I were growing up, my mother once called a family meeting over someone passing gas around grandma. She got herself in such a fret that she landed in the hospital with a panic attack. What could it be this time? I sip my cold coffee and wait.

"Miriam," she starts, "look at this place. This is exactly what I'm talking about. There is dust on everything. Look at the floor; it hasn't seen a vacuum in so long." I glance down. I have no idea why because I know exactly what state the floor is. The idea that it has escaped me seems silly, but I play along in the game.

"What are you talking about? You're mad because my house doesn't have vacuum lines? This is what you think about all day long? Have you tried reading?"

"No. I," she is battling to find words which is unlike my mother. It is then that I notice the sheet of paper in her hands. She also hasn't taken off her shoes or coat, her standard protocol for a visit. I shift in my seat, suddenly uncomfortable. She has always been entirely predictable in her mannerisms, so this is odd for her, and Emma Woods is apparently on a mission.

"What's going on, Mom?" I coax.

"I called a lawyer." The words just blurt out of her body as if it had been taking great restraint to hold them in.

"A lawyer? For what?" My back becomes straight. The mentioning of a lawyer will do that to anyone.

"I asked him if I had any rights to Penelope." She rushes. The words hang in the dead air as she gauges my reaction. I show none because in my head I am counting to ten before I explode. I wonder how the ugly lamp would look smashing against the wall behind my mother and how close my aim can get it to her head.

"Say more, Mother." My teeth clench tight. I can feel the twitch in my jaw tug my ears.

She throws her hands up and falls into the recliner behind her knees. "Miriam, I know you have been through a horrible ordeal. I get it. It will be four years this October, and you are getting no better. You sleep all day. You don't get dressed. Look at your house. It is disgusting. So untidy and in need of repairs. This is no place for Penelope. I've thought it over time and time again. I have referred you to therapists, you go once and quit. I have brought them over for dinner, you ignore them and slop your food. I have asked for friend's advice. I have gone through all the options, and this is the only one I feel I have left. The only one that will help."

If you could feel a color, I would be feeling red. Bright, blaring red. "Let me get this straight," I begin, "You think that taking my daughter away from me will miraculously cure the fact that I lost my husband?"

"No . . ."

"You think you deserve Penelope because I simply have a dirty house?" The scars of my palms are pulsating beneath the tightening of my fists. I can feel the way they press into my fingertips.

"No."

"You haven't ruined my childhood enough that you want to ruin hers even more?"

"Oh. Boo-hoo, Miriam had a hard childhood. Your father left. I did the best I could. You should show a little appreciation." She sighs and lets that anger go, always in control. "I meant that this is the only option I see that would spur you into action. This filth can't be the way Penelope grows up. So," she perks up, "I've made a list, a to-do list if you will, of things you need to complete. If you do these seven things, I will drop the idea. If not," she gets serious, "Miriam, I will contact the lawyer again and put things in motion."

"Everyone grieves in their own way, Mom." Unlike my mother, I lack the ability to hold my emotions in check and maintain control.

I'm interrupted. "Oh, come on. Don't give me that, you don't even try. You let Penelope run around here being the adult. Who got Penelope up this morning, Miriam? Tell me that. Who made breakfast? Who made that coffee you have sitting there?"

"Some people would just call that good parenting, making their child independent." I didn't know anyone knew.

Her blond hair flings around in a fury; her blue eyes turn to red as she rises from the recliner and flails her arms around. "She shoulders everything. She carries you. You are the adult. Act like it." She is shouting at the top of her lungs, no longer in control. I long to hear the shrill doorbell instead. Her words are a bucket of ice water on my anger. I have nothing to say. There's no defense that I can make because it is all true. Penelope has a lot more responsibility thrown at her than typical kids her age, and it is my fault.

I watch my mom wander back and forth, calming herself down, trying to find a different approach to the situation. She's gaining back the control she longs for and desires in every encounter in life. She may not have been the best mother growing up, but for once she has me beat. When Dad left she didn't break down, she just carried on, but this isn't the same. There's closure knowing someone doesn't want to be with you anymore; it may not be comforting, but it is finite. When your spouse dies on you, the fact that they didn't want to leave haunts you, preventing the process of letting go. I can't just cut away as she did, he didn't leave because he didn't love me. I sent him out so some drunk could decide he should leave me.

"Miriam," my mother's voice is softer now, "you need to try. You can miss Ben and Amelia, feel sorry for your loss, but you cannot neglect Penelope."

"Don't say her name." I whimper. I wrap my arms around myself. Two souls lost because of me. "What's on the list?" Blame it on the need to change the subject or curiosity, but I need to know. With renewed energy, as if she has broken the impenetrable, she lists off my fate.

"One, you will go back to a therapist for one-on-one treatment. Two, you will join a support group and go for monthly meetings. Three, you have to donate or store Ben's stuff. You have to do this to move on; my therapist agrees with me. He says that you can't live in a world where all of Ben's possessions surround you in the form of a shrine. Ben is no longer here to enjoy them, so you're only holding yourself back on any progress you could be making by letting them stay in their 'living spot'."

"Just doing what the good doctor says, huh?" Sarcasm has always been my first language, a language my mother refuses to learn or speak.

She shakes her head and ignores my remark. My mother often refers to her therapist in conversation, completely unashamed. "Bitterness doesn't lead to happiness, dear. As I was saying, number four. Number four, you need to fix up your house. I know you have the money so I won't take that as an excuse. I would even give you the money. I'm not talking a whole remodel, though this place could stand for it. You need to do something about the faucet that leaks and the wallpaper peeling. All the walls could use some paint. You girls deserve a nice place to live in, and if this place continues to look like this, you will mirror your surroundings."

"Is that another thing the therapist says?" That one earned me a glare, but considering she didn't retort, I must have hit the nail on the head.

"Number five, you will have a mother/daughter date with Penelope once a week. You will take her somewhere and not just to dinner. You girls eat enough fast food and food you didn't prepare yourself. I'm betting you aren't even planning on cooking tonight, are you? You really should start cooking here at home."

"Is cooking on the to-do list, Mother?"

"I could revise it if the sass mouth continues." She raises an eyebrow in challenge; I raise my hands in surrender. "Good. Number six, you will become more involved in Penelope's school. It's truly humiliating that most of the parents think I'm her mom when I'm there. You work from home, so don't tell me you can't fit it into your schedule. Finally, number seven . . ."

She doesn't continue. Instead, the number hangs in the air like the end of a Hitchcock movie. I wait, not at all longing to ask what number seven holds in store me, the first six items have been entirely unpleasant, except for the mommy/daughter date idea. I can't imagine what item would make my mother pause with such severity.

"Well," she starts after what I'm certain is forever, "number seven is that you need to date." Hurriedly she adds, "I won't put a time limit on this one, it is truly there because I want you to think about it. The other six I would like an immediate response. Penelope is getting to a percep-tive age, and she can see what you are doing. These are her formative years. She may start internalizing or blaming herself to make up for your depression."

This is not what I thought I would be facing when I woke up today. Naively, I believed it was going to be just the same old kind of Friday, precisely like the ones before. But, here I sit, kicked and beaten every way possible at this moment, and my body aches with heaviness. I have been thinly fooling myself for three and a half years. I knew I was putting too much on Penelope, but I avoided thinking of it so I could continue it longer. It looks like I have no choice now. Or the alternative is to lose Penelope. Everything in me desires to throw the afghan back on and give up, but something flickers deep. It's been so long since I felt motivation or a fight inside, I'm not sure if I feel it now. Limply, I hold out my hand for the list, which my mother instinctively places in my possession. I want to tear it apart, destruct the words she has written in that pristine handwriting of hers.

Everything about my mother is pristine, finely pressed clothes, make-up, mannerisms. Her soul is probably that of an old heiress, a time of procedure long forgotten. When my father left, I always figured she didn't love him. She carried on so well without him, maybe she had craved his absence but wasn't brave enough to deport herself. It wasn't true though. My mother just simply didn't and couldn't fall apart. She could deliver a eulogy and not shed a tear. She could walk into a homeless man's cardboard box and still insist it be tidy.

"Leave." I neither tried nor inherited my mother's grace.

"What?" She stumbles and grabs at her chest in a gesture that assures me I have offended her.

"You've delivered your sentence, now go." I am cold and unfeeling, the way visits with my mother always seem to end. I put all the emotions that want to bubble to the surface aside. I become robotic.

She knows she isn't wanted and for the first time, she leaves without having the last word. She said enough when she was here. I look down at the list and place it on the couch next to me; it has the weight of another being occupying the space. I'm going to lose Penelope. I'm not even sure she'll want me to fight; she probably wants to go. I dig my fingers into the coordinating scars of both palms, the reminders of that night. I allow my body the freedom to take over me, as it wanders to the back door leading to the deck. The potted flowers my mother decided needed to be placed out here for life is still blooming. I stare down at a begonia and break the stem off it. The flower twists in my hand, delicate, but with burdensome guilt. I shove the potted plant over the railing. Whoops. I walk back into the house and hang the single flower plucked upside down on my living room bulletin board and stare at it.

My cell phone begins to ring.

"Hello."

"Hello, may I please speak to Mrs. Jones?"

"This is she." I respond.

"Mrs. Jones, this is Principal Murphy at John Madison Elementary. It seems we have a problem involving your daughter, Penelope."

"Oh?"

"Yes, ma'am. It seems Penelope has punched another student and I request a meeting with you at your earliest convenience to discuss the matter." His voice has a scolding tone. I'm not sure I feel like another tongue-lashing lecture on my parenting skills today. I run my hand down my face. Maybe my mother is right, maybe Penelope is not growing up well here with me.

"I'll be there in a half hour, sir." I hang up. I guess I'm going to get that shower today after all.

TWO

John Madison Elementary School is located just ten minutes from our house in the rural town of Herard. It is a tiny little thing, easily missed if you don't know what you are looking for. The elementary, middle, and high school are all housed together on the same plot of land, typical for a small town like ours. Ben and I grew up two towns over. We weren't townies or lifers, we just loved having space to be and stumbled upon our home and fell in love. Most people move on to different states. We just moved to a different town.

I walk through the doors and head straight for the office. I can already see a brooding brown-haired girl sitting just inside the door with her arms crossed. I take in her demeanor. She's hunched over, from her neck to the brown hairline that frames her face, her skin is bright red, and she's scowling at the floor. I can see the tear-stained lines on her face and the wild mess of hair. My Penelope has been to war. I can't help but feel pride. My little girl is a fighter. It is not the physical fighting I am proud of. It's the fact that they have her in here for retribution and she looks resolute to stand by her decision. I wish I could fight like her.

My feet find the rest of their way in, and I see from my peripheral that Penelope looks up then immediately back to the floor. The faded orange and purple swirl carpet is a better view than her mother. She probably just wants to see if I showed up looking human, which I wouldn't toot my own horn but I resemble the other moms for once. Jeans and a nice shirt. Clean t-shirt. My hair is braided since it's wet from my shower. I could pass as normal today. If you took in the sight of me, you wouldn't know I'm damaged. I at least appear better than the office, the obnoxious school colors of bright orange and purple blaring on every available surface.

"May I help you?" The older lady behind the reception area addresses me. She has a small stature enclosed by the sea of school colors tinged with dragon mascot signs everywhere.

"Um, yes. I'm here about my daughter," I raise my left arm and motion toward Penelope, "Penelope Jones. The principal called me."

"Yes, just have a seat. I'll let him know you are here, Miss Jones." I go to correct her, tell her I'm Mrs., not Miss, but she moves fast for an old bugger and is gone before I have the chance.

"What's going on, Penelope?" I lean against the laminate countertop, directing my attention to my daughter. Her gray and black outfit doesn't fit in this bright room, and if it is possible, she sulks even further into herself and refuses to respond. "Alright. If you don't want to talk, you don't have to." She scoffs at me and begins shaking her head. What the heck?

"Mrs. Jones?" The principal's commanding voice interrupts my thoughts. "Would you follow me to my office, please?" I drag my gaze from Penelope to the balding fifty-year-old man in front of me. His furrowed brow seems to be a permanent feature on his face from years of dealing with someone else's children. The stance he takes is intimidating, even to an adult. I can see how this would terrify children into behaving. I merely nod and take up cadence behind him down the hall. When we have reached his office, he motions for me to sit in one of the two blue upholstered chairs in front of his desk. I take my spot in the chair closest to the door for an easier escape as he takes his place behind his desk in a high back brown leather chair that does nothing but points out his height, which can be no more than five-foot-nine. I have had nothing but distaste for Principal Murphy since our big 'talk' during Kindergarten year, a ploy to drag out more details of the accident from yet another interested party. Why are people so fascinated by tragedy? They crave the horrific details, the pitying lines of reality, to satisfy their natural curiosity. He attempted to pry every detail out of me, just short of using a crowbar before he gave up. I imagine this meeting won't go any better.

My fears are confirmed when the guidance counselor walks in, shutting the door behind her. Oh God! Not today. Lawney Towers was the nosiest one yet to cross our path. Weekly, *weekly*, she would call home during Kindergarten year attempting to chat, always ending the conversation with, "So what happened?" What happened?

I smell the turned-up dirt as I approach the tree where everyone is gathered, smoke from the family SUV mixed in. I can hear the EMTs working hard, shouting orders, talking into the radio with the hospital. One male pronounced dead at the scene.

"Mrs. Jones," again Principal Murphy pulls me from my thoughts, "here at John Madison Elementary, we take fighting to be a serious offense. The children are taught that fighting is wrong, so we give stricter punishments to offenders hoping to ward them from the temptation later in their high school years. We feel this policy has worked because altercations have decreased not only here but also in our middle and high school. Penelope is no exception to this policy, being a first-time offender. This is a zero-tolerance policy school. Therefore, I am suspending her for two school days and asking that you take her home with you, instead of finishing out the remainder of the school day today. In the two days, she will miss, she is required to make up any classwork and homework, as well as write an essay on why fighting is not a good idea." He finally pauses in his well-prepared speech, giving nosey Lawney her opening to dive in.

"I wanted to discuss with you, Miss Jones, about Penelope's sessions with me. I believe this altercation is a direct link to some stuff she told me lately. Although it is no excuse for the fighting," she gestures in surrender to Principal Murphy. "I believe it may be the reason. It would benefit her if we got to the heart of the matter."

I ignore her, but her words are indicating she has sessions with Penelope weighs heavily. "Sir, do you know what the fight was about?" I can see the offense on both their faces. Lawney is upset the question is not directed at her; Murphy is upset the question was even asked, considering his speech.

"The children have had a chance to speak their piece about the incident, each in turn here in the office. It seems Penelope wishes not to speak about it at all. I think the two days off will do her good, calm her down from the rage she seems to be struggling with." He gives me a pointed look as if I am not acknowledging the horrible trait my daughter possesses.

"It seems the boy, Justin, whom she punched, made a remark about her father." Leave it to Lawney to be the one to spread the gossip. Good job, Lawn Mower, just what I knew you would do.

"What did he say?" I direct my question at her. People love to feel important, focused on, that their words are the food your ears are starving for. She eats it up. Too easy.

"It was a dad joke. He mentioned something about her father and Penelope couldn't dispute it because she doesn't know much about her father. I wanted to speak with you on that; possibly there could be more communication at home. I understand we all grieve in our own way, but your grief is not allowing Penelope her closure." My gut takes the hit. Why do people want to judge me today? What a lousy job everyone thinks I'm doing with Penelope. I'm in the principal's office because she was fighting; they must be right.

I take a moment to rally, be the mother I always promised myself I would be if ever in the principal's office. Also, we need this show. I can't have the guidance counselor and Emma Woods meeting and comparing notes. "This is a zero-tolerance policy school, correct? Then will the boy be punished as well?"

"He was not fighting, ma'am," Principal Murphy's tongue curls around the last word as if it was a bitter pill to swallow, "he was the one struck with a physical blow."

"She was the one struck with an emotional one. A cruel bullying comment that you deem unfit for punishment because it did not leave a mark you can see."

"Justin was spoken to about his action . . ." I don't let him finish.

"Spoken to? What did you say? Hey kid, don't make shitty mom and dad jokes just in case somebody doesn't have one? And then what? Send him back to class?"

"Mrs. Jones, are you trying to say that physical fighting is less offending than name calling?" He is leaning on his desk now, no longer sitting, in a threatening stance. This will not deter me, I have had a lousy morning, this idiot is about to get the blunt force of all my anger. I allow my body to migrate to the edge of my seat, my hand resting now in a fist upon his desk. I lean in to match him. Game on.

"I'm saying without one you don't have the other. His bullying actions drove the altercation, yet they will not be treated as offending at all. No," I hold my hand up close to his face to stop his near interruption, "you cannot seriously think that I will be satisfied hearing that my child is the only one wrong in this situation. He said something thoughtless and hurtful. Whether the topic was her father or her shoes, is there not a zero-tolerance policy on bullying at this school? Is that not what you have plastered on nearly every poster you have hanging in these halls? I got smacked in the face with four on my way in. Four. You sit there behind your desk and tell me you will take her out for two days and the bully will get nothing? And you expect this punishment to stop her from future bullies? No, I'm sorry, you expect this suspension to stop HER from punching the next bully. So, you protect your bullies in your school, not the victims?"

"I . . . I."

"Is it not true? Are you not a zero-tolerance school when it comes to bullying?"

"Yes, we are." He has become much smaller, not the man I saw out front who could terrify small children. He recoils into his chair. I am not shrinking, I lean further and stand.

"I will ask again, Mr. Murphy," my voice is calm, "what will the boy's punishment be for bullying my daughter here at school today?" He shifts through a pile of papers on his desk, unable to meet my eyes. Lawney, her chatty self, has nothing to say, just mouth agape. No other parent had ever challenged him before, here in his throne, derailing his kingdom. How many kids are continuing to be bullied because of his system, and now are scared to fight for themselves because they'll get in trouble for retaliation?

"After consideration," his tone is much lighter now, "I have decided that, although it is not as severe as a physical altercation, bullying is a punishable offense. Therefore, the boy will be suspended for one school day and write an essay on why bullying is not a good idea. I believe an apology note from each other would be nice as well."

His apology line sounds more like a question; he is asking my permission to tack it on to the other punishments. Match. Point. Game. I attempt not to look smug as I'm thinking over his new proposal. I lean back from the desk. I stand taller because fighting for Penelope feels good.

"I think that is a fine idea, Mr. Murphy." I turn to end this meeting. "Good day." I leave without a chance for anything else. It is clear my voice wasn't exactly at "meeting" level back there because when I make my way back to the reception area, everyone is staring, even Penelope. If I didn't see ghosts daily, I would believe it to be pride beaming on that sweet girl's face.

"Let's go." I wave her to follow me as I head out of the office. Her small shoes are echoing my own on the pavement. I might even hear a skip or two. My high is wearing off, though. She talks to the guidance counselor; they have meetings. She never told me, but more importantly what is she saying to her?

In the safety of the car, after we've buckled in, I lower the radio, so my words are clear.

"You will not go to the guidance counselor and tell her about me anymore."

The happiness on my daughter's face, that sense of pride and wonderment in her mother, flushes fast at the ice of my words. I see the anger that Justin must have seen replace her calm features, but the betrayal must stop.

"Do you understand me?" The words feel hard and final as they pass my clenched teeth.

I expect the simple yes, the one trained into your vocabulary by your mother as a child. Instead, I watch the words bubble up from her chest and burst, "I don't want to be like you, Mom. I want to wake up, change my clothes and go places. I will talk to her if I want."

I'm taken aback; this is not my child. She doesn't shout at me; she is understanding of my grief. That's all she has shown me in the last three and a half years. I don't want her telling Lawney about me. I don't want people to judge my grieving. I don't want my daughter to be turning her head toward her window now. I don't want the tears that are falling from her eyes, silently as if she is too proud to acknowledge herself weeping. But, I can't afford the betrayal. Not with my mother's threat looming, this could only fuel the fire. I can't swallow and ignore the guilt this time. I put too much on Penelope.

"I didn't know you felt that way," I say meekly.

"You wouldn't." Her lip fails her and trembles, letting out an audible sob. I keep my eyes forward, allowing her her grief. I owe that much for what she does for mine. I can't even comfort my child at this moment.

★ ★ ★

"Stupid Justin. He deserved to be punched." I mumble at the can of kidney beans in my hand. After dropping Penelope off at my in-law's house for the weekend, I find myself at the grocery store. This was our ritual, Ben and I. We would take Penelope to his parent's house so we could shop alone. Now, she spends the weekend. Now, he's dead. I slam the can on the shelf. I don't even know why I come here, it's futile, and I don't cook. Penelope makes her lunches now, so I guess there's that to shop for. Man, I suck as a mom. I reach for the black beans. "Stupid Justin. He deserved that punch. He started all of this." I slam that can back on the shelf, too.

"Can I get in there before you make it to the refried beans? Mexican night will never be the same with a dented can."

"Huh?" I look to my right where the masculine voice comes from and standing next to me, leaning against the shelf, is an Adonis of a man holding a shopping basket. Brown-sugar colored hair and eyes to match. Tall, my guess would be six-foot-three, and he's fit. Not gym fit, but manual labor for a living fit. My eyes scan the toned muscles, accentuated by his tight long sleeve shirt. What am I doing? Am I checking him out? Oh my god. No. No. I have no interest in men. No. His eyes are laughing. Laughing at me, because he knows. Crap.

"I would hate to meet the same fate as Justin, but it is my turn to bring the dip to Mexican night." He laughs at the end of his sentence. He has a soothing laugh. If I weren't so startled by my attraction to him, I think I'd try to make him laugh again.

"Crap!" It is only now that it registers why he is filling the grocery store air with that honey-smooth laugh, I was talking out loud like a psycho. To the beans. I was talking out loud and venting my shit to the beans. I place my hands on the top shelf and lean my head into them. I tell Penelope not to talk to her guidance counselor, yet I can't control myself from telling the legumes my problems. "Spilling the beans to the beans." I laugh in my head at my pun. I hear laughter. Am I going insane? Crap. I said that out loud. Honey laugh is the one laughing. Get your shit together, Miriam. Inner thoughts. Inner. As in, don't freaking say them out loud or you'll get yourself carted away to the mental ward. I stay locked in my position, refusing to move, if he is a decent human being he will just grab the refried beans and leave. Why isn't he leaving?

"Leave." I groan.

"No."

I sigh, shifting my head so I can glare at the stranger. Maybe intimidation will work.

"Like I said, refried beans." I look at the shelf, sure enough, I'm blocking the refried beans.

"Fat-free or traditional?" I ask.

"Traditional." I hand him the can, but all he does is stick it in his basket and continues leaning. Staring. "Now, what did Justin do?" I have never seen someone make themselves look comfortable and relaxed against a metal grocery store shelf until this guy. He appears at home in his skin, and he couldn't care less about the people passing us with awkward looks. He isn't even disturbed by the disgruntled shoppers who want us to move so they could continue their bean buying adventures. I want to be that self-assured. He takes my look of envy for confusion because he reiterates to me that I was just telling the kidney beans that Justin was stupid.

"I know who Justin is. Why do you want to hear about him?" I'm back to talking to the beans, refusing to stand up and face this stranger.

"Curious. First time I have ever seen a woman yell at a can of beans. I must say I was intrigued by your crazy display here today." He steps closer when he says this, invading my personal space, blaming the man searching for diced tomatoes behind him. This makes it difficult to breathe. The proximity grants me another blow, his smell, he smells good. What kind of soap is that? I shake my head to clear my thoughts. Not good. I have to stop this conversation. I think I'm attracted to him. I hold both hands up to speak, as well as regain some personal space back. Maybe if I talk with my hands more, he won't want to stand this close.

"I did not yell at the can of beans. I simply told them Justin was stupid." I am giving the world's craziest show of hand gestures as I talk. My motions aren't matching up to my words. Still, he is not stepping back. I look crazier by the minute, and it isn't even working. Obviously, he is turned on by crazy. Plan B, Miriam. I don't have a plan B; I didn't even think I'd need a Plan A. I look down at the floor between us, the one tile he has left to cross, and scratch my head.

"Oh. Is Justin your husband?" Two tiles.

"Huh?" I'm staring at the increased floor between us. I feel lonely now. He laughs. I hope I didn't say that out loud. I brave a glance up, when he catches my eye he points to my hand. The hand that still tangles in my hair, my left hand. Ring. Got it.

"Oh. Um, no." I take my left hand in my right and caress the diamond slowly. Ben. The whole reason for the bullying today, the list my mother made, and why I am fighting my attraction to this man. My dead husband. "I'm not married. I'm a widow." I sigh sadly at my ring. I typically don't tell people that, they start to think I'm a looney walking around with a wedding band on. I'm not sure why I just told this stranger. It isn't even a last-ditch effort to make him leave; I just don't want to lie today. Is that progress?

"How long?" Wow. I usually get the automatic 'I'm sorry' response when I do tell people, followed by their exit because a dead spouse may be contagious. I look into this stranger's eyes and see that he sincerely wants to know and isn't judging me for wearing the band.

"Four years this October." I have verbal diarrhea tonight. The canned goods, now this man. I hope Penelope never finds out because she would give me hell for the hypocrisy. He regards me with a nod as if he understands the ring still being there. What an odd man. I think I'm going to call him Voodoo and keep him at a distance. I am liable to like this one, and what will he do when he finds out I'm the reason my husband died? Leave like everyone else, Miriam. They all leave.

"Justin is a little boy my daughter punched today because he made a dad joke." I shrug. There. Maybe I can cross this off the list, it feels like a one-on-one therapist session.

Voodoo doubles over shaking with a full body laugh. I know I didn't say anything else out loud that I didn't mean to, or even crack a joke. The elderly lady passing by with her cart scowls at him. Merriment doesn't seem to be her style, mine either.

"What is so damn funny?" I hiss. I try to keep my voice low, considering the interest we have piqued in our passerby. He, unfortunately, or is it fortunately, uses this as permission to step closer and lower his voice to match mine in confidence. I'm going to be wrecked by the roller coaster of this entire day, but this soap may be what does me in. Why do you have to smell good, Voodoo? I admit I'm a little lightheaded. I lose all memory of why we are even in this situation, all I keep thinking about is his lips. Wow, they are so full. I smell mint on his breath when he opens his mouth to speak. I wish it smelt of rotten fish because I am only more involved in thinking about kissing him right now. I don't think about any man but my husband. This isn't right.

"You look my age, which means your daughter can't be very old and already she has your temper." He laughs at his quip. He needs no audience.

"I don't have a temper." I bark.

"No?" He cackles louder than before. "I like you. You didn't yell at me for assuming your age. You didn't even care." He stares at my lips. Don't you dare, I will hate myself, and I will have to cause you bodily harm to allow my heart the chance to survive.

"Are all women that vain in your mind?" I hold my eyebrow high in question. How annoying to assume all women are worried about someone knowing their age. Way to be stereotypical, Voodoo.

"I don't know." He scratches his chin, processing this new information. The glimmer in his eye gives him away; he doesn't have to think, has a remark already. Ornery are you, Voodoo? "You haven't told me your age, so I guess I'm still right."

"I'm 31. My name is Miriam. You are boring." He doesn't retract. He only moved back when he thought I was married. I have respect for that. Now it is time to warn Voodoo to stay away. I'm crazy, love, and you can't handle it. No one around me seems to be able to. I begin to walk away, my grocery shopping chore remembered.

"I like the name Miriam." He says in a sexy, flirty voice.

"Oh, God. If you dare say some stupid remark on how it will be the name you are screaming later, I will show you how Justin got his bloody lip." I am still walking away.

"Now that you stole my next line, what else can I say?" He has caught up with me and is walking next to my cart. Still confident in himself. "My name is Oliver. I know you were wondering." I like Voodoo better; it has a sort of anonymity feeling to it. "I will just accompany you on your shopping trip, you know, for the produce's safety. I would hate to see what happens to a banana when you are left to your devices."

A chuckle forms in my throat, but doesn't make it past my lips. It feels foreign, and I can't recall when I last laughed. I refuse to speak again, hoping this terribly fantastic chemistry I tripped into tonight will go away. I want Oliver to leave, though there is a nagging feeling that is praying he stays. The store is not at all large. I at least bank on the fact that this odd set up will be over soon enough should he stay.

We fall into step, and much to my surprise Oliver remains and doesn't push to chat. He just strolls beside me as our shopping continues. I am finding solace in this stranger's silence. His quiet company alongside my cart feels familiar. The same feeling that sitting at the breakfast table reading the paper next to Ben brought. By the time we make the frozen food section, peace has come over me that I have not felt in three and a half years. It's amazing that I should crave silence when my quiet, empty house has haunted me for years.

I act like I'm looking at bread when really I use the time to watch Oliver. I'm not the only woman here doing so, but he seems completely unaware, absorbed in the task at hand. The women around us are looking at him with lustful eyes. He is a perfect ten, but they are missing him. A man who respects a widow's right to wear her wedding band.

He looks up now and then, when he steps away from the cart to grab an item, making sure I'm still there. Shockingly, I am. He isn't smug when he finds me; his face is soft. I have always heard about the selfless deeds of random people. Ben was one of those do-gooders, I know it can happen. Oliver seems different, he knows his place in other's worlds, the pain he can alleviate, and he gives it. I need quiet, and he is happy to give it. Voodoo. He breaks the code of silence when we come to the checkout line.

"I'm not going to ask for your number." It stings just a little, if I'm honest with myself, even when I know I wasn't going to give it to him.

"I wasn't going to give it to you," I state it matter-of-factly, solely for his benefit, I need him to know I can't date. The to-do list be damned. I'm not going to do number seven first, if ever. He just nods in response, he already knew. He somehow weaved his way into my head today, no doubt he knows more about me than I could think about him and all I ever gave him was silence. He doesn't know the whole truth, he never will.

I load my items on the conveyor belt, sending them down to the cashier. Then, I'm at the front where it is all mechanics and muscle memory again; smile, "I'm good, how are you" chatter, swipe card, enter PIN, wait for a receipt, "you too," walk over to the counter, load your groceries in the bags. It's all mundane, the things your body takes over for you and gives your brain a break. It's automatic. I barely register Oliver waiting with his one bag while I pack up my cart. It is not until I'm back at the helm of the steering rod that I see him there. Are we walking to the parking lot together as well? Should I feel some stranger danger? I give Penelope a lecture on it at least twice a week, and yet I am not following my own advice. Instead, I let him fall into step next to me as we head out the automatic door.

Oliver helps me load the groceries into my trunk, a kind gesture all the ladies around us notice. Cute and has manners. He should follow one of them around the store next time because he would have better luck. The thought makes me sad, everyone around me will go on to make their happily ever afters. They'll go home and kiss the love of their life, snuggle in for a movie, complain about the weather. I will go home to an empty house that was once home to my beautiful life.

"See you in two weeks, Miriam," Oliver says as he shuts the trunk and heads off to where his vehicle is parked.

"What? How do you know I come here every two weeks?"

He shrugs. "That's your typical shopping night, or at least it has been for the last few months. Every other Friday night around 6." He is not looking at me, in fact, the darkness of the night covers him well. I can't tell if he is embarrassed that he's been caught.

"Stalker," I shout. I hope he can hear the joke in my voice. Indeed, I'm shocked anyone would notice me. The shell of a human I have become blends into the surroundings anymore. I watch Oliver pull out of the parking lot. He may have just saved this miserable day.

I make the same boring trip home that I make every other Friday, but this time a small smile remains on my lips. I begin to reflect on it, my mind halting at the yellow legal pad list on my coffee table. I'm going to have to decide this. I have to decide if Penelope would be better off living with my mother while I continue to live as a widow barely, or do I start the grieving process everyone seems to think I'm stuck in? I don't have much time to think about it because when I pull into my driveway, another car is parked in my usual spot. My stomach drops. I can't handle much more today.

I get out of my car and walk to the driver side door. In an instant, I recognize the blond asleep in the seat. As my eyes grow warmer, I knock on the window.

"Charlotte."

THREE

"Charlotte." I knock hard on the window of my sister's car to wake her up. She lives about three hours away and rarely visits. I can't say I blame her. If I had the chance not to see my mother as often, I would take it. The last time I saw my sister was over two years ago. I wonder why she is here. The thought sends a panic into my bones. What if something is wrong? This day is already the itchy asshole of Satan, could there be anything worse on top of it?

Finally, I'm greeted with sleepy blue eyes. My sister is the stereotypical vision of beauty-blond hair and blue eyes. All throughout our childhood, I was jealous of this fact, my shit brown hair and green eyes could never compete. Charlotte never made it about competition. Never acknowledged the fact that she was knockout. Instead, my sister would enter a room and make everyone there feel good about themselves as if they were the center of attention. She has the biggest heart and is selfless. I smile as she rolls down the window.

"Ugh, Miriam. You look like shit." And rude. Did I forget to mention that Charlotte has no filter on her mouth? One the many reasons I love her, I guess, just the comments are usually directed elsewhere. She'll give it to you straight.

"Thanks, Char. I'm happy you are here. How's your life?" My voice drips with sarcasm, which is pointless, my sister doesn't care for the tactic.

"Don't avoid," she wags her finger in my face as she climbs out of the car, "it's tacky."

"What are you doing here?" I watch as she uncurls her sleek tall frame and stretches.

"Where's Pea Pod?" Deflection. Her nickname for Penelope floods me with happy memories. When I found out we were having a girl, I immediately called my sister to tell her the name and only her. For the rest of my pregnancy, she would call my belly a pea pod, our inside joke hinting at the name blatantly in front of people. No one caught on, but the nickname did.

"She spends some weekends at Alexa and John's house." I don't know why I feel embarrassed admitting it. She is getting grandparent time, vital to her growing up. "Don't avoid, Char, it's tacky." I reverberate her own words back to her.

"Touché, ducky." She clicks her tongue and winks. "This is where I live." Casual, like she just told me that tacos were her favorite meal. In true Charlotte fashion, she gives me no time to digest this. She lives here? What the hell does she mean? She lives three hours away. In a different state. Not here. She doesn't wait for my reaction. Her mind is made up. My sister doesn't suffer from the usual self-esteem issues girls have, never had to find herself. Nope, Charlotte Woods came out of the womb knowing exactly who she was and what she wanted to be. I loved it. Until now. For the first time, her fierceness was coming into my daily routine.

"Live?" The only intelligible word I could form in my mouth to utter. What a shame, I spend most of my time in my head and yet I cannot articulate words.

"I'm moving in." She says every word slowly, enunciating each syllable. The reasoning was right there in the three words and I was a fool not to see it. I stood, stupefied. "Oh, don't act like you don't want me as a roommate." She gestures with a wave of her hand, letting me know I was making too big of a deal of it, that she isn't here to stir the pot.

"No, I do. I'm just . . . well, I have a lot of questions, Charlotte." Like what the hell, maybe?

"Me, too." I hear her shout from inside her trunk. The entire top half of my sister has disappeared inside the back of her car, and there are only legs and flats remaining. I shake my head. I'm already happy she's here, a whirlwind force of easy-going. "First," she says, popping her head up to look at me pointedly, "you will feed me. I have been waiting for hours."

"Well, you're in luck, I just came from the grocery store." I point to my car. "Help me with my bags, and I promise to feed you." The flash of blond hair as Charlotte falls to the ground and begins bowing before me, makes me laugh hard. It feels awkward and unpracticed.

★ ★ ★

"You said you would feed me!" My sister is whining because frozen pizza doesn't amount to food in her eyes. Picky little bugger.

"I did." I forced a second slice down my throat to make a good appearance for company when in fact I rarely had an appetite.

"Junk. Absolute junk. You got nothing good when you were at the store. Just frozen meals and some lunch stuff." She's criticizing every item in my bags. I sit mortified at my small eating spot at the dining room table. "What do you do for dinner?"

"You just had dinner." I quip.

"Frozen pizza is not dinner." She moans as she saunters back to take up Penelope's usual eating spot. She points at the laundry, "Clean or dirty?"

"Clean."

"Put it away." Easy, Mom.

"What if I would have said dirty?" I challenge.

"I would have said to clean it." She gnaws into another slice of pizza that she disapproves of.

"Why are you here?" I ask, hoping to turn the tables away from the microscope my sister is putting me under right now.

"Keep up, babe. I live here." She smiles through her chews.

"You are frustrating me."

With a left shoulder shrug, she relents. "I heard about Mom's ultimatum and the list. I'm here to help." She picks at her fingernails. "I didn't know it was this bad, Miriam, I'm sorry."

"Neither did I." I feel ashamed. I was going about my days in a routine, thinking I was doing the best at surviving, then in one day all of that blew up in my face. My mom doesn't think I am doing well at all, Penelope is pissed at me, and now Charlotte has taken it upon herself to uproot and fix me. It all felt ridiculous; we are fine. I'm fine.

"Mom sent me the list." It's a quiet whisper, a confession that you are part hoping the other party does not hear. This is the moment where Charlotte takes up arms with me, fights our mother off, tells her she is insane and to butt out. Only this time Charlotte doesn't become the crusader I have known since her birth, three years after my own. She wears a beaten down expression in her body like she's uncomfortable with every word she's about to say. I'm petrified. If I can't have Charlotte, the one who has stood by me countless times when I was wrong, I will lose. There is no way I will survive the list without her. I know why she came now.

"She asked me if I thought it was a good idea. I told her I did." I want to break down. Where was my afghan and my dented concave cushion of the couch? "That's why I'm here to help, though. We are going to crush the list and tell Mom to jam it where the sun doesn't shine." She is trying to smile, reassure me everything is going to work out. I have faith in Charlotte. She looks like she has it in me.

"Ok." I meekly say, tossing my forgotten pizza slice aside. I guess there is no choice now.

★ ★ ★

"Wake up, sunshine!" Charlotte's standing on my bed, straddling my limp sleeping body, shouting obscenities at me.

"Such a potty mouth," I mumble, pulling the covers over my head. Last night I dreamt I was in the accident, watching it all happen. I barely slept, waking in cold sweats every time my eyes dared to drift off. I'd fall asleep and see Penelope crying that I killed her father and waked again gulping for air.

"Aw, still a morning person I see?" She giggles as she sips her coffee. "Rise and shine, sleeping beauty, I have coffee for you, plus you need to shower before we go."

"Leave the coffee on the nightstand and go . . . go? Go, where?" I throw the covers away from my head and sit up in a panic. Saturday after dropping Penelope off was spent sleeping in bed all day, so I know I didn't plan anything. That could only mean . . ."What did you do?" I ask horrified.

"I signed us up for a home improvement workshop. It starts at ten." She is slowly backing away, mug in hand, exactly how you get a dog to follow you with a bone. Unfortunately, it's working on me. I have a fear of letting that coffee mug get out of my sight because it will help keep me awake. I don't want to have that nightmare again. Once both of my feet hit the floor, she seems satisfied enough and stops her cat and mouse game. I snatch the mug from her, so she can't pull any more stunts, spilling some of the contents down my hand and onto the floor. Unfazed I sip at the mug, pulling my eyes to gaze at the clock radio on Ben's side of the bed. Oh. My. God,

"Charlotte Fiona Woods, it is 7:30 in the morning. Saturday. 7:30 a.m. on a Saturday morning. What is your problem? Were you dropped at birth? I'm going back to bed." Before I can reach the threshold of the promised land, my sister does a childish thing and pulls my hair. Ouch.

"No, we are going to class. Have to fix the house, remember? Number four."

She doesn't have to state what number four she's referring to. I, like my mother, have memorized that piece of yellow legal paper's demands, it's burned into my photographic brain. There to remain for all eternity, until I can mentally strike through every single one of them. Charlotte's burning eyes tell me I better humor her today. She's a fix it person, so she is making my life her mission. For her, I will do the home improvement class. Even if it means standing under the shower at Lucifer's hour of haunting in the morning. I flip her off as I cuddle my mug and walk to the bathroom. You love me, coffee, don't you? Yes, you do. Save me from the big old blond meanies. I kiss the cup, my only friend this morning, and get ready for class.

"Why did I need makeup for a home improvement class? Aren't we throwing hammers or some hardcore male crap today? Why did you insist on mascara?" I'm on my third cup of coffee, and nowhere near being less bitter for the day.

"You looked like shit. You need to look better because when you look better, you feel better." Charlotte is looking to mend me. I'm going to kick and scream the whole way.

"I need more coffee." I groan.

"Too bad. We're here. Now, let's go learn how to use tools." She is perky. She is a demon and not to be trusted.

"We're what? I already know how to use tools." I shoot daggers. Charlotte's face falls, she thought she did something to point me in the right direction, but she didn't realize I already know everything we are going to learn in class today.

"Sorry. Well, it'll be a refresher course. Besides, it will help get Mom off your back if you tell her you went to a class to learn how to fix up the house." Always the positive note, and with it, she bounces out of the car with her happy non-broken self. I think about throwing the cup at her.

After locating where it is we are supposed to go and putting some lame looking aprons on, we are ready to start. I quickly find the complimentary coffee table and begin filling up on more caffeine.

"Shouldn't you drink some water?" Charlotte scolds. I glare at her as I sip from the Styrofoam cup.

"Not today, Satan." And with that, she giggles and lets it go.

We are still five minutes from start time, so I look around the room at all the people here, mainly women. I'm surrounded by women who thought makeup was a tool today. Holy moly. They are covered, some I'm pretty sure used a putty knife to slap it on. Am I in the wrong place? We aren't expected to model the hammers, are we? I lean over to whisper the question in my sister's ear when my mind shuts off at the sound of his voice.

"Okay class, thank you for coming out. Today we are going to go over the basics, covering every tool that should be in your tool bag at home."

"Spank me hard." The sight of Oliver is not at all what I was expecting today, my first day tackling a to-do list that holds the outcome of my life in its balance.

"So you aren't completely off the idea of number seven." Charlotte giggles next to me.

"I know him," I mutter.

"How do you know Mr. Yum Yum Jeans?" Oliver's words are lost in the distance as I recant our grocery store meeting to my sister in a whisper.

"Holy shit." That was all Charlotte could muster after I admitted to her that I enjoyed the silence and companionship last night.

"I bet he doesn't remember me. I'll be fine. This will be fine." What a lie I was telling myself. I nervously glance at Oliver, who is standing on a pallet captivating his audience, there's no way he won't know me. He knows my shopping schedule for crying out loud. I understand why the women surrounding me went to such great lengths with their appearances today, and for once I'm glad Charlotte insisted on wearing mascara. That thought threw ice water on me. I can't think like that. I can't want another man to notice me. No. This was wrong. I won't even take off Ben's ring, and now I feel like I'm cheating on him standing here hoping to get noticed. Get it together, Miriam. He is just another man. He is here to show us how to navigate our way through a toolbox. He is not attractive. His eyes meet mine in the crowd. The recognition on his face did not go unnoticed by my sister or me. As he smiles at me, I feel my ribs cave a little. I'm going to blame it on Charlotte's elbow and not the butterflies. He is not attractive.

"Seems he does remember." Charlotte beams as we make our way to our posts. Respectfully, I chose the furthest away from Oliver and Charlotte begrudgingly obliges. I'm not sure what she expects, it looks as though we would have had to catfight and elbow women to get to the coveted front row stations anyway. I had no desire to join in because Oliver is not that attractive.

"Okay, let's screw these screws in and hammer some nails so we can get the hell out of here." Charlotte isn't impressed with my idea, especially when she has a new-found interest to watch me squirm as the man she deems Mr. Yum Yum Jeans comes over to us.

"Hey, Miriam, nice to see you again." He says in that soothing, rich voice that isn't attractive at all.

"Hi." I don't look up, but my body betrays me and wobbles just slightly at the proximity of him. He is not attractive.

"Hello, Yum Yum Jeans. I'm Charlotte, Miriam's sister." As if she called him by his given name, Charlotte extends her hand unabashed. She couldn't care less that he knows her nickname for him or that she finds him attractive. I, however, am hoping the floor will open and claim me, saving me from the utter mortification of standing next to my sister at this moment. I feel my face grow warm, the heat rising from my neck. Oliver just chalks her introduction up to humor, corrects her on his name and turns his attention back to me.

"I didn't know you were in the works of becoming a carpenter." He coos but never leans closer, as if last night is burned in his mind and he knows not to push it.

"Oh, come on Yum Yum. I was hoping you'd be smoother than that." Charlotte has screwed in two of the four screws she has to do and seems to be slowing. I was already on the nail portion of the board.

The row ahead of us starts straining backward, women leaning into backbends to catch a single word of our conversation. They all want to know why the good-looking teacher is bothering to talk to a hot mess like me. Oliver just laughs once again at Charlotte, utterly unaware of the eavesdroppers and unfazed by Charlotte's nickname. I wish I could be confident like Charlotte and Oliver.

"Oh, Oliver? Can you come help me?" One of the groupies ahead of us calls to him. I look up at her, and she has the nerve to glare at me. Why are women so catty over men? Do they realize that they'll die before us? I'm living proof of this fact. Women should not be fighting with each other over men, especially when Oliver has the option to be with any of them here and he doesn't choose it. It is ultimately his decision and not something you can persuade away by baby talking or putty knifing your face. Chemistry is chemistry, ladies. It does not matter if you think you are hotter than another girl. It is a feeling you cannot define by physical aspiration. I mean, if I even wanted Oliver, the chemistry is just not there for me. So, I shouldn't feel a little annoyed that he is being dragged away from my station, right?

"I'm going to kill you later. You know that right?" I take in Charlotte's shit-eating grin as I give out my threat.

"Doubtful." She hardly looks away from the nail portion of her board, hammering like a pro. I want to share in her laughter. I float above my body and peer down at the situation. It is funny. Here we are in a home improvement class, sharing in some sister bonding time and a boy was crushing on me. We should be making jokes. Instead, I see myself from the outside, a wet blanket. I was intent on finishing my project board so that I could be done and go home. I was planning on taking a nap when I got there, an all-day consuming slumber. Charlotte will never allow it, so why was I rushing? I hate myself now; I ruin life for everyone around me. I shove back my sinking shoulders and puff out my chest. I'm determined. I will laugh here because the one Charlotte stole from my body last night felt terrific. She's putting in such an effort for me that I can try for her.

"That's it, wench!" Charlotte proclaims, holding her hammer high. She notices the shift in me, and, being the relentless person she is, she isn't going to let it die out. "Hammer those nails! Screw the screws! Nut the bolts!"

Her enthusiasm is infectious because in no time I'm enjoying myself. I'm privileged to have her in my life, anyone who has Charlotte is. She's sunshine in a dark place, what Bram Stoker spoke about, the light of all lights. We hold up our hammers in unison to clink before each nail on the board. We both already possess the common skills of the class, but she was right to bring me here. Once again, Charlotte knows better.

"You have such a beautiful laugh. What's your name?" His voice is thick and instantly sets off a warning throughout my body. My skin crawls when he takes it upon himself to touch my arm. I draw it back, instinctively, and glower at the assassin of my personal space. I feel Charlotte's hammering cease beside me; this is the kind of man you need back up for.

"Miriam." I was clipped. I want him to sense my disgust and walk away. My level of discomfort is evident, instead of flipping his interest off, it only fuels the fire more. I'm holding a hammer and poised to use it.

"Such a beautiful name." It's as if a serpent has spoken, he is slithering, "It looks like you know what you're doing here. Maybe you'd benefit from more private lessons?"

"No, thank you," I say politely. Bile is threatening to escape my throat, but I'm giving him one last chance to take the hint.

"Oh, come on." He grabs my arm and leans in. He is the worst that women have to face. He thinks I'm playing hard to get and that he can persuade me with force.

"No." I push his arm off.

"Sam. Call me, Sam." He grips my arm tighter and smiles.

"Leave her alone, Sam!" He is next to my side, splitting the serpent and me apart. I chance a look at Oliver's steel arms as he blocks Sam's view of me. He is physically vibrating. I would lie if you asked me if I breathed him in on purpose. I would lie. It didn't happen. I am not at all attracted to this mountain of a man standing close to me, protecting me. I'm not. I swear it. I still wear the ring of another, but I am grateful he is here. Sam holds his hands up in surrender, in a fight against Oliver he knows he would lose. Surprisingly, Sam shows an amount of respect for Oliver that he couldn't afford to lend me. Just like that, he is off to pursue another victim in a row ahead of us. Clown.

Oliver turns to me, grabbing both sides of my arms, making me instantly look up into his gorgeous brown eyes. "Are you okay?" I nod. I am powerless for words in the tight space. I was just having fun with my sister, why do you have to be here? This is too much. He can sense me, that damn heart of his, so he lets go. "If he bothers you again, you come and tell me." With that, he walks away. Nothing more.

"Yum Yum was seething. He likes you." Charlotte says as offhandedly as she can pretend, but I know she is trying to feel me out and see where I stand on number seven on the list.

"I've had enough, Charlotte. Can we call it a day?" I whimper. All the energy has drained from me, no chance of returning. I watch as she looks to where Oliver is standing, watching me. She seems torn, she feels his pain, disappointed that I won't get over that hump and date.

"Okay." She relents. "Tacos?" I feel I've crushed her, but she recovers so well. "Your treat." I give her a forced lopsided smile.

I'd be lying if I said I didn't notice Oliver watching me leave.

FOUR

I let Penelope stay at my in-laws for the extra days of her suspension. She doesn't fight to come home, so I pretend not to notice. Charlotte fills the time picking and fussing about the house or trying to keep me from napping. Everywhere I turn she wants to talk, it's annoying. I use the time mainly to speak about Penelope, not myself. I rehash the whole school incident with Charlotte. For the first time in nearly four years, I have another ear to bend on parenting.

We conclude that Penelope should start a journal. Charlotte thought of it. The journal will help me to understand where she is coming from and possibly eliminate some of the sessions she is having with the guidance counselor. That's what my sister does; she finds a compromise that makes everyone happy. I trust her judgment without question, especially since I don't crave to be in charge. I want a mindless life where someone tells me what to do and when to do it. I just wish I could take all emotion out of these tasks.

Charlotte put away the clean laundry from the dining room table and attempted to vacuum the house. She did dishes and took the trash to the curb, but even she can't tackle the neglect in a weekend. The house still looks empty and dead, even with her bright life inside of it. She busied herself with lists of what we could do to conquer each task. Lists for the list. She avoided number seven until today when she informed me that she gave Oliver my phone number. Casually, over making her morning coffee. No big deal. It is a big deal. I'm mad. I'm still sulking in the car on the way to pick up Penelope.

Sure, Charlotte has a good reason, like she always does. She told me that if Mom asked about number seven, I could show her the man's number in my phone and pretend. Charlotte never does anything with ill intent, I know she means it with love, but she can shove off. I was not feeling the repair everything attitude of my sister today.

I left early to purchase a journal for Penelope, but mainly to get out of the house and away from Char. A new development for me, longing to be out of the house. Possibly my sister is a miracle worker after all. I pull into the Jones' long driveway, my mind taking a walk down memory lane. I drove this long stretch so many times over the years. Ben wrecked his car early on when we were dating, leaving me to be the means of transportation if we were going to go out on a date. It was funny how embarrassed he was over this, even forcing his way into the driver's seat. At least the outside world could think he was the man of the date, that's what he'd say in protest.

I park the car, and for a long time, I sit staring at the brick colonial letting it take me back to simpler times. Times when I worried only about paying a handful of bills, not struggling for a year with the life insurance company to finally pay off the mortgage. Times when I could just walk up to the porch and swing with Ben for hours, not picking out his casket.

I force my way out of my car door and ring the doorbell, something I wouldn't have done in yesteryears. Alexa answers the door with her cheery smile, a part of me hates her for being healthy and sane enough to cope with death in a functioning way.

"Miriam." She shouts my name and pulls me in for a tight embrace. That was the way with Alexa. She hugs everyone in greeting. She squeezes you to inform you of your importance, that you were loved, that she's happy to see you, to meet you, to be in your company.

"Hello, Alexa." My words are only as cheerful as I can muster but she deserves better. She has been nothing but good to me all these years, even after Ben died, she never parted ways with Penelope or me. I'm grateful for her. "How's Penelope?"

"Oh, good. She's good. Come in, dear," She hustles me in the door and calls for my daughter. "She's so pleasant. I just love having her around every other weekend. Thank you for the extra time this weekend. I wish it were under better circumstances." She draws back so that her beautiful gray eyes, Ben's eyes, are piercing me, attempting to see into my soul. Alexa's not a slim woman, but she isn't obese. Her weight matches her wholesome attitude, plump and full of life. She has the mom hair from the '50s still, a true pompadour fashion. "How was your weekend?" She always asks me this upon pickup. A non-subtle gauge to see how I'm doing. This time, though, I have something to give her.

"My sister showed up Friday night after I came here. You remember Charlotte?" She nods. Of course, she remembers. She paid attention to the details of your life as if they were sacred treasure, too precious not to burn to memory. "She'll be living with Penelope and me for a little while, helping out." Her hopeful gleam twists the last blade in my heart. Even Alexa, a God-sent angel, thinks I'm lousy.

"That's wonderful, honey." She brushes my arm in a tender motherly way. It was far from my mother. "So," she changes the subject, "Penelope and I were looking through old photo albums today. We came across her baby pictures today. I swear Amelia and Penelope could have been identical twins. I had to search my other books for Amelia's photo to compare them. Sure enough. Identical." The lump in my throat is hard to breathe with, and the room starts to close in. Amelia. Another victim that night, that night I sent Ben out.

"Hey, Mom." I don't hear Penelope come in the room because I'm counting to keep the walls of the room where they are meant to be. I mentally glue the fragments I can find and shove them back down. Deep down. I have to focus on my daughter now.

"Hey, babe. Ready to go?" My voice is a whisper, threatening to break apart at the seams with every syllable. Penelope looks sad for me. She must have heard Alexa mention Amelia. I press the tips of my fingers deep into the scars on my palms. I need to rally. "Aunt Charlotte is visiting," I say with excitement, my acting skills improving.

"She is?" Penelope's suddenly a kid at Christmas.

"Yup. Let's go." I start for the door. "Thank you, Alexa." I meet her eyes, trying to convey what I know I can't let past my lips. Thank you for taking care of my daughter so I can be a shell of a rotten human being every other weekend. I hope to do better.

We stop for fast food on the way home, which doesn't please Charlotte. After her half-hour dissertation on how fast food is disgusting and she doesn't want it for every meal anymore, she finally takes her place at the table to eat. Over dinner, I tell Penelope about the journal, and it is met with little resistance, unlike Charlotte and fried chicken. She keeps equating the consumption of it to death.

After we ate, Penelope goes to her room to catch up on homework, Charlotte and I stay behind to have a cup of coffee and crumb cake. It's the beginning of a peaceful evening. That is until Charlotte decides to throw a wrench in.

"I booked you an appointment with Dr. Pierce tomorrow. He's supposed to be the best therapist around."

I scrub my hand down my face, pure frustration radiating from my body. Another fight. "Why?" I keep my agitation in check, hoping my sister comes through with her sound reasoning as always.

"Because you have a whole list to do and you need to start." She is sharp but keeps her voice just above a whisper so Penelope won't hear us in the other room. "You can resist all you want Miriam, but you need to do it so you might as well start tomorrow. Then you can take Penelope out." She sits back as her cheery self again.

"I'm going to bed." I push away from the table and head to my room. My head is reeling, and I no longer wish to fight my sister on the list and the things that need to be done. It's not that I'm refusing to acknowledge these things need to be completed, it's just so overwhelming.

"But it's only six o'clock," Charlotte calls in protest.

"It's been a long day," I mutter back.

★ ★ ★

In the morning, Penelope wakes me two minutes before the bus arrives. We go through our regular routine, but this time we have a spectator. For once, my sister isn't butting in. This morning she looks just to be observing. I'd hate to know what is going on in that head of hers. What did she think of Act One before Penelope woke me up?

"Can we go clothes shopping tonight, Mom?" Penelope asks on her way out the door. That's right, our mother and daughter time. I scan my daughter's clothes. They are worn. I haven't been clothes shopping in years; I leave it to my mother and Ben's mother. I don't much care what I look like, but I can't ignore the fact that Penelope needs new clothes. Also, I can't deny that face of hope.

"Sure." And she's off. Have you ever noticed the word sure? The way it is spoken in conversation? It is non-committal as if you are saying yes but letting the person know that it is not your first choice and you are reluctantly agreeing. I press my hand against the window on cue. I lean back into the arm of the couch and close my eyes. Instead of falling back asleep I'm wide awake feeling the judgment radiating from across the room.

"Yes, Charlotte?" I ask, eyes still closed.

"Nothing." I can hear her biting her lip, refraining. "Appointment is at two today. I'll make dinner and have Penelope ready when you get home." With that my sister leaves me to go sit out on the back deck. Finally, I am afforded some quiet, yet my thoughts rage loudly.

FIVE

The parking lot of the good doctors has hit maximum capacity. Apparently, there are a lot of us crazies out in the world. I am a half hour early, blame it on nerves, or a lifetime of being punctual, or even my sister's presence clogging my space in the house, but I had the time to watch people coming and going. It seems Dr. Pierce was not the only therapist at this particular location. The therapists coordinate their schedules well, none of their patients are arriving at the same time. Maybe that helps them to prevent patients making unstable friendships in the waiting room.

I hate therapy. If you had asked me to do this four years ago, I would have agreed. Talking your problems out to a neutral party was once a fabulous idea to me, now it's an intrusion and a real possibility to be deemed clinically insane. I slam my head back in the driver's seat and close my eyes. I should be walking in now.

I get out of the car and make my way to the door, looking back every three steps, plotting to run. Just get through this session and then you will be free to take Penelope clothes shopping. The first session is more like a job interview anyway, so we won't dive into the thick stuff yet. Three more steps and I'm in. The receptionist smiles through her little window. After I tell her my name, she slips a stack of forms to fill out through the crack. Wow, does she need that thick glass shielding her from interaction? That sure makes people feel welcome and safe. I look around the room. Waterfall machine for soothing effect. Sigmund Freud quote on the wall. Typical. I fill out the papers and wait, and it isn't long before the therapist comes to get me himself. Nice touch.

"Miriam, will you please follow me?" I just stare up from my seat, frozen. I cannot move. "Miriam?" I don't want to do this. I can't do this. I can't speak to him for an hour about Ben. He'll ask questions. He'll want to know what happened. This is one stranger I can't just ignore when they ask the details. "Miriam?" The good doctor has the sense to help me out of the chair physically. I don't look ahead as he gently ushers me down the hallway to his treatment room. I'm glancing back at the waiting room door that just closed shut. I'm in freaking therapy.

"Go ahead and have a seat wherever you like, Miriam, and we'll get started." He shuts the door behind me. I'm trying to remember the steps to ward off a panic attack when you feel it coming. I cannot grasp a single one. The room is shrinking in on me, the doctor's voice is a distant sound swirling in my head. He says something about standing. I can stand. Am I standing? Don't worry he says. Don't worry. Is that a step? Counting. Counting is a step. One. Two. Three. Deep breath. Release. Four. Deep breath. Release. Okay. I can do this.

"What brings you here to see me today?" The doctor is coming into focus now. I'm coming out of the panic attack.

"I, uh, I'm a widow." I stutter, tottering on the precipice that threatens to take my sight.

"How long have you been a widow, Miriam?" He keeps saying my name; it must be a trained practice. If they say your name repeatedly, you feel like they care more and are listening, like when you are on the phone with a customer service rep. You should always remember their name and repeat it back to them because you get better service.

"Three and a half years." Walls are starting to close in. One. Two.

"What happened?" There it is. He has a steady voice, sure of his questioning. This is what needs to happen in order to heal, to get to the next level. He knows it.

I'm sweating; the beads are rolling down my skin. I'm on fire, and I can feel my lungs seizing up as they're engulfed in flames. *What happened?* I look at the doctor. Can't he see me panicking? But he isn't there. No one is there. I'm by the side of the road.

They've cleared the wreckage, but the tire marks on the road have remained. The other driver never stopped, but Ben tried his hardest to dodge him. The black peeled into the road tell the story. You don't need an expert to figure it out. I walk into the middle of the street and place my right foot on the starting mark. Here he hit the brakes, step forward on the line. Here is where the car swerved, step forward. Here is where they hit. Only one line now. Here is where the vehicle began to flip. Once. Twice. Sideways marks in the grass to the tree. Here is where it skidded sideways. Hand on the torn bark of the oak tree. Here is where it stopped. The tree is where my life ended.

"I can't do this." My voice sounds like it is coming from somewhere else. "I have to go. I'm sorry." I run to the door, out of the office, straight for my car and I drive fast as if something is chasing me. My ghosts always are.

★ ★ ★

I haven't been home yet; it's been hours. Matter of fact, it's coming up on midnight now. I step out of my car and walk to the front door. After the meltdown at the doctor's office, I drove myself to Ben and I's spot. I let go of so many tears, years of them bottled up, that now as I crawl to face my fate for standing Penelope up, I have no idea if I'll even be able to talk. I'm hoarse. My throat is raw. I spin the flower that I plucked from the field where Ben and I would picnic. I unlock the door noticing the living room is dark.

"Where the hell have you been?" The ugly lamp flickers on and illuminates the irritation in Charlotte's face.

"Therapy didn't go well." I take in Charlotte's countenance; she is more than pissed, she is disappointed and let down. So much worse.

"I thought you died. No text. No call. Nothing." She screeches. She shifts her gaze to Penelope's bedroom to reign in some self-control, one of us has to be an adult. "Penelope waited and waited." Tears are flowing down my sister's face. She is fighting for Penelope the way I should be. She wants what is best for her and I have been abusing that thought and replacing it with my selfish desires. "She cried for hours, Miriam. Hours!"

More cries escape my body as I fall to the floor. "I can't do it, Charlotte. It's too much. You are pushing too hard."

"Someone has to push you."

"The car, oh God, it was wrapped around the tree. It was so bent and curved around that tree, Charlotte. They couldn't get the passenger door open. They couldn't pry anything open." I'm bent over, my sobs echoing off the floor. "You pushed me too fast, Char."

I hear the footsteps in the distance, not just Charlotte's coming to comfort me, but Penelope's coming to the edge of her door and listening. It only makes me cry harder. I'm a terrible mother. Selfish. And I can't get past it. Penelope is better with my mother or maybe even Charlotte, but it was certain she isn't going to be happy with me. I'm failing, fumbling with the idea of healing but not actively committing. Why can't I? Logically, I know that I need to do it, for my daughter, but I can't get my heart on board.

"It's too hard, Charlotte. Too hard." My wailing has died down, and I hear the retreat of Penelope's feet. Back to bed. "You can't push me, Char."

"Fine, Penelope is better off with Mom anyway." She bristles. I shoot my head up.

"What do you mean?" I don't believe what I'm hearing. My stomach drops to the floor.

"Look at you. You're a mess. You can't even walk her to the bus stop in the morning, and it is only down the driveway. You can't get out of bed without your seven-year-old daughter waking you. You're useless." Charlotte's never mean like this, but looking at her stance and the toxic poison flowing from her mouth you'd think she's a pro.

"I'm not useless." I stand up. "You don't understand."

"I do. You want to be selfish. So, let Penelope go live with Mom then you can wallow in your inability to try."

"Penelope doesn't need to live with Mom." I start moving about the room and picking things up off the floor, righting the pictures that are crooked, busying my hands.

"She'd have a better life. You can't even keep the house picked up when you are here all day." I grab the magazines off Ben's chair and throw them in the garbage can. I long to throw Charlotte's head in there. "Except you're not here all day, even when you are." She's hot on my heels as I grab the clutter surrounding us. "You are a shell, Miriam. You aren't even a person anymore."

"Shut up!" I grab all the dishes from the dining room table and put them in the dishwasher. Charlotte is at my side, berating me.

"You just want to sit and mourn your husband while you have a living breathing daughter to take care of. Someone still here to love. You're selfish."

"I'm not selfish. I love Penelope." I turn the dishwasher on and start throwing away the garbage on the counter.

"I can help you pack her bags for Mom's tomorrow then I will leave town, too."

"She is not leaving." I grab the broom and start sweeping the crumbs off the kitchen floor. After I'm done, I grab hold of the garbage can and lift the bag up. I seal it off and toss it in the garage that's off the kitchen. "She is not living with Mom, how dare you say that."

"You're right. She's not." All the fire drains from my blood when I take in my sister's smug face. She is resting now, at the dining table, tilted head propped on her arm. She's staring at me like she holds a secret and she's waiting for it to come to me. I have all the pieces.

"What?"

"You'll fight for her." There isn't an ounce of mean left in her. I'm not sure how her fire died that quickly.

"Of course I'll fight for her. What are you talking about?" I'm confused at my sister's sudden change in demeanor. I don't realize what just happened until she waves her arm around the house.

"I cleaned up." It was the dumbest thing to say, but it's all I can muster. While my sister was tearing up one side and down the other, I finally started to take action. For Penelope. "Oh no, I cleaned Ben's chair." It's too late to take the step back, but I feel guilty for not taking the time to appreciate it when I was doing it.

Charlotte comes up behind me and squeezes my shoulders. "I'm going to bed. Penelope left her journal for you to read on the coffee table." She kissed the side of my face and walked away, leaving me in awe of myself. I did it. I took a step. When Charlotte threw the reality of my inaction at me, subconsciously I reacted. Without thinking, my decision for Penelope and I was made. I don't want Penelope to live with my mother. I'm going to do this.

I walk over to the coffee table sure the next step won't be as easy, I know whatever she wrote is going to rip me in two. As I reach the table, it dawns on me that there's a genuine possibility that I'm too late. I finally started to fight for Penelope, but is she done fighting for me? I lunge at the journal, desperate to find out the ending to the story.

April 12ᵗʰ

Today my mother never came home for our date . . .

SIX

April 12th

Today my mother never came home for our date. That made me sad. I thought she was going to come home, but she didn't. She forgot me. I try to be a big girl for her since Daddy left. Everyone has told me to be a good girl for Mommy because she is going through a lot. I thought I was good. Maybe she is mad at me for the fight at school. I don't like Justin. He always picks on me. Friday he said a mean thing about my Daddy and I didn't know if it was true. I was so mad. I hit him. Mommy doesn't talk about Daddy. Aunt Charlotte said she might someday. I was going to ask her some stuff tonight, but she didn't come home. I hope she didn't leave me. I'm not mad at her. I know she is sad. I try to make her happy. Maybe I can't, I'm sorry. Just come home, Mommy.

I place the open notebook to my chest and cling to it as if it were my child. It is. It's her words, the words I never knew she had in her. The way she feels. I never took the time to ask her how she was feeling. I thought I was shielding her from the hurt that consumed me day in and day out by not telling her about Ben. I figured it would be best for her to keep her happy memories of her father, rather than know he was in pain. No mother wants to relay that to her child, but instead of just hiding that from her I hid all of him from her. I am the reason he isn't here for her, and I took the last bit of him she could have away. I can't remember being four; I guess I just assumed that she would. It's clear to me now that she doesn't. Otherwise, Justin might not have gotten punched in the face.

My tears have stained the last page of her words. *Come home, Mommy.* I'm home now. I'm no longer holed up in this empty house letting it haunt me. I'm craving to get out, to love, to laugh again. I look at the clock, one in the morning, the witching hour of the weary. I have to be honest with myself; the act is getting old. I want to be like Charlotte, selfless and giving. Why wasn't I striving for it with my daughter? She wants to make me happy, and she thought that entire process relied on her being a good girl. I hate that. Adults always do that, tell kids to behave for their parents because they're having a rough time. We expect so much from tiny humans. We want them to burden so much of the load. It is impossible. They are just learning this stuff that isn't their responsibility. It isn't Penelope's. It's mine.

I rise from the couch and go straight to her room. I don't know if she will be asleep, but it doesn't matter. I need to hold her, not for my selfish reasons this time; I need to hold her for her. She requires me to be the parent; she will no longer carry that load. Not from this second forward. She won't be going to live with my mother. I was going to pull it together. I didn't know how and the thought threatened to send me back into my old shell, but I couldn't let it. Not this time.

I climb into her twin size bed, behind her tiny frame, and wrap my arm around her middle. I breathe in her hair and take in her warmth. She is alive. I'm alive. We can't act like we are dead anymore. Years of checking on Penelope through the night inform me that she is not asleep right now, just pretending. She wants to know if I love her when she isn't awake, and if I need her when I think she isn't looking. I squeeze tighter and kiss her sweet mess of brown hair.

"I will try harder," I whisper. "I love you." My tears fall across my nose and down the other side where they hit her pillow. I can feel her body start to shake with silent tears. Tears of relief. She is resilient. How amazing children are to continually hand out their pure love when we have done them wrong over and over. We abuse that. When they talk, we find it insignificant, chalking it up to just gibberish. We don't listen with rapt attention as they do us. We are all assholes when it comes to children. In the darkness of Penelope's bedroom, I resign that I won't be that person anymore.

She eventually cries herself to sleep, and I am left in the silence holding her. Silence. It seems to be a forever post in my life. Whether comfortable or haunting. This time it feels empowering. A resolve to fight. Contentment in the decision. Hope for the future. This space does not haunt me. I'm reminded of the peace I felt in the grocery store with Oliver. If I'm going to move forward and fix things I will need good people around me, supporting me. I wonder if Oliver will be one of them. It is not every day you find people that you can be silent within this noisy world. That must be the secret to life. Find those you can enjoy out loud and in silence. A small grin touches my face. I wonder if Olive likes coffee.

I reluctantly leave my daughter's bed. I step back and admire the soul that encompasses my child. She is an angel on earth, a role model for forgiveness and love. I make my way back to the living room, in search of my phone. I find many missed calls and texts from Charlotte. I gave her such a fright. So much so that she thought the worst. I didn't think to consider what may have gone through her head. I make a mental note to make it up to her. My sister is a soulmate, a being that completes me, I have abused her knowing she wouldn't leave me. I notice a missed text from my mother that says I need to call her. I shudder. I hope she doesn't decide to take legal action because I flaked on Penelope. How many strikes do I get in this process? I hope she gives me a few.

I start a new text to Oliver. Courtesy of Charlotte's stalking, she put his number in my phone once she found it out. It is four in the morning now, but I send it anyway. *Can you meet for coffee?* I wait impatiently for his reply; I want instant gratification. I believe people should be up and waiting to respond to me should I decide to reach out. I need to work on that. I reason with myself that people have lives and I need to start remembering that. The phone still lights up. I send out thanks to the universe.

Dear God, woman. Not at this hour. 6. Brightons. Now go away.

Apparently, my new friend is not a morning person either. Time to shower.

★ ★ ★

"You look like shit." I hear his grumble before I take in his face. I won't dare let on that I knew he was here before he came over to the table. I've been here since five this morning waiting for him. I couldn't stay home any longer. I was motivated and making a friend is what I need to get done today. I didn't want the newfound resolve to get stale in the house of the living dead. I left Penelope a note to say I would be out when she woke up, but I'd see her after school.

"What?" I say in reply, pretending I didn't hear him. I'm giving him a chance for a better compliment.

"Aren't girls supposed to wear makeup and dress up on a first date?" He didn't take the hint.

"This isn't a date." I groan.

"Sure it is." He walks away to get coffee. He needs caffeine before this goes any further. I follow.

"People don't grab a cup of coffee on a date. How lame. And you didn't shave so it can't be a date." I rattle off the reasons, shrugging my shoulders, keeping my eyes trained on the ground.

He chuckles. "Well, I was going to get razors today since it is my day off, but I was forced to have a first date over coffee. And yes, Miriam, people do have dates over coffee."

"They do?" I finally met his eyes. They are more than just brown. The outer edges are the darkest shade of chestnut you can imagine, but as you move closer to his pupil, the color fades to a light ocean blue. They hold a distinct feeling of depth, wisdom placed in the shade at birth.

"How long have you been out of the dating scene, Grandma?" His face falls when he catches his own mistake. I let him go. I did pull him out of bed to ask him to be my friend.

"This is terrible. What happened to dinner and a movie?"

His smile returns just in time for us to move up in line. It's busy. Considering this is the time most folks stop for morning coffee on their way to work. Brighton's is an amazing coffee shop, my favorite; I'm glad Oliver picked it. They make a delicious breakfast sandwich. I at least waited until he got here to order one of those, but I won't lie, I'm on my third cup of coffee.

"See, coffee is the perfect first date," he starts, "You can dress casual. It's cheap. It's always an interview anyway, might as well be comfortable."

I look at him in horror.

"What?" I watch him attempt to solve the confusion on his face by backtracking over his last statement, but I can't hold it in and wait.

"You're one of those first date guys!"

"Huh?"

"Lots of first dates?"

"Yes," then the realization hits, "Oh God! No. No, I don't do the one night stand thing. I'm just bad at first dates, that's all." He smiles, then the smile falls, "That didn't sound much better, did it?"

"It was honest at least." He's saved by the cashier greeting him with a smile and asking to take his order. I snicker behind him like a mad woman, causing him to smack his hand back at me playfully. Why is this so easy? I gave the cashier my order as well, refusing to let Oliver pay for it. We walk over to the pick-up counter and wait for our coffee and sandwiches.

"Thank you." I break the silence.

"For?"

"I needed that laugh."

"Obviously, I mean you do look like shit." He waves his thanks to the barista as he sets our orders up for us and we shuffle back to the table.

"I'm not the least bit surprised that women aren't jumping at you for a second date." I hiss. He laughs, caramel smooth. My laugh is out of practice and comes in a cackle while his is well-rehearsed.

"So, why did you invite me on this non-first date at six in the morning looking like a frumpy mess?" He sips his coffee.

"I went to therapy yesterday," I start my speech, but I'm talked over.

"Wow!" He spits coffee on the table "You're worse than me at first dates. You can't tell people you are crazy off the bat."

"I talk to beans, so I thought you knew." His eyebrows raise as his he bobs his head.

"Good point. Continue." He waves me on as he settles back in his seat after he's cleaned his mess up.

"This is not a date. I text you at four in the morning asking you to coffee then I show up looking a frumpy mess. Me saying I went to therapy surprises you?"

"I love when a woman berates me over coffee. I will never go on another coffee date with anyone but you, they would pale in comparison." He makes me blush. I wasn't expecting it. "So, you went to therapy, and it made you think of me? I'm flattered."

"It didn't go well." He just hums in response, "Oliver?"

"Yeah?"

"I need a friend."

"Ok." He bites into his sandwich and watches me.

"That was me asking you to be my friend." I pick at a chip in the polyurethane table. How embarrassing. I just asked someone out loud to be my friend, and I didn't even do it right. I had a whole speech prepared; I memorized it. This isn't how it was supposed to go. I had a fail-proof paragraph to recite that he couldn't say no to. I chance a look when I hear him smack his lips.

"That was me saying okay, Miriam." He smiles to the side and shakes his head. "You'll need someone as wonderful as me to talk about in therapy." We laugh, our eyes meeting as we enjoy each other's company. They linger there for too long. It's as if Oliver is looking into my soul. It's not there.

"What's the worst pick up line you've ever heard?" I blurt out; I have to stop the intimacy. He leans back in his seat, amused at the random person in front of him, this crazy woman he has just decided to be friends with. He obviously has poor judgment.

"Hi." He finally answers after pondering my question.

"Hi?" Did he not understand the question?

"Now, I can go home and write down the first words the man of my dreams ever spoke to me."

"Blech." I physically shudder. "That may have been the tackiest line I've ever heard, and someone said it?"

"Yeah." I'm a little jealous that a woman had enough courage to give him a pickup line, even a dreadfully lame one.

"Did you sleep with her?" The poor guy burns his tongue on his coffee.

"What? No!" The people in line for coffee are watching him with piqued curiosity, this man who has spit his coffee twice. Oliver is wiping his face with his napkin, the rejected coffee from his chin and neck where it has dribbled down. I follow the drip as it makes its way down his throat until he catches it. I never thought a drip of coffee would be so fascinating.

"Why not?" I ask. Still staring at the spot where the drip stopped. I wonder if he smells like coffee now. I bet it would go great with the smell of his soap.

"Can't perform under that kind of pressure." He chokes out, barely able to contain his laughter.

After my coffee with Oliver, we promise to meet again. I'm sad to see him walk across the parking lot to his truck and before I can stop myself, I'm running after him. He is equally shocked when he turns at the sound of my pounding footsteps. "Be careful driving." I breathe out and jog away.

Once I get home, I see Charlotte waiting for me at the dining room table with a warm greeting this time. She smiles when I walk in and kiss her forehead. I lift her up by her arm, silently demanding she follow me, and she does so without fuss. We walk hand in hand to the living room and retrieve the to-do list from its hiding spot in the magazine rack. I pull her with me to the kitchen, where we hang the list on the refrigerator together. A daily reminder.

"Okay, let's do this," I say. She smiles.

SEVEN

I have been sitting on the floor of my bedroom, staring at the contents of my shared closet with Ben for the past half hour. The coffee in my cup has gone cold. Still, I cradle it for warmth. I never turned the light on, so only the sun from the window illuminates the room. As fate would have it, the morning sunrise is making the closet glow, particularly Ben's side. The side I have to deal with today. I sip the cold coffee. Terrible.

I haven't opened the door to Ben's side since I picked out his clothes for the funeral. It sits, like the day he left, still in the same order. Disorder. There is no system to Ben's set up; he would just hang clothes wherever. My side looks like a magazine article, all by color and sleeve length. His side screams teenager. Jesus, Ben. I sip my coffee again. It's the worst thing I've ever tasted, but I won't move from my spot.

"What are you doing?" My light flicks on then Charlotte's groggy voice fills the space. She slept in this morning, which is strange for her. But she isn't dragging me to any home improvement classes this Saturday. She looks worn, beaten, which is odd given the pleasant day yesterday. I was waiting, dressed, and at the end of the driveway when Penelope got home from school and we had a lovely family night. Charlotte cooked. I even mentioned cleaning out Ben's clothes today and was met with warm, encouraging faces. Penelope and I still needed to have an extensive talk about things, and start mentioning Ben. I look from my sister's face to the closet in silent conversation. Her gaze follows. She gets me when no one else understands she hears the words in my head. She turns off the light and plunks herself on the floor beside me with a loud ungraceful thud.

"Headache?" I ask.

"Yeah. I slept wrong. Is that fresh?" She points at my coffee cup.

"No," I say in disgust. "Tastes like shit." My sister quietly retrieves my coffee and shuffles to the kitchen, mumbling about getting up to find some ibuprofen anyways, leaving me alone once again with the clothes of my husband. Belts. Lots of belts. I wonder if you can make anything out of belts. I'm sure I could go online and find a ton of DIY crafts.

"Here." Charlotte returns with two hot cups of coffee and sits, leaning her head on my shoulder and slurps her cup.

"Why does your side look like you suffer from perfectionism?"

"It's a color system."

"You can't even do your hair in the mornings, yet you have a color system for clothes?" She chuckles humorlessly. "Ben said screw the system."

"That he did, my friend. That he did."

We stay in silence on the floor for probably another half hour, drinking coffee and staring into the abyss that is my closet. People you can be silent with together. I lean my head on top of hers, a position from our childhood. My mother always thought we were trying to mold our minds together silently. She didn't want to believe we just liked each other, siblings weren't supposed to be like that.

"Mom?" Penelope's small voice at the doorway breaks both of our concentration; we didn't hear her coming. The doorway swallows her tiny frame, but her presence is felt immensely. She is the most adorable kid I've ever seen, rubbing her eyes, her hair in tangles and piles everywhere. She must do laps around her bed at night to get that kind of hairstyle. She has her duck pajamas on this morning. I frown. I can't remember the last time I saw Penelope in her pajamas in the morning time. It is quite unusual that I am the first one up today, before anyone else. I pat the space on the other side of me for her to occupy. She does without complaint and lays her head in my lap. I stroke her hair with the hand not holding coffee.

This is how we stay. The three of us jointly connected, never once uttering a word, speaking only through our souls. Silence has been a staple of my life these last few years, a haunting grip that pulls me down a dark drowning hole. Lately, I've been changing that demeanor, making silence a solace. Like all good things, they must come to an end, and the screeching doorbell sounds. I glare over at my sister, but she's already up and making her way over to the doorknob. The intruder on this moment is none other than the infamous Emma Woods. The tornado drops her off in true destructive fashion. She doesn't wait but a second before she is screaming about me.

"Hey, Grandma's here," I say sarcastically. Penelope giggles in my lap and it is pure childhood. I want to tattoo that feeling on my whole body, on my soul.

My mother stops her muttering about how I'm probably still asleep when she finally turns the corner and catches sight of Penelope and me.

"Mom." I regard her coldly.

"Miriam." She says in return, matching my tone. "What's going on in here?"

"Going to clean out the closet today." I don't look at her; I continue staring at Ben's side of clothes.

"Oh." There's too much delight in her voice for my sanity. "I have boxes in the car I could bring in." She doesn't even let me respond, just skips her merry little way out the door to retrieve them.

"Lock the door, Charlotte," I half jest. She can't move fast enough though; my mother is already back in the house with loads of cardboard in her arms.

"Have you started yet?" She's deflated after placing the boxes around us to see nothing has been pulled from any hangers yet.

"Yeah," I say. She does another sweep of the area, sure that she has missed something.

"Where?" She finally can't hold it in.

"Up here." I point to my head.

"Oh. Okay." She's trying not to burst. My mother is trying to be supportive. She turns her attention to Charlotte, who has returned with a cup of coffee for my mother. "Oh, Charlotte, honey you look wonderful." She's in pajamas. I'm actually dressed. "Miriam, you could at least do your hair, you know?"

"Yes, Mom. I know."

"What was Daddy's favorite shirt?" If the room hadn't been silent, I would have missed Penelope's question. The amount of courage she had to muster to ask it broke my heart. I stand up, reluctantly making her move off my lap, and walk over to his side of the closet. It doesn't take me but a second to find it. It was Ben's most prized possession; I even debated about burying him in it. His Ozzy Osbourne concert t-shirt. It's worn, almost paper thin now, but it was soft. I took it off the hanger and gave it to Penelope.

"Here. You keep it." Her eyes lit up. "That was Daddy's favorite singer. You can go find the CD and listen to it if you want." She was up and running now, ready to soak in any part of her father I gave to her.

"That is not suitable music for a child." My mother shrieks.

"Shut it." I bark. "Out!" I point at Charlotte as well when I say it. I need to do this alone. Charlotte understands like she always does. Pride outweighs the hurt in her eyes, she wants to fix it all for me but knows she can't. By taking this step alone, I'm showing her that I'm okay. My mother, however, is having a hard time dealing with the fact that she can't get her hands on the project and take over. I shut the door on them. The sound of my mother snapping about me to Charlotte echoes in my ear.

I know every shirt in this closet in detail; I know the stories behind him. The gray polo that he hated was his only dress up shirt, my favorite. It would cling to his arms tightly and he had to stretch at the sleeves just to make the shirt comfortable enough for him. He only wore it when I forced him to go to the theater with me. I would sit next to him in the seat and watch him tirelessly pull at the sleeves. I could have bought him a larger polo, a more comfortable one, but I secretly loved watching how he didn't fit in. Not because I wanted to mock him or bring him down, just because it reminded me how much he loved me. The theater wasn't his scene, but he went there for me.

I took the gray polo from the hanger. It felt almost like a sin to do so. For the last three years, I have left his stuff alone, a shrine to the dead out of respect. Now, I was breaking that wall. I lifted the shirt in front of me and let it encompass my face. It didn't smell like him anymore. Nothing did. I raised it back up, at arm's length, turned it around and opened the bottom of the shirt, pulling it over my head. It was big on me all over, hanging off my body as if I were wearing a blanket. I caught sight of myself in the mirror over the armoire. I am a widow.

I turn back to the hanging clothes and become possessed. I tear at every shirt and send hangers flying and clattering everywhere. I throw them behind me in a wild motion, tears flying. I punch the tower of jeans until they fall around me. A denim snowfall in April. I toss his shoes in the box near the door, and the belts hit the wall.

The hyperventilating sounds amongst the commotion must have sent a distress call to those in the living room because they burst through the door to find me in a tangled heap of clothes. I'm gasping for air in between my cries. My husband won't wear these clothes anymore. He will never pull at these sleeves again.

"OUT!" I scream. I don't need them. I have to do this myself. I have to do it my way. I feverishly sniff every shirt, searching for a trace of his scent. It's gone. He's gone. I can't even remember what he smelled like, and nothing is close enough to remind me. I know I liked his smell, I try to summon it up from my memory. It's gone. Memory fails me.

★ ★ ★

I emerge two hours later, with boxes all packed up and clothes tucked away, and the gray polo in the back of my own drawer. I'm keeping it. I point weakly at my bedroom. I don't want to carry all the boxes out. My mother's more than happy to do the rest of the job for me. Charlotte is just pleased to help me.

I make my way over to lay next to Penelope, drained from the task I had completed, longing to snuggle into her. She's the last bit of Ben I have that is smiling and breathing. She's soaking in words from all her dad's favorite CDs. I bury my head in the nook of her neck and sigh. I wrap my arms around her. It's that touch that isn't enough and all you need at once. So, you hold on tighter, longer.

"This one is my favorite so far." She leans her head on mine, much like I do with Charlotte. "Which one is yours, Mom?" She has chosen an old rock ballad.

"I don't have a favorite, babe." I know I'm disappointing her, but I haven't listened to music since Ben died, telling her I have a favorite would be a lie. I lay there with her letting the music play while Mom and Charlotte load the boxes off and head to Goodwill. The next CD is a mix. We're about halfway through it when it clicks over to a song that steals my breath.

Penelope notices the change in my body language. She shifts to catch a glimpse of me. I probably look like I've seen a ghost. This song.

"What is it, Mom?"

"This song, baby," I whisper.

"Can you tell me about it?"

"I don't know if I can." I want to cop out. I want to hold it in, but she needs to know her father. I hate emotions. I'm typically a cool-leveled person. I don't react. Lately, I've been all over the place. I hate crying the most. I can usually turn it off, numb myself to the act. There are all kinds of little tricks; biting the inside of your cheek, pinching your arm, or even thinking of something unrelated and irrelevant. None of the methods will work if I tell her the story. Not for this song. I try to push the tears that are falling back with my fingers; nothing is working.

"It's okay, Mom." She's telling me I don't have to share. She's letting me have an out. I won't take it because I am moving forward when I go back to that day. I give her Ben.

It was my graduation party. Everyone besides Ben and my friend, John, had left. John was an outcast, much worse than myself. People often walked past him in disgust, his appearance and level in society offended the popular kids. He wasn't even well-liked by the "freaks" of the school. But I liked him. He was nice. He was talented; the other kids didn't know it. He followed his own beat. I never believed in making people feel horrible just for being different. So, I was always kind to John. As an adult, I can see why he was so threatening to everyone at the time, he knew himself, liked who he was. Contentment such as that annoyed a generation that got to the next level by kicking others down.

There we were though, in the backyard sitting on the wooden swing just talking. My mom and dad had headed inside so it was just us. I sat in the middle.

We enjoyed an unguarded conversation as John and I always had. I was a little nervous how Ben would take it. We talked about parents, how they drove us crazy, how they let us down at times. Each one of us takes turns without interruption, without judgment. We consoled each other and formed an alliance.

Somewhere in the conversation, we all glanced at the stars. They drew us upward.

Silence fell upon us as we enjoyed the splendor. No charade to perform, no need to act cool. John was the first to break our quiet.

"Do you think there are extraterrestrials?"

I inwardly cringed for a second, Ben hung out with a cooler crowd when he went to school, so I didn't know how he would respond. The question would have been okay between just John and me. I felt our comradery was going to shift with the new change in subject.

"I think that sometimes," Ben spoke a quiet kinship with John. He didn't judge him. He didn't make him feel uncool for asking, calling him names or telling him that he was crazy. He didn't even hesitate.

I agreed that there were things we didn't know of or couldn't explain.

Our eyes never left the stars. But much like Grace Potter, I can't look at them anymore without pain.

EIGHT

Almost a week has passed since I cleaned out Ben's side of the closet, and I have yet to move anything over. I struggle with the guilt of wanting to and it being disrespectful to do. Penelope mentioned clothes shopping again. I told her I would pick her up early from Alexa's this weekend and we would go. That satisfied her. Now, I need to decide if I'll put clothes on that side or not.

I'm sitting in the grocery store parking lot, it's the first time I've ever waited to get out. I should wait for Oliver, right? We are friends now. He knows my shopping schedule. Is it too intimate though? I should just go in because I can meet up with him in the beans again, right? He was behind me that day, so maybe he doesn't get here at the same time I do, perhaps he is a little later. I should have thought of that and drove slower. I don't have another minute to decide because he raps on my window alerting me he's here.

"Hey! Ready to shop?" He smiles big. I made the right decision waiting for him. I nod in agreeance, and we begin our ceremonious strides into the building. I have to see if the familiar quiet was a fluke last time or if it can be recreated. I'll die if it was a fluke, I need that peace tonight. I crave it. We get one cart without even discussing it, and it feels familiar. As we walk through the entrance, I have to breathe to stop a panic attack from coming on. It could have been a one-time thing, and I'm making this all up in my head.

"What do you do for work?" I ask. If there's a possibility that the quiet won't work, I can always chat.

He taps on the cart to the beat of a song I don't know. "I'm a handyman. I run my own business and teach classes from time to time for my brother. He's a manager at the improvement store you were at."

"What's your middle name?"

"Don't have one." He shrugs.

"What's your last name?"

"Moore." He's loading up on oatmeal. He's not even asking any questions back. I hate when people do that. The narcissism of today's world allots for less back and forth conversation; we hope for someone to ask about us and make us the starlet that we never ask a single question back. It is downright rude and bad manners. One strike against Oliver tonight.

"Do you know how to fix a leaky sink?" I blurt out. We are right next to the produce, and he's picking between packages of green peppers. He just starts shaking his head. Oh, I guess plumbing isn't one of his handyman jobs. I look at the corn in front of me. What else could I ask? He doesn't seem in a talkative mood tonight. I think my previous narcissist thought can be ruled out.

"Stop thinking so hard; it's just corn." He shouts at me.

"I was just thinking I need to call a plumber, that's all." I shrug and pick up some corn, even though I don't need it. I don't know how to cook corn. I better look it up because it looks like we are having some this week. Charlotte, determined, gave me the task of preparing real dinners this week.

"You can't ask me to fix your sink, then ask a plumber." He frowns at me, sauntering over.

"You shook your head no," I say in defense.

He softens, "I was shaking my head because you are the most random person I know. I never know what is going to come out of your mouth. I can't prepare for it. I can fix your damn sink." He is holding on to the handle of the cart with me, leaning in.

"Well," I say, trying to gain some footing, "fix my sink, then." I push the cart away, and he lets go and stays standing in his same spot. "It drips. It's on my to-do list."

I've gotten a reasonable distance away when I hear him shout, "Only want me for my brains. You do know I have a body, right?" Everyone is staring at us. Well, not us. Me. Everyone is staring at me. The heat on my face could rival a Florida summer day. I whip my head back and flip him off. He's just smiling. Cocky ass smile. Two can play.

"Yeah. Yeah. You're a Greek God in modern times making women all hot and bothered around you, but you fix sinks better." I shout back. The old ladies nearby are chuckling. I gain a beautiful alabaster pink shade on his face for the remark. Worth it. He shakes his head at me and marches over to where I'm propped against the cart, waiting. When he reaches me, he instinctively puts his hand on the helm of the cart and leans in to gather my attention, so I hear his whisper.

"What is it with you and the canned good section?" I can tell he is on the precipice of laughter. I look to my left. Kidney beans. Again. I can't help the crazed cackling escaping my body. I think I'll buy some kidney beans today. I throw two cans in the cart.

"Thank God, I'm starting therapy again. I seriously am crazy, but if it doesn't work these bad boys will be in my cupboard waiting for me."

"I like you." He says. A simple admission. It could mean anything, from the innocent I like you as a person, to the intimate I'd like to fall in love with you. It sobers me up.

"I'll text you about the sink."

"Okay." He is curt, smile completely gone. Those are our last words. He sensed my shift at his admission, and he isn't foolish enough with his heart to pry further. I don't blame a smart person like that.

★ ★ ★

I don't usually go this way home. It isn't on my way at all, it's thirty minutes out of the way, to be frank. I'm not even here to pick up food this time; Charlotte won't allow it anymore. She has banned fast food from the house, all except the occasional taco from a restaurant Charlotte deems worthy. My car still hasn't made it back on to the road that will lead me home.

I'm parked in the church parking lot. There are so many churches nearby that I didn't need to go to this particular one. Here I am. The church holds a support group meeting for the grieving every second Monday of the month. It isn't even the second Monday of the month. It is the middle of the month, almost the end. They won't even be holding a session here for another three Mondays. I have no intention of going to that meeting. My car just took me here. The steeple is gorgeous atop the church. I wish we had Ben and Amelia's funerals in such a beautiful church like this. Maybe it would have made it easier, coming out only to look up from the window of your car and gaze upon a marvelous thing like this church. I bet when it rains it's still beautiful.

The newly painted red doors look inviting on the front of the pale white building. It is adorned with spring wreaths on either side of the doors. Daffodils line the walkway to the entrance. The buildings grown up around it pale in comparison; it still holds its essence. The white brick hint at a pure virginal aspect, not in an unattainable way. Not like some churches. No, this one contains hope for a clean slate. A fresh start.

I put the car in drive and head home. I'm already later than I said I would be.

★ ★ ★

After our shopping Sunday afternoon, we come home to Charlotte cooking a large dinner. I'm not sure my sister understands that there is just three of us sometimes, she cooks like an Italian mother feeding the village. We chomp down as much as we can, then Penelope puts on a fashion show for us with her new clothes. I plan on staying up late and doing laundry so she can wear her new clothes at school tomorrow. I don't long to go to bed all day now. All week I've woken up, got dressed, and walked Penelope out to the bus after we've had breakfast. So this is life? This is what it was meant to feel like.

Penelope and I offer to do dishes since Charlotte cooked, and she gladly props her feet on the dining room table while we get to work. She looks worn today. I feel guilty. I've been putting all the housework on her still, not taking on my share. She uproots her life to come here and help me then I make her do all the work. She cooks a lot better than me. I won't be taking over that chore anytime soon, but dishes I can handle.

"Where does this go?" I'm holding up a colander at Penelope. She points to the cabinet.

"This?" Whisk. Another point.

I lift the grater and draw a blank on its place of residence also.

"That goes in that cabinet." She says as she points, then turns around to rinse off the plates for the dishwasher. I look at the clean dishes in the dishwasher that I said I would unload and I have no idea where any of them go. I'm frustrated.

"This is bullshit." I slam my fist on the countertop.

"What?" Charlotte runs in rubbing her eyes. She must have fallen asleep.

"I don't know where anything goes in my kitchen." I flail my arms around me for emphasis. Penelope shrinks at the sink, Charlotte shrugs. Nobody wants to say the truth to me. I haven't done dishes in three and a half years. Penelope or someone else has. I haven't taken her clothes shopping for that long, my mother and my in-laws have.

"It's okay, Mom." Penelope begins, but I cut her off.

"No, it is not. I'm rearranging the kitchen. I will know where everything is." I'm determined. "And then I'm going to get some paint because these cabinets are an eyesore, and I'm going to install new floors, and I'm going to do the walls." My excitement is radiating, changing the somber tone the kitchen was beginning to hold. We start to bounce off ideas for the kitchen with each other, Charlotte's sleepy state forgotten. I rearrange the cabinets and familiarize myself with everything once again.

Two hours later, Charlotte is writing our ideas in a notepad, and we are giggling at the silly ideas Penelope is coming up with for the flooring. I feel pleased at this moment. I feel healthy. I am alive.

"Since I live here now, can we please discuss the sink in the bathroom? The dripping all night is sending me over the edge." Charlotte whines.

I laugh at her. "I asked Oliver to come fix it. He won't be able to for a few weeks, though, so you'll have to hang in there." The mentioning of Oliver seems to perk up my sister a bit. The prospect of Oliver fixing the sink gets her evil matchmaker tendencies cranking. It, however, does not make Penelope happy.

"Who is Oliver?" The inquisition of my seven-year-old daughter is punctuated by her hand on her hip. This is the same girl who suggested pink and purple cabinets five minutes ago with a fit full of uncontrollable giggles.

"Just a friend. I asked him to come fix the sink." I broach it carefully and watch my daughter stare at the to-do list on the refrigerator.

"I'm going to take a shower and go to bed." She stomps off, out of the kitchen.

After a few minutes of both Charlotte and I looking at the spot that she once occupied, we both simultaneously look at each other. There is a weird vibe left in the room, something we never thought of addressing or questioning. Would Penelope be okay if I ever started dating again? That was quite foolish of us not to think of, how my daughter would feel at the potential of someone filling her father's shoes.

"I guess Penelope isn't ready for number seven." Charlotte mumbles.

"Makes two of us."

NINE

'Being entirely honest with oneself is good exercise.' Out of all the Sigmund Freud quotes the waiting room wall could house, the one chosen has to be the most ridiculous. It is one of those wall deco stickers in black stuck against the light blue wall. Is there a catalog for therapists to purchase this kind of décor? It's like the doctors in the practice are trying to remind their patients what they're here for before going back into the tiny room. You are here to divulge your secrets, the sins of your personality, the things you can't escape but avoid. I'm not sure it's good exercise, though, you leave here wanting to jump from the bridge after that. And there is one half a mile away from here.

I was back at therapy, ready to try again and give an honest effort. This time Charlotte didn't make the appointment, I did. The doctor is going to have to do things on my terms if we are going to get anywhere. I have a real possibility of another panic attack in five minutes, and the waiting room décor is starting to wig me out. Zen garden in one corner, trickling water in another. I never thought I'd be happy to hear the good doctor call my name.

My journey down the hallway behind Dr. Pierce is riddled with the shrinking feeling again as if the walls are going to squeeze the life out of me, but I shove it down. Not today. I am in control. I am here for Penelope. It makes it easier to breathe saying Penelope's name in my head. She will become my new mantra, my meaning for living. The doctor keeps looking back frequently, me being a flight risk and all. Fast learner, I appreciate that. He even decided to switch rooms on me this time. The new room gives off a more welcoming vibe and the demons squeezing my lungs ease up. The walls are painted a mellow color, light orange, unlike the deep red of the last one. The furniture is bright. Even the sun is shining through making the room glow. This must be the happy room. I bet they put a lot of thought into the decoration of the treatment rooms.

"So, Miriam," he's apprehensive when he speaks, questioning how he should approach me this time, "I want you to feel safe in your therapy, so I thought we could go over what is expected here first. I have to push you in some areas, and I will stay back in others. It's your job, as we go along, to tell me what areas are hot subjects for you and what is okay. It's my job to tell you the same about myself, what behaviors are okay with me from a patient and what is not. Your exit last session was because we didn't do our parts, and I apologize and hope to change that. Somethings are out of our control, but I appreciate that you respect my time and commit to your therapy. Your turn."

I commend this approach, seems Dr. Pierce has put in a lot of thought and effort on his part just for me. "Okay," I start to feel confidence grow in my chest, "I don't want to talk about the details of my husband's death just yet."

"Okay." He jots it down. "Anything else?"

"I don't talk about Ben or Amelia."

"Ever? Or not now?" He asks, pen poised in the air to put my following words down on the chart. That was the actual question, wasn't it? The turning point in all my progress, to finally stop running daily. I could ignore those demons all day; I had been the last several years, becoming a pro at avoidance. Was I ready to stop, turn around, and face the dead?

"Um." I think about it. It won't be progress if I say never, but I can't promise the doctor it would be anytime soon. "Not never. But not soon."

"No one knows until the moment. If you mention them, I'll let you lead. I won't push you."

"Thank you." I sit back on the couch, a weight off my chest. I might grow to like therapy after all.

"I am okay with your run out last time. I don't suggest making a habit of it, but I understand what happened. You had a flashback, didn't you?"

"Yes," I whisper, scared it may trigger another.

"Next time you feel the panic attack coming on, I want you to breathe and focus on counting or on a picture of a wide open field with no fences."

"Okay." He understands.

"So, let's begin this session. What do you feel like talking about today? What's something you hope to accomplish when you walk out the door?"

"I hope to make it to the end of the session." I blurt. He chuckles making me feel fond of him. "I'd like just to get the feel of doing therapy. This isn't my first time, but I've felt rushed before." I'm honest with him, something I always felt was taboo even in therapy. If you let too much truth in, they are sure to see the crazy and lock you up. At least that is what I've come to believe.

He sits back and takes in what I'm saying, and what I was not. His chin rests in the crook of his first finger and thumb as he strokes his left cheek in thought. I'm not going to be a simple patient for him, and I have the real possibility of getting stuck and making no progress. I hope he is up for the challenge.

"I think we can manage that if you promise to at least try for me. Push your boundaries a little more each time you come in. I won't push you, but I can help guide you. I think you are capable of doing it on your own every week. You came back after the panic attack and made the appointment yourself, that shows progress."

I release a sigh of relief. Holy crap. This doctor is impressive already.

"Wait. Every week?"

"Yes, I think that is best until we come to a good point where we can taper off. When you don't need me as much."

Oh okay. Not permanently. I can do this. Every week isn't indefinite. I won't be crazy forever, will I?

"What shall we talk about today, Miriam?"

"Charlotte." I smile. "Let's talk about my sister." I spend the rest of the hour regaling the doctor with stories of my sister, and we even discuss my mother, acknowledging that we will eventually need to spend more time talking about my issues with her. Possibly my challenge for next week, as the doctor said, I need to push myself.

When I get home, Charlotte and Penelope have already had dinner and are on to a small aunt and niece nail painting party. Penelope is painting Charlotte's nails a dark blue, one of her favorite colors, and doing a better job than I ever could at the age of thirty-one. She has the knack for girly stuff, probably passed down in the genes from whoever gave it to Charlotte. They are being carefree, laughing about silly noises you can make with your mouth. I admit I'm a little jealous sitting here in my corner of the world being a voyeur to their interaction. I'm still decompressing from my therapy session, so I chose to be a silent observer.

"Will you get the door?" Charlotte asks, annoyed with me since I missed the first time she asked.

"Oh, sorry. I was in my head there for a second." I say as I stand, heading for the door. I'm not sure what guest to expect at this time of night. When I pull back the door, I'm face to face with an unfamiliar woman younger than Charlotte, but not by much. "Hello," I say.

She fumbles with her hands, rolling them repeatedly as if her speech is failing her. I look for any sign of trouble, but she is not bleeding, limping or crying. Her porcelain skin isn't marred by any slash wounds of a knife or even tears. Her makeup is well in place in a thought out way that tells me she took great mind of her appearance today. Her hair is light brown and down in wavy curls. Her makeup has a flick in the eyeliner, helping to bring out the natural almond shape of her eyes. She chose a green shadow that draws out the brown flecks in her eyes. Her clothes are wrinkle free and casual, another thing she must have thought out. However, her confident appearance does not line up with her nervous body language.

The pause in the conversation has drawn a crowd around me, the members of the manicure brigade have come to my side to get a peek at what is going on. I'm still not sure myself what the stranger on my stoop wants. She is biting her lip and looking around the driveway, the yard, the porch, the wall, anywhere but my face.

"Can I help you, sweetie? Are you okay?" I am worried about this woman who came calling so late in the evening.

"Are you Miriam Jones?" She squeaks out. Her words are rushed as she forces them out of her body, demanding they don't hold much meaning to them so that she may get through the speech she has practiced.

"Yes." I draw out my words, worried where this conversation is leading. She doesn't look professional enough to have any legal business here.

"I'm Gabrielle Novan. My father," Before she can get the rest of her sentence out I hold my hand up stopping her. The last name hit me like a bullet train in the heart. *Mike Novan, 60, was allegedly drunk when he veered over the center line of Briar Road colliding into the SUV of Benjamin Jones, 30, causing the vehicle to careen off the road where it flipped twice before crashing into a tree on the passenger side, killing Jones and his passenger . . .*

"No." I'm shaking my head and starting to close the door. "No." Her father took it all.

"Mrs. Jones, please, I just want to speak with you." She's pleading with me. "I want to talk about that night. I want to tell you . . ."

"No," I shout. I slam the door in her face. In that beautifully done up face that is now dripping with tears. The makeup she intended to wear to face the widow her father made, is now ruined. Her pathetic father, who couldn't just call a cab home. She thought about her outfit, what would be appropriate to wear to meet the family her father destroyed. She thought about her hair, what style would make a good impression. She thought about her speech, no doubt practicing and memorizing it. I suspect she chose her words carefully, debating over 'like' vs. 'as.'

"Who was that?" Charlotte asks. When I meet her quizzical eyes, I catch a glimpse of my confused daughter clinging to her side, and realize my outburst frightened her. I bend down, arms wide, inviting Penelope in for a hug. Her grip is tight and warm; it is alive. It isn't dead and cold like the hands that touched us at the funeral. The pity hugs, touches, kisses to the head we received from an insurmountable amount of people as they formed an assembly line around our chairs. They all wanted to say their piece, show their love, and offer their condolences, then leave before the disease of a dead spouse could rub off on them.

"That was the daughter of the man who wrecked into Ben," I whisper loud enough for Charlotte to hear me from her standing position, but soft enough that I manage to get them out without the accompanying tears. Penelope's body goes stiff in my arms, but the grip never falters. She knows her dad was in an accident, so many people said it around her, but she doesn't know that someone else caused the crash. She doesn't know it was me not just Mike Novan.

"Do you think you should have shut the door?" Charlotte approaches carefully, but it wouldn't matter how she came with the question, she would get the same reaction.

"I did. I do." I snap my head up to hers. "I don't want to hear what she has to say right now."

Charlotte doesn't take the bait to fight back. Instead, she looks proud that I know my boundaries. I let go of Penelope and tell her I'm sorry. I don't want her to be disappointed in me.

"It's okay, Mommy. You'll get there." I carry her off to her room for bedtime. She believes in me, and that's all I need. You may not always make the "right" decision on your path back to a healthy state of mind, you might not even make the popular one, but if you know in your heart that it will set you back if you chose to do it, then you made the correct one for you.

I read Penelope her story and tuck her in with three goodnight kisses. I shut off the light and make my way to the living room, to face my sister, except she's passed out on the couch. The night's events must have worn her out; I feel entirely drained myself. I pick her up and carry her to bed. She feels light, or maybe I'm just getting stronger from carrying the weight of the world on my shoulders.

With Charlotte and Penelope both tucked in and lightly snoring, I'm alone in the house. I stare out the picture window in the living room. In the quiet that encompasses me, I let myself admit that I'm curious what the speech would have sounded like had I allowed Gabrielle continue.

TEN

"**S**crew you, phone," I scream as I slam my hand on the nightstand in protest. I will not answer it. The vibrating stops and I'm satisfied. I lift my head to glance at the clock, five in the morning. Anyone who calls at that time deserves to be ignored. I nestle back into my pillow, hoping against all the odds to return to my dream of living in a mansion with lots of books surrounding me. I start to drift off, smelling the old leather binding of the books when the damn phone goes off again. Alrighty then.

"Whoever this is, I hope you choke on the next item of food you put in your mouth," I answer without looking.

"Would you like to go for a jog?" Oliver's baritone voice sends shivers down my spine. He's groggy sounding as if upon waking he thought of me.

"Is there a murderer planning to jump out and stab you on the trail?" I quip.

"What?" he laughs, but it's uneasy. I can hear the backpedaling his mind is doing. He didn't realize I wasn't a morning person, and that is no exaggeration by any means. I once dumped the entire contents of Ben's top nightstand drawer on his head because he asked too many questions when I first woke up.

"If they are then sure, I'd love to go. I want to watch anyone who calls me at five in the morning to go exercise die a slow torturous death."

"I hadn't realized you wouldn't be up. I thought you were getting

Penelope ready for school." He's meek.

"At five o'clock in the freaking morning? What? She is seven years old. What the hell does she need two and a half hours of prep time for?"

"So, no run?" He chances.

"I don't run. If I'm running, it is because someone is chasing me or I'm chasing to kill someone."

"But it'll be fun." I hear him trying. He wants to be with me this morning, and I'd rather eat an entire box of rusty razors covered in bird shit and dipped in acid before running for fun.

"Hang up."

"What?"

"If you know what is good for you, you will hang up this phone."

"I see I've called you at a bad time. Next time I will try later with a coffee and a doughnut."

"Bye."

"Bye, Miriam. Um, sweet dreams." I click the phone off and slam it back down on my nightstand. I can't help smiling to myself because the cute boy thinks of me when he wakes up. Crap. That's not good. I groan into my pillow.

"Mommy?" I hear the croak of a tiny voice in the doorway of my bedroom. I lift my head off the pillow and whip my hair out of my eyes.

"Yes, baby? You okay? Nightmare?"

"Who was that on the phone?" she's skeptical, at the tender age of seven she is a fine detective.

"Just Oliver, baby. Sorry to have woken you, go back to sleep. You can come sleep in here with me if you want." I throw back the covers on my side of the bed, inviting her in, but warmth is not at all what I am met with.

"He calls you?" She is on high alert.

"He wanted to know if I wanted to go jogging." I feel like I have to justify my calls to a seven-year-old, but it is just her and me now. And Charlotte.

"Are you going?" She crosses her arms in a scolding manner. Whoa, sassy.

"Are you kidding me?" I laugh at the idea of running.

"Good. Keep telling him no. I don't like him." With a sharp turn on her heels, she trots off down the hallway to her room. I shift the covers sheepishly back onto the bed. I need to have a talk with my mother about number seven. I don't want to date anyone else, that's why I got married in the first place, but I don't think the idea sits well with Penelope at all and I'd hate for Oliver to end up with a shiner like Justin.

* * *

The steam of the shower clouds the mirror in the bathroom and puts a sheen of moisture on the walls. I bury my face deep into the cascading stream of the water, allowing it to combine with my tears as if I weren't crying. When people see a woman who doesn't cry or buckle we immediately equate her with strength. Little girls long to emanate her. Men ask their significant others why they can't be more like her.

Instead, she has them all fooled. While they shower her with praising words, complimenting her strength and ability not to let things get to her, she is dying inside and just hiding it well. But at night, when she steps into the crashing spray of water, she'll sink down to the cold tile. Covered by the sound of the pounding water, and masked by the curtain, vaguely protected by the closed bathroom door, she'll let her body begin to shake. Ever so slightly she'll shudder, as she battles the breakdown. She'll allow the pain to fall about her only for a short while, and even in the solitude, she will fight because she fears being sought out. A small noise will escape her lips, and it will strangle her, she'll pity it. She wants to give in and cry but scolds herself that giving in is a weakness. She knows she has to knock it off before she is discovered, before her cover is blown.

So she'll push herself back up from the floor of the shower, thrusting her face into the cascade of hot water. There her tears will wash away, mixing with the darkened water from her makeup until it reaches the drain. Washed away from history as if it never happened, because to everyone else it never did, and she carries on that way.

I attended the book fair at Penelope's school today as a volunteer. I tended to my duty behind the cash register and even chanced to make a friend with another mom. It went well, not a single glitch or hand strangled the life from the day. Nothing to report that would lead to the mess of a woman clutching the shower wall, drowning in a waterfall. I had lived a full day on my own today, without my husband. I was the picture of healing on the outside, so the world accepted me with open arms because I looked like I was coping magnificently. Here in the shower, I show my truth; I am broken. My right shoulder can still sense the weight of the woman's hand who came over to tell me how sorry she was to hear about my husband. I shift so the water can wash it away.

My back still bears the weight of the many hands that informed me they were happy to see me again. I wash them away. They never showed at my door when my husband died, because death could be contagious. But they were all there today, acting as my support team. What a fraud. It hurt my heart. It bothered me more than the women who stood on the sidelines whispering about me and pointing, at least they were honest. I was a pariah. I didn't fit in.

In society, we idolize the person who has the strength to make their loved one's death a stepping stone that moves them on to bigger and better things. We, however, look down upon the grieving who simply cannot "get over it" and move on. Being alive should be reason enough to celebrate, they made it another day. Even from the privacy of the bathroom surroundings, I know that it isn't enough. It's not enough to just breathe. I know I need to move on. But it isn't fair. Those women today got to go home to their spouses, maybe even hug them a little tighter because of the sight of me. I didn't.

I planned the rest of time with Ben. I didn't plan until the end of his life or mine. I planned for forever. I got a measly six years of marriage. Six. Six years of inside jokes, laughter, love, waking up next to him, falling asleep next to him, hearing about his day, telling him about mine, taking pictures with him. It wasn't enough, but I was not the judge in that. I was not the jury. I didn't get to make any decision on the matter. I didn't get to voice my opinion. Fate took it upon herself to strip parts from me that I needed. I was dead but walking. Now I am trying to revive myself, and it is so damn hard.

A wave came over me after the book fair, and I hadn't the heart or strength to talk to Penelope or Charlotte tonight. I set my idle hands to the task of boxing up the rest of Ben's things. Trinkets he kept. Some I placed in Penelope's room, the rest I put in a box for donation. I thought about saving some for myself, but considering I spend too much time wearing a hole in my side of the mattress, it would be best if I just cleaned him from the space. It hurt like hell. Or worse. I can't imagine hell being the worst feeling. In the Hell that everyone describes, you are dead. Death only bothers the living. This was worse than Hell.

I'll never be anything more than Ben's widowed wife. If I date or remarry, I won't even have his name anymore. I have no ties to him. Nothing beyond the grave. Just like every person who explains the Bible, 'til death do you part, I am no longer married to Ben nor will I be in the afterlife. Penelope will always be his daughter. He will still be her father, of that they cannot strip her. It is set in stone. She will only ever have him to be responsible for her existence, to identify with. I won't. I have been holding on to something I cannot even have, and it hurts.

I turn off the shower, the water has grown frigid, but I don't step out just yet. I stare at the knob that I turned with my left hand, my ring still shining at me. I am no longer a wife. I am a widow. I am just me. I'm no longer Mrs. Jones. I am the former Mrs. Jones. I now have to say things like, "my late husband." I struggle to swallow past the knot in my throat. Closing my eyes, I lean my forehead against the cold tile of the shower wall. I blindly reach for the shower curtain and throw it open. I stand, for several minutes, allowing the remnants of the shower to drip from my hair tips to my toes.

I lift my head and move to the opening of the shower and grab my towel. I dry myself off and cocoon my goose-pimpled skin in the terry cloth. I slide my hand across the glass of the mirror when I step out, clearing just enough space to see my eyes. Hollow. They used to be so filled with life; if you look at our wedding photos, you would think I wasn't the same person from just my eyes alone. I walk out the door, ignoring the glances shifting to me from Penelope's bedroom as I pass by on my way to my own. Once I cross the threshold, I shut the door and head straight for the foreign side of the bed. Ben's side. I haven't touched or dare let anyone sit on this side for three years. I'm surprised it doesn't gobble me whole when I collapse upon it. Beds don't hold feelings though. They don't turn into cursed objects with the power to strike out those who rest upon it. They are not holy ground. I shift my body so that I am laying on my side facing Ben's nightstand. I should say the extra nightstand. I cleaned it out tonight. There is nothing left of him in it. I lay my hand on the top and slide it to the wall, where the alarm clock once perched. Not anymore. Nothing remains. I stare at the grain, memorizing the design.

Before my eyes close in sleep, I slip my ring off and place it in the top drawer.

ELEVEN

"**C**an you hand me the Phillips head?"

Underneath my bathroom sink, Oliver's shirt has been pulled upward just a little by the raising of his arms. It is enough to leave Charlotte and me ogling from the safety of our bench, otherwise known as the bathtub ledge. The sliver of skin peeking at us contains a manly trail of hair leading to a destination somewhere below the waistband of his jeans. It also suggests that maybe Oliver does spend some time in the gym, the coveted "V" most people work endlessly trying to obtain, is present on this man.

My sister was surprised to see a man following behind me when I came back from grocery shopping this evening. She was even more pleased to know she didn't have to help carry in groceries, as of late she had been acting like those bags weigh a hundred pounds. I even caught her pretending to be asleep one Friday so she wouldn't have to help. I don't understand why it is a big deal, the putting away part is my least favorite, not bringing them in. None the less, Oliver was a fine gentleman and offered to assist. He's Charlotte's favorite even more now that he is under the sink fixing the faucet drip she can't stand.

Neither of us hears his command. When he slides out from under the sink to inspect if we're still nearby, it is evident that we've been caught. Charlotte is not fazed and continues to ogle Oliver's ridiculously muscular body openly. I, however, do my best to cover my guilty look.

"What was that?" I ask I attempt to keep my voice calm, failing miserably. I sound just like Penelope when she was a toddler, and I caught her rifling through the magazines in the living room, tearing pages from them. Her voice became high pitched, letting me in on the not-so-secret secret that she was lying. The evidence was right in front of me, but she denied to the end. Much like I am doing now. Like mother like daughter.

Oliver is kind enough to laugh it off as if I had just not heard him because the built-in vanity muffled his voice, and again repeats his request for a Phillips screwdriver. I promptly hand him the tool, and he rolls the top portion of his body back under the cabinetry, never once taking his eyes off me. Eyes like Oliver's can see into your soul, the intimacy of it leaves you feeling naked. Exposed without a wall to hide behind. I don't want someone to look at me as if they can read my secrets; I don't want to know my own secrets. Though they can strip you bare, his eyes have a sense of calm to them. Maybe he can see my secrets and accept them, not run. He has been watching me intently tonight ever since he noticed my ring missing at the grocery store. He didn't say anything, but I've caught his gaze landing on my bare finger fifteen times now. I'm not sure what else his eyes hold; is it hope? I ignore it because hope is the last thing he should have for a girl like me.

When Penelope saw my empty finger this morning, however, she immediately copped an attitude that would terrify a thirteen-year-old, and from what I've heard they are fearless. It is apparent, although she is slowly getting a stronger parent back, she is having a difficult time with the changes of me moving forward. I am as well, but it doesn't bode well with my mother to show my outward struggle with all this advancement, so I keep it hidden. Fake it until you make it. Penelope was not as good of an actress. She showed a lot of distaste towards Oliver the last time he was mentioned, so I left the stone unturned and didn't mention he was coming over tonight when I dropped her off at Alexa's house. He is just a friend, but I'm assuming that the fact that he is male won't convince my daughter. One thing at a time, I'll deal with the ring first.

I take my seat on the bathtub ledge again next to my sister and lay my head on her shoulder. Charlotte's head nestles on top of mine almost immediately. She has been so quiet the last couple of days while I cope with boxing up Ben's stuff. I'm starting to miss the annoying way she butts in and throws her decided opinion around. I had a crazy idea last night of telling her so but thought better of it. For now, I'll enjoy our time in the bathroom, staring at my friend's stomach which he doesn't bother to cover up when he lays back down. The bastard.

After a while, Charlotte's head begins to feel heavy upon mine. It is a relaxed weight one can only accomplish in sleep. I kick Oliver's leg to gather his attention, which I'm granted without hesitation. I motion my eyes upward toward Charlotte in question. With a nod, he confirms my suspicions. A small smile spreads across my lips; my mind plays back to the days when I would carry her off to bed after she had fallen asleep in my lap while watching a movie. We hardly fought, rare among siblings, but it was true for us. Our personalities weren't always as opposite as they are now, I used to be more like Charlotte. Not since the accident. Back then we were so similar that we enjoyed the same hobbies, movies, music, and so much else it was hard to believe we were two separate beings. She is three years younger than I am, but I would always invite her to join my group of friends when they were over, she did the same. People around us just knew they got one when they were with the other.

Sadness sweeps over me because you can't have the old days back, the good days. You can't just place yourself into that mindset and time on a whim. Charlotte and I drifted as life turned to ugly adulthood, leaving us with little free time or faith. I asked her what had happened with her boyfriend, Arthur, but she didn't want to talk about it, always turning the conversation focus to me. She was selfless by nature, but I could tell it was a diversion tactic on her part. I needed to start being selfless as well, starting tomorrow I'm going to start focusing on Charlotte, Penelope, and Oliver. Start asking them more questions, find out more things, and make them feel important.

I mouth for Oliver to help me. He sets down his tools and effortlessly lifts his body from the floor, not even a single groan which is common among men who work so hard with their hands and bodies. He lifts Charlotte up in his arms and off my head, motioning for me to lead the way. I take my place in front and whisper a warning not to hit her head on the doorway. He held a kind of crooked adoring smile, but I don't look for long, the twist in my chest warns me of the damage I could do to him. Don't do it, Oliver. You don't want me. I focus on Charlotte because she looks so small in his arms. I'm grateful for the way he is caring for her as if he knows how special she is to me. My mother said I used to pray every night for a baby girl. "God must have really liked you," she would say. My mother hated being pregnant; she even blamed Charlotte on my prayers. After she had Charlotte, she immediately told the doctor to tie her tubes. She wasn't a bad mother. You can't ask much from a person who doesn't have it to give, she was never meant to exceed at the job.

We get Charlotte in her room and settled under the covers. Oliver steps back watching as I fuss over tucking her in and making sure her pillows are settled comfortably under her head. My sister brought out a maternal nature in me. I brush the hair off her face. My mother would have left you on the couch to sleep if you dozed off there, she wouldn't dare try to carry you to bed. Hell, she wouldn't even throw a cover on you. I kiss Charlotte's forehead and follow Oliver from her room, closing the door behind us as we cross the threshold. I spin around and land right into a hard chest. Oliver.

Before I can finish uttering an apology, he has his hand in my hair tilting my head back. His other arm instinctively wraps around my back, further assisting in tipping me backward. He doesn't stare into my eyes for long. He swiftly plants a gentle kiss on my forehead and lets go. He turns around and walks back to the bathroom, where he quickly finishes packing his tools.

Why are forehead kisses more than regular kisses? Why does your whole body tingle inside? A kiss on the lips can be misconstrued as lust, but a forehead kiss always means you care. Oliver cares. I want to follow him, find out what the heck that was, let him care for me until I'm healthy again. I want to damage and ruin him so that I can feel love again. It would be one-sided, I could never love another man, only Ben. I want to just feel it for me. I want to give in to being selfish, but I promised myself not to be. So I stay.

He walks out while I stay standing in the hallway.

Oliver cares.

* * *

My mother showed up today, unannounced, unwanted, and ultimately unfazed by my attitude. Her yellow legal pad ever present in her hand, as she wanders around the house like a cat on a hunt. Yellow. The color yellow was starting to set off a rage inside me. Yellow is meant to be a warming color, energetic, positive, but Emma Woods manages to make it an intrusive blast. She thinks it is her right to be my judge, jury and now my social worker? Walking about my house with her pen and pad poised in hand while doing her surprise inspection. And Sunday was supposed to be a day of rest.

Charlotte is seated on the corner of the couch glaring at my mother. She is the only one who could take up such a manner with Emma Woods and have an actual effect. I can feel my mother's unease radiating across the room, one measure of Charlotte's body language has her second-guessing her mission here today. Which is what exactly? She wipes her finger along the bookshelf, and I can bear it no longer.

"What are you looking for? Is dust on the list? Did I miss that? Is that a clause somewhere?" My mother expects the reaction from me; she doesn't recoil from the venom spewing in her general direction.

"I am just making sure that everything is going well over here, it is part of our agreement, Miriam." She must be joking, but that is unlike her. She doesn't have a sense of humor.

"This was not part of our agreement, Mother." I spit the last word out as if it were a sour piece of candy puckering my mouth in disgust.

"I have to make sure you are keeping to the list, that there is a change going on here. You didn't seriously think that I would watch you pack Ben's closet and assume you were doing everything else, did you?" With that, she walks herself into my bedroom. I stomp after her and my trusty sidekick, Charlotte, is not far behind.

When we cross the doorway, we take in the sight of my mother looking around like she is a house inspector making sure the general state of the room is safe for purchasing. It gives me a small bit of pleasure to see her face falter when she takes in Ben's empty nightstand. Short-lived joy as I realize the nightstand would never look that way if my mother had never given me the list. How long would it have taken me to come to this place on my own? I can't bear to answer even myself, though I know the answer.

"I'm pleased to say things seem to be improving." My mother's prim voice is back in place, and it's taking all I have and Charlotte's firm grip not to punch her face. She takes my silence as something other than restraint, missing the fact that she makes me prone to violence. "I don't hear the sink dripping anymore."

"Oliver fixed it." I grit out. The mention of a male's name perks my mother right up. I messed up.

"Oliver?" she hums, "Is he who you are seeing? I notice you aren't wearing your ring anymore, dear." Now it is dear. Now I am worthy of a term of endearment because of a man.

"Stop." Charlotte's voice is flat and even, a tone nowhere close to a yell but a warning all the same. "Go home, Mom, that's enough." My mother is shocked, she's not used to this behavior from Charlotte, and it hurts. My sister is the peacemaker, born into the job by my mother's favoritism for her. I see her weary eyes from this journey with me has caused her patience to run thin. I can't say I'm proud of it, though at this moment I'm thankful for it. I don't want to strip my sister of her qualities in character that have afforded my mother and me to exist on the same planet in a non-violent harmony, but I'm shamelessly giddy she has chosen my side today.

My mother nods to her. Recovering. Always poised. "I hope you can continue all the progress you've made, Miriam." Her voice is tender when she says it, she truly means it. She walks to the door and leaves. Finally. Charlotte doesn't linger on the moment or look to rehash it; she has perfected the art of knowing when to speak and when not to. An art most people don't bother attempting. Instead, they fail to miss another's body language and cues favoring to press on for their selfish attempts to quench their curiosity.

"Let's have some coffee before we get ready to pick up Penelope."

She says as she walks towards the kitchen.

I am still trying to master cooking as per Charlotte's request. It's been a while, and the saddle is rusty, but no one makes a peep when they are munching on a burnt under-seasoned lasagna at dinner time. They even make sincere compliments on my attempt. I could let the intrusive thought that my failing at dinner meant I would fail at everything, the nagging feeling inside my head begging to take over, but I won't. I'm looking at my progress, at the effort I've made, thanks to the good doctor and his teachings. I bet he will be pleased to hear it at our next session. I'm required to keep a thought journal and work on identifying what automatic thoughts I have and how they are dysfunctional to my progress. Together we are working on how to change the thought process to better handle the feelings that come with the daily situations. I won't dare let him touch on the accident, so this keeps his idle hands busy with healing me.

I believe in Dr. Pierce more than any other therapist I've attempted to see. Looking at my beautiful family here tonight, gathered at the table, I feel happy. Something I haven't had in a long time. He knows his stuff. I'll have to swallow my pride and tell him. I was in full acceptance of being a broken, unfixable person. I might have to rethink that. We clear the table and begin a relaxing game of cards. It has become an almost nightly ritual to play some game after dinner. I look forward to it. I would once curl right back up in bed or the couch after eating some fast food for dinner.

However, the game isn't bringing spirits up tonight. One trip to the bathroom has turned Penelope into an investigator. "What is this screwdriver for?" I'm met eye-to-eye with Oliver's Phillips screwdriver, the one I didn't hear him ask for because I was too busy ogling him.

"Um, that looks like Oliver's. He must have left it here when he fixed the sink the other night." I start shuffling the cards and dealing the next round, hoping the heat from my right side is a weird body malfunction and not the rage of a seven-year-old. I was wrong. My body is fine.

What transpires next can only be compared to an exorcism, I imagine. Penelope throws herself straight into a fit, one so monumental she begins to curse, words I didn't know she learned yet. I sit there at the table watching the rampage unfold in her face and body. I freeze. I honestly don't know what to do about a tantrum. Her arms fling wildly, colliding with anything and everything on a surface in the dining room. She throws the cards all over the room, toppling over the chair, and breaking her glass. I glance over at Charlotte for assistance, but she is not stepping in. She points to me. Crap. I look back at the angry demon that was once my adorable peaceful child and decide to let her ramble on a bit longer while I delve into my mind for every parenting article I ever gleaned.

It is scary, the calm that comes over you before you take on a storm. Other moms must know what it is like because other moms are not as useless as I am. But I have to do it. I've come too far, and Penelope needs me, though I don't think she'll agree in a second or two. The feeling of every emotion slowly drains from my body. I know where she is coming from, but I have to come from a place of authority and love. I hold my hand up for her silence, which I am quickly granted as she falters in surprise.

"You will NOT speak to me like that," I start, "I run this house. I am your mother, and I deserve respect. If you want it in return, then you will show it. Clean up this mess, now! This is unacceptable."

"Mom, I was just . . ." She pleads, but I must be firm. Today is a new day.

"Now." Her eyes are wide, a doe caught in the headlights as a car comes tearing around the bend. She doesn't move immediately, not until my face helps the words sink in. I watch a small glimmer in her eyes return, not tears, a spark. She nods respectfully and makes her exit to the kitchen for the dustpan and broom.

Kids like routine and boundaries, don't let them fool you, it's what makes them feel safe. They want to be free, but they want to know how far they can go. They want to be able to fully trust you'll stop them before they hurt themselves or others. In short, they want to know you won't allow them to become an asshole.

"As for Oliver, you will respect him." She pauses in her cleaning, resuming after a noticeable deep breath.

"I don't like him." I hear her mutter.

"I don't care. You will respect him." After her mess is cleaned, I tell her to go to her room for the rest of the night. The slamming door told me we would live to fight the Oliver battle another day, but I had won this one. Charlotte winks at me from across the table. This wasn't monumental on any parenting scale, a typical day for anyone else, but for Penelope and I this was the beginning of a better start. She was no longer the parent. That gleam in her eye was a child's and not an adult trapped inside. She got to be the kid again, punished for her wrongdoing. It was my responsibility to save us both from drowning. It can no longer be up to her.

TWELVE

The church parking lot has twelve cars: four red, three white, one silver, one blue, one green, two black. My car is one of the four reds; this should make me feel surrounded, supported, unified. Does your vehicle color choice have any significant meaning, an insight into the purchaser's mindset? Can you tell someone's personality by the color of car they drive? I think back to the day that we purchased my car, had it been a purposeful choice?

It was fall time. I know that for sure because I was bundled up and freezing waiting for the salesperson to come out and stalk us. I was confident they would jump on us like leopards, it was a Saturday after all. That was the only day of the week that Ben could go with me. I wouldn't go alone because I wanted his input. I was nervous to negotiate. Ben was better at it. He was poised and patient, never showing his cards or emotions. No one could read him, except for me and that was only granted by the years we had spent together.

We finally got the attention of a salesman and told him the car we wanted to have; I had done my research for months. I knew what I wanted. It boiled down to two on the lot, one black and one red. Why had I chosen the red one? I pinch my eyes shut harder to see the picture in my memory clearer. *"I want the red one." "You can have whatever color you want, dear." "I want the red one; it looks like fire."* I blink my eyes open. Fire. I wanted to feel alive in the car, to go fast as if I were blazing. Back then I longed to be put in the flames, to dance in the heat as it licked the sides of me with no fear. I was always alive and in the moment. I was drowning as of late. The flame had died out. It only remained in the color of the vehicle I drove. Cherry fire red.

I look around the lot. Even though I'm not that same girl, my car still stands alone. It's the only one that is bright and vibrant. Every other red is dull or burgundy. I bet they didn't choose it because they felt like fire. I convince myself that I'm just stalling. I better go into the building and get the first meeting over. I always hated support group. This one would hold a meeting every first and third Monday of the month. They have every intent on making you a participant in your healing. Some groups just meet once a month, other more severe groups once a week, I didn't choose either of those. This was the furthest one from the house, no chance of the town gossips loafing around the cellar.

I'm not a rookie at this. I'll go in the church and find the room, sit in one of the chairs either in a circle or rows. I'll listen to everyone tell their story, and everyone in the group will empathize, maybe give feedback if they feel so inclined to do so. In other groups, it's mainly the leader who speaks. I remember one thing for sure, I can pass on my story today. I don't have to share. It isn't a requirement, though your progress will be stunted without it. I remind myself that coming here was a big step for me, but I haven't stepped out of the car. Come on, Miriam, get in there.

I step out and stroll to the door. I'm in no hurry. I make it there, and as expected, the entry sign tells me which room will be conducting the Loss Support Group. Basement. Always in the dungeon, in the dark, down closer to Hell to divulge your truth and fight your demons before rising back up the stairs at the end of the night. I shake my head and carry on down the stairs and hallway to the entry of the room, stopping at the door. *Loss Support Group.* The sign on the door is clear that this is where I'm supposed to go. My brain is sending the command signals, but my hands won't listen, the muscles refuse to lift and pull open the doorknob. I can't do this.

I can't run. I throw myself against the wall opposite of the door instead and stare. Maybe for motivation. Maybe for answers. I have been dealing with Ben in my household, clearing stuff out and making myself move forward, but this is public. Hello world, I am a widow. I know what it is that I'm scared of saying out loud, I know what is going to break me, so I push it down. Bury it. The tears in my eyes blur the words on the paper sign. Loss. Behind that door, I will be bombarded with everyone's story, with everyone's loss. Twelve cars' worth.

My peripheral vision catches sight of someone coming down the stairs before the blood rushing in my ears quiets enough to hear them. Another latecomer. Another loss. I wonder if they refused to walk in for the same length of time I did. The meeting starts in three minutes according to my watch. I look at my shoes, hoping I won't draw any attention to myself, that I'll deter this person's interaction. I'm studying the laces on my Chucks when I feel the body plop beside me, grazing my elbow.

"Going in?" I look over at the woman intruding my bubble. She has a kind face, relaxed and open. I notice she is wearing scrubs. She must have just got off work at a hospital. Her dark hair slicked back into a ponytail, her face clear of makeup. The darkness of her skin makes the scar on her forehead more noticeable under the fluorescent lighting. I push my thumbs into my own scars. There is peace in hers; mine feel angry. From experience I surmise that this must be the group leader, the patience and training etched in her demeanor. She's also in no hurry to make meeting time and seems too healthy to be one of us coming to learn how to deal.

"I don't know," I admit. She nods and looks at her shoes and dusts a piece of lint off her pants.

"You know," she says fixating her stare on the door now, "you make no progress in the hallway."

"The hallway is progress. I made it out of the car." I huff.

"That's a cop-out."

"Excuse me?" I snap. She just shrugs, still looking at the door. She doesn't reply, and I'm ready to unleash on her when finally she drags her attention to me. Her auburn eyes scream of the depth behind them, the hell they've gone through, the clawing to get back out and away from what they've seen. They hold my attention.

"You can always do better than the hallway. The hallway is just another waiting room where you wallow in your pain. You don't have to talk, just sit. At least in there," she points to the door but never loses eye contact with me, "you'll be distracted by someone else's pain." She pops to her feet with ease and extends her hand.

She has to be the most curious group leader I have ever met. The others always made an emphasis on telling your story and healing yourself. No one has ever suggested I spend my time in the circle distracting myself with other's misery. I'm intrigued to see how she will run the meeting, and against my better judgment I take her hand and head through the door. It clicks behind me, and I know there is no turning back. No more waiting room.

"Hello everyone!" my hallway friend begins, "My name is Miranda, and I'm your support group leader." Just as I thought. "We meet every first and third Monday of the month unless I tell you otherwise, which brings me to the first order of business, this stupid phone contact sheet." She is met with groans. "I know. I know. But we have a few new faces, so go through the motions with me, huh? Check your name and number, make sure it is correct, or add it if you are new. This is the way I would contact you if we have a group meeting cancellation." She hands off the sheet to the girl nearest to her, she doesn't look a day over eighteen, and I start to panic inside. This feels like a huge commitment, and I'm not sure I can take the step. Deep breaths, like Dr. Pierce told me. I can do it. I sign my name and number when the sheet comes to me, and keep passing.

"I will start with my own story, like always, to get the wheels rolling. I was fourteen when my mother passed away. My father was abusive and hardly home. To deal with it, I took to drugs and alcohol young. When I was seventeen, I went to rehab for the first time. It didn't work, and I continued going in and out of rehab until I was twenty-six. We would discuss the beatings, the verbal tirade, the drinking, the using, and my abusive father. We would discuss everything but my mother. I didn't want to talk about it, deal with it, or raise a voice to it. I would always come out clean, fall right back in, climb out. Rinse. Lather. Repeat. One night I was with my father, he was drunk and decided to slash my tires. We argued in the most violent way, leading him to slash my forehead." She points to her scar. Her story is one she repeats twice a month, but even so, she needs a moment at this part. A pause to regroup. "The blood loss was great, but the choking made me fall unconscious. I was ready to die. Get it over with. That was until I saw my mother. She was that last picture I saw, and she told me to fight. When I woke up, I was in the hospital; I had beat the odds. My father was finally behind bars, where he needed to be to get clean. I started to go to counseling for the death of my mother instead of the abuse of my father. It was difficult, to put a voice to the pain I was really feeling. The abuse was simple, but the loss isn't. Not to me, and obviously not to you. That's why you guys are here tonight, that's why we are all here."

I glance around the room, but I'm the only one listening to Miranda, and she's directing her words straight at me. They've all heard the story before, but it was my first time. I understood the tranquility behind her scar now, her confidence to show it. She had made peace with the demon that put it there. I look at the palms of my hands, the raised ridges in each showed nothing but bitterness and hurt. There was no calm. The glass had shattered my skin the same as that night had shattered my world. The scar tissue was hard and unmoving. Sometimes my hands ached when I stretched them out, the reminder was profound and buried to the bone. I was dealing with the things Ben had left behind, but as Miranda had said, I wasn't giving a voice to the actual pain.

As the meeting took off, we started with the eighteen-year-old closest to Miranda. She had lost her boyfriend to suicide, and her story was hard to make it through without tears in her eyes. One after another, I heard stories of losing fathers, mothers, grandmothers, best friends, and a son to war. When the circle came to me, I quietly placed my hand up to pass. I had to give it to Miranda; no attention was drawn on me on her part, she quickly moved to Rick next to me as if it were no big deal. I think she was the only counselor to do that, not just for myself but for anyone in the group. Miranda was rare, and it made her good at this job, I could tell already it was her calling.

Rick finished his tale, the death of his wife. It hit close to home for me, and I couldn't help but divert my eyes to the floor, to my shoes, anything so that I would not give myself away. Rick and I may not be able to ever sympathize on the same level, but I feel the tightness of the shoes he is wearing. I was thinking of Ben when Rick finished his story, telling us every day was hard without her here. He turned to alcohol to cope and now was addicted. His eldest daughter didn't want anything to do with him anymore. I thought of Penelope. I had to stop my downward spiral before she became Rick's daughter's age before she could hate me permanently.

"If she doesn't have to share, then neither do I." The defiant voice of the man next to Rick brings me back to the present. I look over at the man. He has his arms crossed hanging on his belly just below his long white beard. He has a skully cap on, all black clothes and heavy biker boots. I didn't see a bike out in the parking lot during my vehicle count, so I assume this man is without his hog tonight. His beady little eyes fixed on me, wearing the pissy look of a toddler who was told to eat their peas or no dessert. His bushy white eyebrows furrow to the center, drawing deeper wrinkles in his forehead. Always has to be one in the group.

Miranda's voice breaks in. She is attempting to appease Henry, Mr. Hell's Angels, "You don't have to share if you don't want to, Henry, but you cannot blame her for your lack of sharing. Blame does nothing for personal growth, and you know it. It's a sorry excuse for a shitty personality." Definitely not like other counselors.

"She's too good to tell us her problem?" He never takes his eyes from me. I began to bite my tongue to hold the sarcastic bitch inside me. I don't think I can dance too many rounds with Henry, giving his stature and girth. He was a big boy and wearing more studs than I could ever manage in an outfit.

"She is going at her own pace, Henry, this is her first time. Do you remember your first time sharing? I bet it made you nervous and stripped you bare. Let her be." Miranda's voice was low, but warning, the practiced skill of a mother, and I begin to wonder if she has children. She could definitely dance with Henry; I'd even place my money on her.

"Probably sitting in here just soaking in everyone's misery, getting high off it because she doesn't have her own. Or maybe she is using ours for something. I don't trust her." He speaks as if I'm not here as if his evil brown eyes aren't glaring directly at me.

"I do have my own misery." I muster.

"You ain't getting nothing 'til you fess up, missy." With that, he turned his tantrum elsewhere, and the eyes of the room drew themselves to me. They want me to put up. I just shut up. Miranda hopelessly tries to get the group back on track, but three of the last remaining five participants opt out of telling their stories. I have ruined group, and I surely don't feel wanted. I no longer looking forward to coming back. There will be a mutiny. This was the first group where the leader didn't push me, the members did.

Miranda came to me afterward, encouraging me to come back in two weeks. She said it would be okay, but when she spoke she subconsciously touched her scar. I wonder if she realized it, her tell when she got nervous. A fall back from her strength, remembering the ones who cut her skin. The scar will always come back to haunt you; it never dies. It knows just how to thrive in hostile territories such as tonight.

THIRTEEN

"Take your screwdriver and just leave."

Let all the records state that I had the best of intentions tonight. I even talked the idea over with Charlotte, who gives the most solid advice, and we were confident that after a minor bump or two everything would be harmonious. Neither of us could have predicted the red face and tears being displayed, or the violence of the screwdriver being chucked into the air and landing in a dead aim at Oliver's face. She was going to be okay. We were going to have her meet Oliver just for a small second as he picked up his screwdriver on his way through. Instead, Penelope is lunging like she is six feet instead of four at a grown man who has the decency to look nervous.

"Take your screwdriver and leave," Penelope shouts it again at Oliver, who barely made it past the threshold of the front door before the assault began.

My mouth doesn't work as fast as my arms do, so I scoop Penelope up and haul her off to her bedroom kicking and screaming the whole way. I don't even leave the stunned audience in the living room with a bidding farewell. I slam the door behind us and deposit my mid-tantrum child on to her twin size bed.

"What the heck was that?" I shout. I am shocked at her actions. My daughter's violent outburst at school was one thing because it was a bully, but this was an unprovoked attack on her part. Crap. I hope Oliver wasn't hurt, that screwdriver hit him dead in the nose. He'll probably have a black eye for sure come tomorrow morning, all thanks to my daughter. But why?

"Nothing." She has contorted her body into the fetal position, protection. A shield. She isn't going to be giving up any information easily. I want to scream bloody murder at her, ground her, send her to the timeout chair, or something. I know I lack in parenting skills due to my history, but even I'm aware of the punishments on children. I stare at the ceiling to center myself, calm the storm raging inside, and buy time as I figure out how to talk to her so she will give up the reason for this assault. I can hear the bed rustling as she digs herself deeper into a ball and hiding. I look and see her body slowly shaking with the battle of control over her tears. It softens me immediately. This wasn't an unprovoked attack in her heart. Something put anger and sadness there.

"Penelope, what's wrong?" I climb onto the bed next to her and begin to slowly stroke her hair, a soothing technique I learned from Charlotte.

"You don't love me anymore." Heartbreaking words spewed out in broken sobs. My heart stops cold. I didn't love her, was she crazy? I love her more than anything in the world, more than life itself. I would give anything for her. I was fighting for her. Didn't she see that?

"I love you more than life allows. My heart is so full of love for you. Why do you think that?" Her body can't hold her despair much longer, and she goes limp, melting into the bed succumbing to it. I rush to snuggle her from behind, holding on, hoping my love will flow through my touch and reassure her. Penelope had convinced herself with all her soul, that I didn't love her. I could see it in the way she carried the burden now telling me, letting what she believed to be the elephant in the room out.

"You like him. You don't want me anymore." The confession is a weak whisper, more to the pillow than the air between us. I don't know where the lines got crossed, or what put it in her head that I would ever love anyone over her. She was wrong. I needed to right it now.

"I want you more than anything. Why do you think that Oliver has taken place over you?" She remains facing away from me, consulting more with the pillow. It's easier to confess when you aren't making eye contact. I let her have it because it makes it easier and keeps her talking. She picks at the thread hanging off the seam of the pillowcase. She's working the courage up so her voice doesn't break.

"You are getting better for him. Not me. You even wrote a list of things to do for him." A new rage of tears rakes through her body. I can't bear it any longer; I turn her face toward mine. She won't just hear my words. She needs to see them and feel them. Her wet emerald eyes meet mine with resistance.

"I am not getting better for Oliver." Every word is slow, deliberate. She pinches her eyes shut, I patiently wait for her to come back to me because she has waited for me much longer. When I am afforded eye contact again, I continue. "I didn't want to tell you this because it's grown up stuff, but Grandma came over with that list that's on the fridge. I did not write it. She threatened to take you from me if I didn't do it. I started it out of fear I was going to lose you, but now I don't do the list for you anymore." She flinches, but my words are like salve we both need to draw the hurt out of our wounds. "I do it for both you and me now."

Penelope stares at me, mouth agape. My admission surprises her. I didn't want to tell her why I had gotten better. I don't want to ruin the grandparent relationship she does have with my mother, even if I can't stand her. I didn't want to scare her into thinking that she could be taken away and split from me. I also carried my fear that she would be happy to leave me, take the first bus out of crazy town. The list on the refrigerator was on display in plain sight, so it was foolish to think I wouldn't have to explain it.

"I am trying to give us a better life, to be more present and here for you. I know I haven't been a great mom since Daddy died. I'm messing up at every turn, but I am fighting now. I am fighting for you. For me. For us. No one else. Everyone else is second if they're lucky." I kiss her forehead and pull her into my embrace. I never want to let go of her.

I have reaffirmed her faith in me by strictly being honest. That's something we forget to do to others, share our flaws so they might love us for our loose ends. I have been hiding for the last three years, not only in my house but inside myself. I have pretended to my daughter that I was okay until I couldn't anymore and then I just ignored it. I never talked about Ben or Amelia. I didn't want anyone to think I was too depressed to have Penelope. Little did I know, my inactions were speaking louder than my admittance ever would have had I just said it.

Penelope jolts back, causing our embrace to be shorter lived than I wanted it to be. I longed to hold on for forever. "Why would Grandma do that?" She is throwing anger in my mother's direction now, precisely what I didn't want because of the downfall it would bring in their bond. She needs all the family members she can get, and my mother may not have strong points with me, but she loves Penelope with all her heart.

"She did it to help me. Don't be mad at her or decide you need to go to war with her, too. You are too young to be throwing punches," I pause, "or screwdrivers." My mother did ultimately hand me that list for my benefit. It is a hard list, I won't lie, and I'm still not fond of the idea of number seven. However, I wouldn't be here talking to my daughter in this manner or had any of the experiences in the last past weeks, if my mother didn't kick me in the pants. For that, I am thankful, although I will never say it out loud to her.

"I'm sorry for being so mean, Mom."

"I'm not the one you need to be apologizing to. You cannot just throw screwdrivers at people. I understand where you were coming from with your anger, now that you have shared with me, but it wasn't right. No more. From now on, you come to me and talk it out." This may only be my first months back on the job, but I don't think I'm doing too shabby. That sounded like a parenting magazine article response.

She nods to me. "I want to go say I'm sorry." Somehow, with no effort of my own, I have an amazing kid. Even in the midst of my shitty parenting years, she has prevailed. I can only hope that the next years of me being present will take her even farther.

I help her clean up in the bathroom and throw some cool water on her face. She may just be a child to some, but I want her to have her dignity as well. She deserves it. It's just her and me now, my partner through life. If she could afford me the sanctuary of our house for my dignity, I can give her five minutes to collect herself. She gives a thumbs up to me on her appearance. She feels ready to go back in the living room. Hopefully, Oliver hasn't left yet. What if he just turned from this crazy house running? I didn't even think of the possibility that my kid throwing tools at his face would sever our new friendship. Dammit. I need friends, too. I just made one in Oliver. I pause in the bathroom before opening the door, silently pleading he hasn't fled.

Not when I was talking to canned goods, not when I said I was going to therapy, and not when my daughter threw a screwdriver at his face. We turn the corner for the living room, and I see he has taken up residence in my concave portion of the couch, his elbows are perched on his thighs, and he is directing his attention to Charlotte as she is telling a story about when Penelope was born.

"Miriam took none of the drugs, insanity to me because just the thought alone puts me in pain. She didn't, and she pushed out that nine-pound baby." She looked over at Penelope. "Bigger than a pea pod." She winks at my daughter and puts her at ease. She's letting Penelope know her apology will be well-received. Apologizing after you have done wrong as a child is inevitable, but that doesn't mean it isn't hard to do. It can feel downright embarrassing as if you are backing down from a fight. Defeated. There would be times still in the future that Penelope would go through that feeling, but tonight two beautiful souls in the living room are putting her at ease.

"Hey there, Rocky. You have to give me Justin's number now so we can commiserate over that right hook." Oliver has a bright red mark blaring at us on his face, but a huge smile directed at Penelope instead of anger. I think Penelope and I both sigh with relief. I gently nudge her forward, a silent cue to make amends properly, she doesn't falter.

"Oliver, I'm sorry I hit you. It wasn't very nice of me. I thought Mommy was going back to the doctor for you. I thought she took off her ring for you and it made me mad. I was wrong." She was remorseful and humble, the perfect apology. She stood tall, facing him, even though she was in the wrong she didn't shrink. She was a better adult than most. I was just hoping to let her be a kid some.

"Hey," He speaks softly, "I understand. Next time I'll duck, okay?" He laughs, and so does Penelope. And that's how the rest of the evening goes. Oliver stayed for at least another two hours. We all sat around laughing, telling stories. With Oliver no longer a threat competing for her mom's affection, Penelope seemed to fall for his charm. Voodoo.

When Charlotte went to help Penelope get ready for bed, I walked Oliver out. We lingered on the front porch, evident that neither of us was ready to end the night, staring off at our shoes. Oliver has an infectious personality. It's no wonder people want to be around him, like the girls at the class vying for his attention. My cackle was turning into a practiced laugh, and the pitch wasn't as rough and dry anymore. I had Oliver to partly thank for that. The cold air wasn't the only reason I was pulling my sweater tightly around me; I needed protection. I couldn't lie to myself anymore. I'm attracted to Oliver. Not just in a physical sense either. I want to be around him and hear him talk. I want to have him listen to me speak. That was all too dangerous. If he finds out everything about that night, he won't stick around. And if I tell him, I'll already be too far into trusting him for it not to hurt me.

"I want to apologize for Penelope hurting your face."

"You know, Penelope is a lot more eloquent than you." He chortled.

"Shut up. I'm trying to say I'm sorry."

He leans his forearm against the pole on the porch and stares out onto the road. A few cars pass by, I move and mirror Oliver's posture on the next pole. It is clear he isn't going just yet, and I am all too eager to soak up a minute more of him. We hold our comfortable silence, a signature now for us, for a few minutes longer. He is the first to break it, but he speaks in reverie to the road, not to me.

"I never threw a screwdriver, but when my dad came around to date my mom I was pissed enough to. I threw out obscenities my mother didn't even know I knew. Words that to this day when I say them, I still taste the soap she used to clean my mouth out." He snorts at his joke, bowing his head, the memory clear in his mind. He turns to me with a serious look in his eye and says, "You're a good mom, Miriam." I roll my eyes. "No, I'm serious."

"That's not the popular opinion around here." I pull my sweater even tighter and examine my shoes again, embarrassed to admit they were right. Oliver won't let me look away though. He comes over grabbing both my shoulders and calls my attention to his face.

"She came out and sincerely apologized to me. She even explained herself openly when she didn't have to. She could have just said sorry, that's it, but she explained her feelings to clear the air. You did right with her." I feel the sob in the back of my throat forming, and I swallow it hard. That is the best damn compliment I have gotten in a while, and it is etched on his face that he wholeheartedly believes it.

"So what happened with your dad?" Change of subject. Diversion tactic, so I can gain control of my emotions.

"Oh," he drops his arms from me and leans his back on the post, "they're still married to this day. But, now it's dad and me who team up against her when I'm over for dinner on Saturdays." His boyish charm is fixed back on his face. I have a hard time believing Oliver can be serious for a long consecutive time.

"No, I meant your . . ." I let the air fill in the words I don't say.

"Oh." Oliver understands. "He passed away when I was young." He did understand where Penelope was coming from. No wonder he didn't fault her for her actions or see them as a lack of my parenting. Dang it, Voodoo, who sent you? I peer onto the road, and I can feel Oliver's eyes on me. He is giving me his full attention. I usually shrink under that kind of microscope, but he does it with an honesty that makes you hold your head high. He isn't scrutinizing me; he appreciates my scars and human flaws. When Oliver watches you, you shine.

"My mom only dated a few times after our father left us. She had too long of a qualification check-list to settle down again." If we are sharing wound stories on dads, I guess I can share mine.

"What about you?" he asks.

"I'm not always fond of lists," I say dryly.

"No. Do you see yourself dating again?" His eyes might be hopeful, but you could pass them off as curious just the same.

"I don't know. I've only been not sucking at this mom and widow thing for a little while now. One thing at a time, you know?" I shrug.

"Yeah." He nods and grabs his keys out of his pocket. "One thing at a time." He squeezes my shoulder and walks down the steps to his truck.

I watch as his headlights disappear on the road. I pray he drives safe so that maybe I can shine in his eyes again.

FOURTEEN

Charlotte had gotten it in her head one morning that we needed a massive birthday celebration for the three of us. Penelope, Charlotte, and I all have birthdays just a few days shy of each other. They were coming up quick. In fact, from the day Charlotte got the idea she only had a week to plan before the first one, Penelope's. I knew I shouldn't let my daughter's birthday go by without doing something since I'm trying to recover to the land of the living, but Charlotte had a tall order. One week? Impossible. There was a sense of urgency in her eyes that I couldn't say no to, so for the last week we have been busting our butts and following my sister's orders.

The party is today. Charlotte has invited family, Penelope's friends and parents, and of course Oliver. I didn't have an extensive guest list to hand her. I refused it for days until she made it for me and just asked my okay. It was pathetic to see the number of people who wanted to deal with and celebrate me written on a piece of paper. You could have fit it on a post-it and still had room. All that was on there was Oliver. Naturally, Penelope and Charlotte were my people as well, but they live here. Charlotte knew better than to put Mom as a name on my guest list, though I'm sure she was tempted after seeing how small my number was.

I asked if she planned to invite Arthur, her boyfriend she left to go live with her crazy sister. She brushed me off and avoided it for days until finally, she confessed it didn't work out between them. When I asked why the only reason she would give me is that she didn't want to hurt him anymore. Vague. I'll let her slide, for now, I'm not the pushing type like my sister is. I'm not even sure it would work with her because she has mastered and probably owns the rights to those skills.

I find myself in charge of a lot more than I ever wanted to be for this party. Charlotte woke with a horrible headache, so I sent her to bed with some ibuprofen to sleep it off. It felt like a fine decision at the time, a kind and nurturing one, but now, standing in the kitchen trying to finish off the food for the party I was longing to whine to my sister to help. I hate parties. I hate planning. I always knew I was going to fail at being this kind of mom, not for lack of effort, instead, I just lack the grace and calmness. I was currently staring down at a dark brown mixture in a saucepan that was meant to be white. I burnt the marshmallow mixture for the Rice Krispies treats. That's how bad I stink at this.

I set my head on the cool tile counter and counted to ten. I am going to ruin the party that Charlotte worked so hard for. I close my eyes, refraining from tears just yet. I have to regain my strength and try again. Just then, I was enveloped by the warmest and surest of hands, my sister. My stone. She kisses my forehead and puts her head down facing me on the counter.

"Whatcha doing?" Her tone is bubbly and warm.

"I burnt Rice Krispies treats." I almost burst into tears.

"You are awful at this." She says the insult so lovingly, you would think it is a compliment from the heavens. "Go blow up balloons, huh?" I rise from the counter and nod. She strokes down the sides of my arms and yanks me into a hug. "So, you rent out a place that puts the party together for you from now on. No need to cry." I laugh into her sleeve. What would I have done without her here after getting that damned list from Mom? I wouldn't have made it this far, I know it.

So, I do as she says and blow up balloons while she finishes the food for the party. I am turning thirty-one tomorrow, and I can't cook cereal bars, but my almost twenty-eight-year-old sister can. Oh well, I am going to rock the shit out of blowing up balloons then. It's the least I can do.

We spend the rest of the afternoon getting the house ready for the party, and when our family and friends arrive everything is perfect like

Charlotte wanted it. She is running around from person to person, greeting them and being the best host. I am more than happy to stand in the corner and observe her grace. My empty house is filled with people, with love, with laughter. My heart feels full today as well. From the safety of my corner, I watch Penelope tip her head back in a fit of laughter playing a game with her friends. She helps one of them up without hesitation when they stumbled. She makes sure everyone has a drink if she goes to get one for herself. Eight years old. Maybe Oliver was right.

I watch Charlotte sitting in the center of a group of adults, her arms moving in timed theatrics to her story they are all enthralled with. She makes eye contact with everyone, making all her listeners feel important and that they belonged here. Her blond hair is bouncing around, carefree, as she speaks. She has everyone's attention, and they are all glad to listen.

I catch sight of my mother, sitting in the corner alone. She is also taking in the general splendor of the party. Her eyes light up when she sees Penelope running and laughing like a child should. The smile that creeps on my mother's face isn't smug; she is genuinely pleased. I note she is absent a pen and pad today, though she had eyed the state of the house upon arrival. My mother's list started this journey, I'll give her that, but the smile on Penelope's face is what will continue it. I need to heal, to grow, and to move on. I am never going to admit to my mother that her list was what I needed.

"Aren't you supposed to be mingling at your birthday party?" His deep voice is right beside me. I didn't even know he was here yet. I draw my focus to him, he is smiling lazily, and the sneaky suspicion creeps in that he has been watching me for a while.

"I am. I'm talking to you now." I take a sip of my root beer to cover my smile. "So, do you always come to birthday parties empty-handed?" We slip easily into our playful banter with no introduction or warm up.

"Nope, I set Penelope's gift on the dining room table." He thought of her. I can't hide my smile now.

"What did you get her?"

"Boxing classes." We both burst into deep belly laughs, bracing on the railing for support. I'm so glad he was on my guest list. His humor cripples the bad days and makes them weak at invading my heart and mind. When the happy tears clear from my eyes I catch sight of my daughter smiling up at me from down in the yard below the deck. Such a turnaround from their last meeting. That smile is meant to settle me, but it does the opposite. Penelope was my last chance of holding off on Oliver. My reasons are waning since I cleared Ben's stuff, no ghosts gobbled me up when I admitted to myself that I like Oliver and my daughter now liked him. Penelope's agitation was the last thing telling me not to try; now it was gone. Damn him for being easy to like.

I switch from hot to cold and leave him spinning. I quickly excuse myself to the kitchen without so much of an expression except a grim line in my mouth. Just like at the grocery store, I don't give him a warning. When his kindness gets too close, I cut him off. Cold turkey. I can tell he had feelings for me, any idiot can see it. He is in a vice, and I just tighten the grip. I am the worst kind of person because I crave the high of his attention, but I'm not willing to give anything back.

Charlotte is by my side in minutes. She must have witnessed the whole scene on the deck. I should be elated that the boy I like likes me back; shouldn't I? People like me, the ones who send their husbands out and get them killed, don't deserve happiness twice. I ruined my chance. I should live the rest of my life punished for it. I look up from the sink to my sister's face, she knows. I don't have to say it. I never do with her, but I can feel she's about to tell me something I don't want to hear.

"You are not ready yet. You won't be until you accept all that happened that day of the accident. You have to say it all out loud and set it free." Before I can make my rebuttal, or have Charlotte make her case further, the doorbell rings. Saved. I immediately volunteer myself to greet the next guest. When I reach the door, the confused look on Charlotte's face finally registers. Everyone who was invited is here.

"Gabrielle." With that one spoken name, the wind is knocked out of me. Why is she back? I have thought of her countless times since the night she first showed up on my doorstep, wondering what the speech would have been had I let her continue. I tried putting myself in her shoes, but my anger still left me bitter. It wasn't her who crashed into Ben's SUV, but her father. I spent nights lying awake, curious to know what she would say. This is her chance.

"I'm sorry, Miriam. I need to do this. I have spent the last three years blaming myself for what happened that night. If you shut the door now, I'll just keep coming back. I have to do this. I have to say it. I have to say it to you." She is pleading. Her appearance is a bit more haggard than last time. She didn't carefully assess every flick of eyeshadow this time to meet the widow her father made. This time she is wild, a bit crazy, a version I can identify with better in this whole ordeal. She came raw and unedited.

"Listen, now is not a good time . . ." Charlotte starts, but I cut her off with a wave of my hand.

"Go ahead." That's all I say. Those two words, go ahead. Destroy me with what you are going to tell me. Bring me back to that night and pray it doesn't cripple me again.

"I just started therapy a few months ago." The lump visibly forms in her throat, and I can tell that she is debating running back to her car. For the first time, I see how hard this was for her. How hard it must be to be related to the man who destroyed a family. My wall for her crashes down. "I blamed myself. My father was an alcoholic. A mean one. I used to pray every day when he would head out to the bar, that he would hit a tree coming home and die." The last words are hard for her to let pass her lips, a weight looks like it has lifted off her chest, but the burden of her thoughts will forever remain with her. I know the outcome of her story because it is forever entangled with mine, but still, she continues. "I never wanted him to kill anyone else, but it's all my fault. I wanted him to die."

Her admission of guilt stuns me, no one but her father was the cause of the accident. Her father and I, for sending Ben out. Wait. I was doing the same thing that Gabrielle was doing. I was blaming myself for the accident, not the one who caused it. I know why the therapist probably sent her here, they weren't getting it through her head with words. They want me to do it, but I haven't tried doing it for myself.

My hand drops from the door, and before I realize what I'm doing, I'm hugging Gabrielle with all my might. That's an awful cross to bear, I know because I too drag it around. She was trying to get free of it, opening up to her therapist and baring her soul. I could only speak of Charlotte, Penelope, and my mother to my therapist. I haven't ripped my envelope open, but I refuse to seal up Gabrielle's. She was trying to heal as well. I squeeze her tighter to me, repeating over and over in her ear how it is not her fault. I feel the burden shed from her shoulders. This is no longer her scar to wear.

After a long embrace, we say our goodbyes, the words we don't say are well understood by us. I watch her walk to her car, bid her drive safe, and then I watch her pull away, on to a better life. I can't tell if I feel heavier or lighter after hearing Gabrielle's truth. I am thankful I listened this time. I feel an odd contentment flow over me. There is a possibility yet.

"Mir?" Charlotte's voice sounds weak. I turn just in time to catch her as she faints.

FIFTEEN

"Leukemia."

I say the word out loud to my reflection in the mirror and try to let it sink in. A wave of nausea washes over me, and once again I am bent over the toilet purging everything in my body. I stand back up, flush, wash my mouth out and try again. It's a bad taste in my mouth, the word. Toothpaste won't cure it. Mouthwash won't freshen it. The water will never help me to swallow it. I look at myself again.

"Charlotte has leukemia. She's had it for a while now and didn't tell you." I whisper, hoping it helps. I throw up again.

There is nothing physically left inside my body for me to dispense, but that doesn't stop the motion. A nurse has come to tap on the door to see if I'm okay, to warn me if I have a stomach bug to go home and try not to pass it on to my sister. My sister. My sister has leukemia. My sister is laughing at the nurse for checking on me. The nerve of her. She knew this whole time, every moment. Ever since she parked in my driveway, she was aware. Aware of her . . . I stop myself. I'm going to need to come up with a word for it because the word they've given it makes me sick. I look around the hospital bathroom for inspiration. Bedpan. I'll call it bedpan because it sounds just as shitty. I can't stay in this overwhelmingly tiny tiled bathroom all day, but the room outside is just as bad and threatens to swallow me whole. I'm stuck. Forever wedged between what I have to face and what I'd rather pretend is not there.

Everything was going splendid. I don't understand. The party was great. I listened to Gabrielle. I had no ominous feeling unsettling me. No warning. My intuition is shit. I'm blindsided, hit from behind, and Charlotte knew. We took her to the hospital, Oliver and I, while my mother stayed behind to watch Penelope and clean up the party. The party. No wonder Charlotte had a sense of urgency to make it big. She knew it would be the last . . . oh God. I throw up again.

I rest on the bathroom floor. It has been a blur of nurses and doctors since we came in. Everyone is paging each other, talking in hushed tones, the smell of hospital permanently staining their clothes. They work like machines; they know what to do and how to do it. They don't surprise you with their mannerisms or procedures because it doesn't stray far from the same line whether you come in for a cut or an awful disease. You still have to be registered. You will always be introduced to your nurse and doctor. They'll even run labs. They'll even give you a blanket.

Blanket. I slump forward so my head is resting on my knees. When they put that blanket on Charlotte, she looked so frail, and my knees buckled. Why hadn't I noticed any strange symptoms? Why hadn't she told me she needed to go to the doctors? Why didn't she go? Why had I been so selfish as to not pay attention to her? I know I won't find my answers here on the floor of the bathroom, Charlotte's private bathroom. Her private bathroom on the oncology floor.

All the medical jumble they have thrown at me tonight has gone way over my head. I was staring at Charlotte the whole time and never lost eye contact. I couldn't read her thoughts. I just knew those were the saddest eyes I ever saw. It was like she was sorry for me, not for herself, but for me. Her eyes held more pain they I had ever seen in them. Charlotte has the most dazzling eyes; life sparkles from them. One look at those eyes and the bad wish they were good and the good wish to be better.

"Doctor, I can solve all your lab tests right now." She said as she grabbed his hand to silence his chatter, "I have recurrent adult AML, and I'm almost positive I have fallen out of remission again." His eyes looked upon her sympathetically. It made my spine shiver. Remission, like a horrible shark lurking under the water only to grab its prey and drown it out of nowhere. Charlotte looks at me. "Leukemia, Miriam." Chomp.

An innocent internet search later and I sprinted for this bathroom. I could stay on this floor forever, or I could go to my sister, who was probably terrified that I was slipping back into my old ways. In all honesty, I want to because it is comforting to be numb. Much better than facing life's lousy events head-on with no airbag. Airbag. Those don't always deploy.

I stand up. I wash my face. I dry my face on the towel. I head to the door. One step. Two steps. Turn the knob. I've made it out of my prison cell, now to put my big girl pants on and face the prison sentence my sister will be given. Charlotte had come to me when she knew I needed it, void of selfish thoughts or single care to her well-being. Even now, as I take her in, she is scooting her frail body over to make room for me to lie down beside her. Charlotte is ready to comfort me when I should be at least doing that for her, but she doesn't need anyone's pity. I'm a terrible human being because I let my sister cradle me as I think about my sorrow instead of hers. How can I make it without her if she can't fight this?

Charlotte spends three days in the hospital; I spend them all with her, even my birthday. We never talked about the pink elephant in the room. In fact, we hardly talked at all. I only address her issues of comfort; a glass of water, another blanket, the remote control, or a pillow. I can't offer to ease her mind about cancer because I can't ease my own. Besides, she doesn't look at all at war with it. The day of her release, her birthday, we get the discharge papers and the directions to book all the other chemotherapy appointments the doctor recommended. The words are a blur, they flutter into my head and never go out either side, but that doesn't mean I have digested or savored them. I tuck them away in a drawer, neatly where I won't have to think about it.

I help Charlotte slip on her clothes and pack her things from the room. She has regained some strength back from the fluids and drugs they have been pumping into her, but the truth is screaming at me from her bones. She is sick, and I haven't bothered to notice. Our bond has been unbreakable since birth, she came out of my mother's womb and straight into my heart. I couldn't love her more if I tried, she was my precious baby. I never let my mother be alone with her those first years. I would be present during all the night time feedings as well or sitting in the hallway listening. I had an immense sense of duty to protect her from the moment I met her in the outside world. I had known her kicks and the symptoms she handed my mother during pregnancy, but nothing equaled the first time I finally put a face to the reason behind my mother's swollen belly. And now, I have let that precious baby I loved so much down.

They wheel her hospital chair down to the parking lot, where Oliver has brought my car around. He has been a rock these last three days, solid and sturdy. He surely didn't budge when I tried to get rid of him. He knows I need someone to do the meticulous things of life while I search for a way to cope. At least he has a great sixth sense to know how helpless I am. He is never failing and always pleasant.

I lean against the edge of the bricks that contain the hospital's landscaping and place the roses one of Charlotte's well-wishers bought her on its edge. Roses. Tea roses. I pretend to admire the flowers while I observe the interaction between Oliver and Charlotte. He is helping her into my car and taking great care in doing it. It looks like an effortless dance, giving that much attention to someone's needs is just built into Oliver. It isn't taught or practiced; he just has the kind of soul that isn't fulfilled unless it is in the service of others. He shuts her in and searches for me.

He regards me like a rabid animal because he doesn't know if he should run or if I am going to. I imagine what I look like, lost in my thoughts of misery and sorrow. I hold up my finger, signaling I needed another minute. As he walks to the driver's side, I catch my sister's eyes on me. Curious. Everyone is interested what the widow will do now. It's funny that Oliver is driving my car, I can very well drive us myself. I scoff and look at my feet. No, you can't Miriam, and he knows it. Bastard. I look to my left at the vase full of flowers. They are full from the plant food in the water, bloomed to capacity. Yellow roses, tips brushed with pink as if an artist accidentally placed it there, saw it was a good idea and kept going. I pick up the vase and head to the car, Oliver left the door open for me. Before I duck inside, I pluck one of those buds and stick it in my purse.

Once home, Charlotte tells Oliver to leave her on the front porch. She wants to breathe in fresh air after being cooped up in that stale, pungent hospital room. I observe him tuck the blanket around her legs and squeeze her shoulder goodbye. He calls out a birthday wish as he heads back to the driveway. I linger in the car, waiting for a chance he might help me to the door as well or just to avoid my sister for a minute longer. Oliver comes over to retrieve me, but I feign strength.

"I'm alright. I just need a minute," I say. I'm not convincing, they aren't polishing my Oscar for me, but Oliver is kind enough to let my lousy acting pass.

It's not until then that I realize Oliver has not said many words to me at all since the party. I pause and take him in. He is looking off into the distance, attempting to find a tree or a landmark to focus all his energy on. Anything but me. It makes my heart ache. I haven't even given him my full baggage claim ticket, and he's calling it quits. Lately, I have been dangerously toying with the idea that Oliver would be the one to hear everything and not walk away. It was a foolish dream. I kept pushing him away. He should go, right?

"I'll see you around?" I can't disguise the desperation in my voice any more than the unexpected way his eyes lose focus on the tree. I'm hoping he'll hear everything I'm not saying in those few words.

"Of course." It's barely audible and drips of sad resignation. He'll be back, he'll try again, even though he knows I can't be what he wants. He's going to torture himself until he can shake me, but the fear in his stare from the open driver's door of his truck tells me he doesn't think he ever can. Again, I watch that truck leave my driveway without telling him a single thing.

I plunked down next to Charlotte on the front porch, gripping the vase in my hands. After witnessing our exchange, I wait for my sister to do what she always does and say the right thing at the right time. I wait for my house to go back to the happy mood she bled into it, filling it with her light and positivity. I wait for this nightmare to be over. I don't expect her crushing words.

"You can't let me fade out like Amelia; you have to acknowledge me when I die." With that, Charlotte gets up from her seat and goes into the house. Happy birthday, Charlotte.

SIXTEEN

A gray sky backlights the church, all that remains after a day of intermittent storms are thick clouds, heavy with grief. It's a blessing the sun isn't out at this moment. The day has been dreary, and it fits perfectly. I sat on the porch until Penelope came home, made her dinner, kissed her and Charlotte goodbye and came here. I came here with resolve.

Charlotte knows she's struggling, it's evident in her words to me that she doesn't feel she'll last long. Her last effort here on this earth will be in vain if I don't get myself together. How will people know her if she dies and I am too broken to tell them? They'll imagine she never existed or isn't worthy to talk about. She will only live in my memories, while everyone around me tip-toes, hoping not to send me spiraling down. That's what happened with Amelia. They all grieved her, missed her, embraced her memory and held her in their speeches. I've thrown her memory to the darkest part of my mind, a place I don't visit because it hurts too much, but I can't let her keep fading. I can't have Charlotte fade.

I push the car door. It's hard to open, much like my heart, groaning with the effort. Every step to the front door is determined. I decided this afternoon while watching the rain fall that I was going to open the wound and let it bleed out until there was nothing left to drain. The story of that night will always need to be spoken. With Charlotte's illness coming to light, I feel as if I don't have much time left to share it. I was sharing Ben with Penelope, telling his stories and describing his smile, but I never speak of Amelia. I slap on a regular face and hold back the crazy her death threatens, afraid I'll lose Penelope.

Now, I'm going to lose Penelope if I don't speak. I could convince myself with a million reasons why I shouldn't walk in this door. That's the thing in life; you are never ready to face the hard stuff. It's a frequent cop out anymore, "we aren't ready for kids" or "we aren't ready to buy a house." You'll never be ready. There is no preparation, always another thing you need to do or get in order before you are prepared. The best is to jump in, have it thrust upon you, learn as you swim. To hell with it, I'm jumping in the deep end, and I plan to drown so I can live.

My footsteps echo off the wall, bouncing in my head like a cadence. *I love you, Amelia. Don't worry. You're still here with me.* I turn the knob to the room without hesitation, no more waiting room. The heavy door slams behind me, no turning back. This used to be a storage room for the church, it still is, but it holds a dual purpose now. It serves as a refuge for alcoholics, addicts, and grievers to meet and share their pain.

I'm early, only one other soul was in the room aside from me, a man whom I learned last time had lost his son in the war. I nod my hello, for a mere second I wonder what he thinks of the girl who refused to share her story. I think about how long it must have taken him to share his own. It probably took him a while, but like most, he did it at home before coming to the group. Not me, I was forced into this by ultimatum.

Henry's next to walk in, his eye roll provokes a violent feeling inside of me. I want to throttle him, punch him deep in the throat until he knows the meaning of real pain. I'm here for Amelia, not Henry, so I swallow the notion twice because it sticks in my throat. I'm entitled to be in this group as much as everyone else; I have crawled through hell on my knees as well. I stare into Henry, hoping to see his soul. Instead, I make him uncomfortable and he nervously shifts in his seat. Squirm, Henry. Everyone else files in, but I never let Henry escape my vision. Miranda's voice finally calls my attention away. She's surprised to see me after last week's escapade.

"Alright, looks like everyone is here. Miriam, it's great to see you again." She locks eyes with me, silently questioning my changed countenance. I want this on my own accord before she offers the chance to start. I don't want to wait anymore and possibly chicken out. I raise my hand.

"I'll start." My voice's small but heard. Henry looks pleased with himself as if he's the reason behind it all. I toss daggers at him. My eyes hold nothing but pain and death, it's all I can feel now. I see around him that the others who sat out last time because of me perk up. Some don guilty faces, as if they're all pushing me before my time. I am being pushed from somewhere else, beyond the grave.

"Are you sure?" This is out of context for her because she usually does her story first.

"I am."

I've been home alone all day, struggling to stand with only three hours of sleep underneath my belt. There were no consecutive hours of sleep either, so the coveted REM cycle never came. Penelope's sick with a terrible cold, leaving her with the worst disposition all day long. I can't blame her because I would be grouchy, too. I am grouchy in fact, striving to be super mom and not let it show. I speak with tenderness when I deliver my words to her, though my body aches with a deep tension to finally have her stop whining.

After many weak attempts, a steam in the bathroom to break up her congestion, medication swiped on her chest, humidifier on, head propped up, and medicine administered, she finally has fallen asleep. I finish checking on her and sneak out of the room when I notice the clock. Ten more minutes and Ben will be home. Today, I need the break.

I get on my knees and crawl on the living room floor over to Amelia, who is content to stare at herself in the mirror. I lay my head lightly on her tiny chest to see if I can hear any congestion, because once one child gets sick so does the other. Damn, there's a bit of gurgle in her breath. I sigh. There will be no sleep tonight as well, and it's already an hour past her bedtime, and she's refusing to be put down. Anytime I take her to her crib, she screams in deafening tones. I resolve myself to the living room, hoping a good cuddle and rock will help her pass out. I pick her up and take her to the couch, the cries begin and threaten to wake Penelope. I quickly set Amelia back on her mat, my tears flowing. I'm exhausted, at the end of my rope; I just want some sleep.

Ben walks in to witness the blubbering mess. There was once a time in our marriage that I would check my makeup before he came home so that I looked nice for him. Silly really, Ben didn't care. Today is different. I have not showered, I smell awful, I'm pretty sure I forgot to brush my teeth, and my hair is disheveled. He throws his briefcase down and rushes over.

"What's the matter, babe?" He's tender. He's the kindest person I know, always so sweet to me when I don't deserve it. I want to be a super mom, raise the kids effortlessly while he's out making money and live in a harmonious 50's movie. He works long hours to provide for our family, never complains, and I can't make it a whole day with the kids.

"I can't get her to sleep. She won't go in her room. She screams so loud. And I finally got Penelope to go to sleep. She's going to wake her up. She won't let me rock her." I'm flailing, the volume of my voice increasing with the stressful words. I'll be the one to wake Penelope. I throw my face into the couch cushion behind me. "I'm sorry. I'm sorry. I'm the worst mom ever." I need him to hear my apology. I want him to know I'm trying.

I'm engulfed in Ben's warm arms; he always radiates heat. It can be the dead of winter, but snuggled up to Ben you hope for the air conditioning. He's vibrating. A small snort burst through his nostrils. He's laughing at me. I can't believe he is making fun of me at a time like this. I lean my head back ready to scold him and leave his ass with the two kids, see how funny he thinks it all is after a couple of hours, but a glimpse at his face and I too succumb to the laughter.

"You know, honey, you don't have to parent alone. I'm here." He kisses my forehead and soothes my mind. Ben's a great father. He loves to be home with the girls. Never complaining that work was too hard so he can't help with bath time or the night shift. He is forever my partner and never my jury.

"Can you take her for a drive?" It usually works to put Amelia to sleep when she's being difficult. I fear my sleepy state on the road with her. Ben nods without hesitation. Eager to help and cure whatever is causing his wife's face to leak.

"Go lay down. I'm going to take a ride with Amelia." He winks at me as he bends over our six-month-old daughter who coos with joy at the sight of her daddy. "Want to go for a ride with DaDa?"

I help load them up and kiss them both goodbye and goodnight. I'll be asleep by the time they get back. I watch Ben's SUV back out of our driveway, and something in my heart begins to hurt and make me nauseous. Must be the lack of sleep, but still. I start to clean up before heading to bed, quitting two minutes into the task and deeming it futile. I lay down in bed and set my cell phone on the nightstand along with the monitor for Penelope's room. I lay there with my eyes closed finding it hard to fall asleep, to shut off my mind and this strange nagging feeling.

When I open my eyes, I realize I must have passed out because it has gotten quite late. Something doesn't feel right. I check Penelope's monitor and her light snoring assures me she isn't the cause of the notion. I swiped my arm to my left. Empty. I jump up on my bed and peer out the window because it has a clear view of the driveway. Empty. My heart sinks in my stomach. I grab my phone. No missed texts. No missed calls. I call Ben, but there is no reply. I dial his mom's number. She hasn't heard from him, and he didn't stop over. I tell her to come and watch Penelope. She doesn't have time to respond because I hang up and continue trying Ben's phone the whole time I get my pants and shoes on to leave.

It doesn't take Alexa long, the panic in my voice evident. I set out the door the second her car enters the driveway. I'm already in my car before she is out of hers. I roll the window down and shout that Penelope is sleeping. I must find Ben. I know the way he goes when he takes Amelia for a drive to fall asleep. I keep trying his phone the whole time. He must be out of service or dealing with a flat tire, or something. There is something to explain this. I'll find him and help him change the tire, or maybe he ran out of gas, he never does like to stop.

I drive around the bend in the curvy road and catch sight of flashing lights. I scan the area, desperate for something that will disprove my gut. There's a blue car in the middle of the road. I'm no good with car names or types, but I know it isn't Ben's. Thank God. Police car. Police car. Firetruck. Ambulance. No.

No. No. No.

Mangled in a tree off the side of the road, I see black. Black SUV. License Plate. HMV-9876. Dammit. That does me no good. I don't know his license plate number. I don't even know my own. Who remembers their license plate number? It can't be his. I would know. Something inside of me would click, right? This is probably what delayed him, this accident. The battery on his phone must have died, and he took the long way home, that's what happened. I start my three-point turn, sure to find the route Ben must have taken, when I see it.

An Ozzy Osbourne sticker in the upper left corner of the back window of that black SUV that can't be Ben's. No. My heart drops. The world is standing still at this moment, but everything is moving fast. I throw the car in park, bolt out the door. I notice the EMTs working around a tree fifty yards from the SUV. A cop is running toward me but I reach the driver side before he can catch me, and there he is.

Ben. He's slumped over to the right, and his face isn't visible, but I know him anywhere. I know every part of his body. I've cataloged every inch, and that is his neck, his shoulder, his shirt, his ear, his blood. The chill in the October air cuts through me, and I fear I'll never be warm again.

I'm able to reach in; the window must have been down. On closer inspection, I see it was busted. No. This is awful. I gently shake him. "Ben! Ben!"

"Ma'am, I'm sorry but you can't be here. Please, go back to your vehicle." The cop is firmly pushing me toward my car. He thinks I'm here as an onlooker, just a rubberneck gawker who stumbled upon the scene, but he is wrong. I'm involved. I'm the reason.

"Like hell I will! That's my husband!" I shout. I'm battling him, every muscle in my body is combating his guidance. I stare now, into his eyes, letting him know I mean business. Ben tells me I have the meanest eyes when I'm mad and, I use them on the officer now. I'm met with no resistance behind them, just wide eyes and an open mouth. His hand goes slack against my upper arm, and I use it as my chance to break in the direction of the SUV again, not allowing myself time to comprehend what those tragic eyes mean.

"Ben! Ben!" He isn't moving. He must just be unconscious. He'll be okay. He's just unconscious. "Ben, you're going to be okay." I'm stroking his hair; it's matted with blood, the usual softness gone. In fact, he is covered in blood. Oh, God. I see it inside his ear, in his hair, his neck. Where is it coming from? "Where are you hurt, Ben? Where is the bleeding coming from?" I'm searching him over, trying to find a wound to explain all this blood, and the horrible feeling in my stomach hits me again.

I place my hands on the edge of the driver's window and hoist myself half-way inside. The glass cuts me, and I jump back. The pain hardly registers as the blood pours over my fingertips and drips down to the earth. "Ben!" The officer is back again, pulling me away from the vehicle.

"Come with me, ma'am." The tone of his voice has changed. He is not the officer demanding the gawker to go away; he is softer. I hear the training in his voice; this is the part where he delivers bad news. This is his voice for it.

"NO!!" I shove his arm down. Shouldn't I be arrested by now? This is assaulting a police officer, is it not? I run from him. I run all around the vehicle, catching sight of the damage. The massacre. The front of the car is crumbled in, pushing upwards to the heavens. The side by the tree is bent in, the car shaped like a U. Everything is bent, broken, or scratched badly. What happened here? I run my hand over the side fender just before it meets the tree and find a flower stuck in between the metal. I pluck it from the carnage prison and hold it tightly in my hand. The blood from my cuts soaking the petals. I can't get into the passenger side.

The officer catches up with me and is no longer gentle, he roughly grabs my upper arm and pulls me away. He is successful, dragging me against my will, but the need for answers causes me to fight. I yank him backward, throwing him off balance in a game of tug of war with my body as the rope.

"Ma'am, you need to come with me. Now!"

"Ben?" Half-heartedly I call out, hoping my husband will perk up and respond, tell me what has happened and that he'll be okay. *"Will it all be okay?"*

"I . . ." He is at a loss for words, but he needn't have them.

I smell the turned-up dirt as I approach the tree where everyone is gathered, smoke from the family SUV mixed in. I can hear the EMTs working hard, shouting orders, talking into the radio with the hospital. One male pronounced dead at the scene.

That's when I see it. The car seat. Amelia's car seat was ejected from the car. Oh god. No. I break for the tree. I must get to my baby. I have to hold her, tell her she's alright. She has to be alright. Unfortunately, I make it there before the officer can stop me. Oh, I wish he did. My baby girl is gone, and the last sight of her that I'll ever know is of her sweet small frame marred with blood and debris. I listen for cries, but there are none. I hope for cries. There are none.

The tears cascade down my face uncontrollably. I'm sitting still, but my body is about to fall over from the weight of the night hitting me all over again. Someone is there to catch me; it's Henry. Through my blurred eyes I see his face, it's softer now, and his apologies are ringing in my ear. They can't reach me. I'm listening to the coos and giggles of my baby girl as they suddenly flood my mind.

I can see her beautiful toothless smile. I can feel her hand grasping around my finger. I feel the weight of her in my arms once again. I won't let it fade again.

SEVENTEEN

The crunch of the gravel echoes through the car as I turn into the drive. I didn't let the radio play this time. Music has always been a salve to me, something to dive in and cover my wounds with. The day I came to terms with my father and his new family, music saved me. I gave up the techno bubblegum pop I had been listening to for a heavy acoustic sound, thriving on the lyrics of the pained. I stayed on the floor for hours in my room, letting the words of a tortured artist seep into my soul. I relinquished my ears to those musicians night after night, their lyrics bringing tears to my eyes and goose pimples on my skin. The pain they suffered to make a song, build my strength. The day Ben and Amelia died, I let the music go with them. I no longer sat motionless for extended periods of time wearing my headphones, eyes closed, losing myself to the power of song. I instead let the silence of my depression lull me into a numbed state of mind, body, and soul.

I will never hear Amelia say, "Mommy." Her sweet voice will never register in my memories, only her cooing. What song is out there to glue those pieces together? I know there is enough pain and suffering in the world that inspires these great works. Looking at this house in front of me, I'm hoping to find something, now that the wound is open and bleeding. I haven't spoken about Amelia since the day I laid her in the ground. Funerals of older relatives you aren't familiar with, or fond of, never prepare you for a child's funeral. I insisted it be a double ceremony because I didn't want Amelia to go through it alone without her father.

They warned me it would be hard. They tried several times to change my mind, but I believed it was best for Amelia. I still do. They never prepared me for the little casket.

I went through the motions. I was poised as the perfect grieving mother and widow, but I was dying on the inside. I bound my chest to stop milk from coming in, crying all through the night because of the physical pain, the ache reminding me of what I lost. I would not feed my daughter again; she no longer required nourishment. I wouldn't hold her in the middle of the night when she cried. During the day, I composed myself. Our house was surrounded by mourners, every single one sorrier for themselves than the next. They spoke of their pain, their loss. Those who hadn't bothered to meet Amelia in the six months she was alive, grieved the hardest. No one suspected or watched for the signs of a breakdown.

No matter how they cleaned them up for the final viewing, I only saw the blood of the accident. It took me a year to conjure up a living image at the sound of either name versus the accident scene. The casket choosing for Ben wasn't surprising, I had helped my mother pick out my grandmother's four years prior, so I knew what to expect. Amelia's casket choosing, there's nothing to equate that. The director took his time, talking slowly and delicately as to ease the complication of the task. I picked it out. That tiny box. How can something that small contain a human that was so big in my life? The pine box was a deep cherry color with wooden trim outlining a design of cherubs along the lid. I chose a stone cherub to watch over them along with a joint tombstone. She would look down on them in their final resting place, constant and rigid.

Penelope sat so still at the funeral, everyone remarked on how good she was. She was four; she shouldn't have sat still. She held my hand the entire time. Everyone hugged us, rubbed our backs and patted our hair, but we never lost our connection. My leg bounced harder and harder at every contact from grievers. I sank further into myself. The chairs we sat in made the living envy the comfort of the dead. I stared at the tiny box next to the full-grown man's coffin, tried my best to do the math in my head and come up with dimensions. It had to be off because she couldn't be that small. I worried they crammed her in there.

Was she even in there? I once read a person's rant about how they think the funeral company doesn't put the bodies in the coffin. They dig up the coffin once the family leaves and replace it with a plain box containing your family member. She was convinced she saw the same coffin, same dent, that she chose to bury her father in when she went to bury her mother four years later. Presented with the boxes before me, I would have to agree with her theory. There is no way that small box fits my baby. She isn't in there.

I stood up during the preacher's speech, drawing a hush in the assembly and breaking the link between Penelope and me, and walked to the caskets. I went to Amelia's box and lifted my left arm next to it in measurement. I knew just how long she was by the way I held her. She fit. This man-made creation held one of my two creations, next to it laid my husband who gave me my children.

What happened next, I don't personally recall, not even after all this time, but I've heard stories. They all mimic each other so it must be true. I grabbed hold of the box and screamed, some called it gut-wrenching because attendants chose to leave. Charlotte told me that the resounding "No" came from deep within my soul and she'll never forget the sound. I don't remember a thing. They say once they pried me off the box long enough to continue with the service, I seemed okay again. Charlotte called it the eerie silence. As the caskets lowered, I broke free, climbing on top of Ben's box screaming for him not to leave.

Days later, I woke from a heavy drug-induced rest to find myself in the psych ward. Terrified they would take Penelope away, I told the doctor everything he wanted to hear. I pretended to grieve. When I came home, I discovered my mother had taken it upon herself to redo the nursery. It was now a guest room. She had removed every trace of Amelia from home. She thought she was helping me cope. She didn't want me to come home to an empty nursery after being admitted to the hospital. I punched her that day. Square in the nose. She had to have it reset. Penelope didn't talk for three months. I never spoke of Amelia again.

Now, I'm here at this house, the last place on earth I ever thought my car would steer. My mother's home. She's facing the possibility of looking upon that same kind of coffin, Charlotte's, and I had just verbalized the loss of my daughter. I need to console her. I need her to comfort me. It is my mother who pushed this progression on me, the one who started my journey back among the living. I want to share in my bittersweet accomplishment this evening, and I want to mend the bridge that has been slowly burning around us. I see the front porch light turn on. It is not the time of day that my mother usually has guests. I'm sure she is curious who in the world has taken residence in her driveway.

I shove the door open and let my feet continue the resounding crunch of gravel to the sidewalk. Along the path, my mother has planted different shades of red flowers, her favorite color. I pluck a bud and stuff it in my pocket, stealth-like so she won't throw a fit. The moment I come into view of my mother's eyes, the steel door opens, and only a screen door separates us physically. She makes haste at removing the last barrier, but hesitation clouds her eyes. It isn't like me to come over; I can only imagine the possibilities for my visit running through her mind. Does she think I am delivering the awful news of Charlotte's departure? I make quick to erase her troubled mind, with a shake of my head.

"Mom." My words take effort to push past the burning of my swollen throat from crying at group.

"What is it, Miriam? Are you okay? Is Penelope okay? Is Charlotte . . . ?" She is frantic. The idea of me coming to her has her desperately nervous.

"Mom." My vision blurs, and wet release falls down my cheeks. "I told them. I told them about Amelia."

The woman that has been the constant roadblock in my life, the head I butted with the most, comes to me without fail and clutches onto me. Years of my childhood and even my adulthood have been spent wondering if my mother truly loves me. She always favored Charlotte, and I never minded that. But did she love me, too? She grips me so tight in this hug that we become synchronized. She has been rooting for me this whole time. She doesn't want me to fail. She doesn't want to take Penelope away from me, it was a scare tactic to motivate me in a positive direction, and it worked. It is working. I realize it as I hold her just as tightly. I've lost hours of my life thinking horrible, hateful thoughts about her, but she was the one to start this for me.

"I love you, Mom." She never says it back.

It is well after midnight by the time I make it home. I look at my phone to discover three missed text messages from Oliver. He wants to get coffee with me again. I send a quick message back to let him know I'm not up for it tomorrow, but maybe Wednesday. I turn the knob of the front door, letting myself into the dark house. Charlotte and Penelope have retired for the evening. I'm glad they didn't wait up for me. The vibration from my cell phone echoes in the living room.

Oliver. He keeps waiting for me. I let myself think of the possibility of becoming romantic with Oliver. His personality has shown me nothing less than kindness, but would he be able to handle all this pain? He didn't flinch when I spoke about being a widow, but what about when I tell him I lost a child? He is excellent when I talk to beans or talk about therapy, but what if he knew I spent days on the psych floor of the hospital? I guess I'll have to dive in Wednesday and see because he says the day works for him.

The words from tonight strangle me all at once with no warning in the dark of the living room. I shared Amelia with the world. Amelia is dead. Ben is dead. And Charlotte is probably dying. I lost a child. I am a widow. I am fighting to keep Penelope with me and to make a better life for her, but all I want to do is stay numb. Do I drown or do I swim? As the proverbial water fills my lungs the decision that should be quick isn't coming. Matters of life and death always require a split decision. Fight or flight. Adrenaline fills every crack and you fight, or you run. Why isn't it coming now? What do I do tomorrow?

The logic in my mind screams that fighting is the only thing I can do, I can no longer run from the past. Penelope and I will never get anywhere if I remain frozen in my pain and stop talking about Amelia and Ben again. I will only drag her down and drown her along with myself. I just wish I could tell that selfish part of me, my heart, to listen for once. It wants Ben and Amelia back. It has no logic; it only has emotion. It is begging me to remain still, to hold on to the pain and the suffering because it will keep them alive. It will give them the oxygen they need, but it will suffocate me.

I bleed for those who have bled out, and I refuse to cauterize the wound and let them fade into the black. I can't pretend the accident didn't happen and that it hasn't forever changed my life. I spend nights begging for God to replace them and take me instead. In the living room tonight, I am still sending that same prayer up, but my mind is fighting back with logic for the first time. It is screaming the lunacy of such actions.

It takes me another hour to calm down. I crawl my way with the aid of the wall to Penelope's room. She is sound asleep, tangled in the sheets as only a child can be without the fear of neck pain upon awakening. She looks peaceful, and my mind is shouting for me to pay attention. 'Look at her; she matters now. You can't save Ben and Amelia. It isn't worth another life. You'll take her down. Don't do it.' I let my mind win for tonight. I kiss Penelope on the head. I promise my heart only one more day. Tomorrow is your last day.

I turn my phone off, committing myself to a full day from sun up to sun down to just indulge my heart in its selfish ways. I make the rounds to Charlotte's room, planning to plant the same goodnight kiss on her forehead as I did to Penelope, but when I do, she isn't there. A quick search of the house finds her asleep, sprawled out on Ben's side of the bed. My heart doesn't hurt to see the space taken like I always believed it would. Instead, it rejoices that Charlotte is there. She is still here, and she will be closer tonight. I change into my pajamas and climb in beside my sister, facing her limp sleeping body. I take her hand in mine and squeeze, three times for I love you, and I let the exhaustion of the day seep into my bones. One more day, heart.

EIGHTEEN

Charlotte shakes me in the morning to wake me for the day when my alarm never goes off. I fling a half-hearted swing in her general direction and mumble incoherently about my heart needing the day. She doesn't understand me at all, and after several more failed attempts, she launches her hands up and shouts at me to get out of bed. I roll over and fall back asleep.

The next attempt at a wake-up call is from Penelope. Although her attempt is much gentler than Charlotte's leg pulling, it still doesn't work. I promised myself this last day, and I was going to give it to my heart for closure. Was it selfish? I guess one could argue that it was, but it was easy to when you know that it is your last day. I wish I had known it was Ben and Amelia's last day because I would have told them to stay home. I would have apologized for being so selfish, asking for him to take over when I could have dealt with the fussy baby and had them both alive instead. There were so many things about that night that I would have done differently had I known.

The last three years, I've done nothing but think about the past and how I would have done it differently. I have let myself wallow in the fact that I was at fault for sending my husband and daughter to their death. I allow the pain to paralyze me to the pillow. Iit took my mother threatening to steal Penelope away to get me moving. It even took a while after that. I can't do it anymore; I know that. Today is my last day in the depths; tomorrow I will not be returning to that black hole. This is the promise I make to myself and a message I try to convey to my sister and Penelope.

"But you've been doing better and not sleeping like this," Penelope whines at me. My heart hurts listening to the pleas pass my daughter's lips, but I am committed.

"I just need this day, baby. It's my last day, I promise." I throw the pillow over my head, ending the conversation. I don't even want speaking to be part of this day, but I have to communicate that this is not a bad thing to my daughter. I watch from under the slack of the pillowcase as they both reluctantly leave my room, worry etched deep in their faces. Part of me wants to follow them, the living part of me, but the dead part of my soul begs for selfishness once more.

I move my head upwards to angle my view toward Ben's old side of the bed, where Charlotte slept the night before. I don't hurt like before. I look upon it without my heart feeling empty. I miss his scent the most, nothing holds it anymore. I wish that would have been public knowledge, taught to me at some point in my life, the scent of someone you love will eventually fade. It won't last years. I wish someone had shared that truth with me at some point.Maybe it would have done better to prepare me for the loss of the memory.

I thought about Amelia's scent. After the time in the hospital, I came home to that lost nursery. In its place was a strange room, one I was sure never belonged in my household. The walls were no longer the peach color I had painted them when we found out our second child was a girl. They were a hard gray, cold and lifeless. There was no crib, baby clothes, diapers; there was nothing. The room that I was more than positive I had left as a baby's room, was now turned into a guest room. The confusion set upon my face prompted my mother's confession as the culprit behind the operation. She said she thought it would be best, considering my delicate state of mind after the funeral debacle. I punched her. The one time I ever laid hands on my mother. I took her action to mean she wanted me to forget Amelia, but not Ben seeing how she never touched a single item of his.

My relationship with my mother has always had its moments, but we share an understanding that neither one is the other's cup of tea. Our personalities clashed regularly, so from teenage years on I just made it a point to stay out of her way. It wasn't until Penelope came in my life that my mother started to hang around and we managed to form a tolerable relationship. I would never hold my child back from the possibility of having a grandparent that loved them just because of my feelings for her. My mother was never a malicious or physical threat to my child, any rejection on my part would only lead to Penelope's resentment toward me. I'm glad for last night being a turning point in our relationship. God forbid my mother ever have to deal with the reality of losing a child, but I hope now she understands the helpless feeling that comes along with the potential of it. She will be able to come to terms with my healing process from a different place and have more understanding now.

I conjure Amelia's face in my mind, and it is still there clear as day. She had gorgeous blue eyes and brown tinted spackling of hair on her head. Penelope was born with a full mess of hair, but Amelia was near bald when she came out. By six months old, she was sporting just a sprinkling. It was the softest hair you ever ran your palm across, especially right after bath time when the grease of the day was out, and it fluffed up like a duckling's feathers. Her baby chub was still ever present on her face, her baby acne wholly gone. I could get in there and run my nose along her cheek and feel only softness. She adored cuddles. I never wanted to put her down because she was the most observant baby, showing her everything I was doing became a game for us. She was perfection.

"What the hell are you doing?"

I must have fallen asleep because the sound of my mother entering the room never registered. I open my eyes to see her red face, the leering eyes of the Devil herself beaming down on me. She's practically foaming at the mouth, and I missed the question because I was dreaming of my sweet baby girl's face.

"What?" I venture. It is quite foolish to tempt a charged-up woman, but I'm not playing dumb to get her goat, I just didn't hear what she said. This must have been an impossible realization in her mind because my question set her off pacing, allowing her face to become redder. I sit up in bed and take a chance look at the clock. It was close to 2:00 p.m. I fell asleep. But that is the only task I assigned myself for the day, so why do I feel guilty? I charged myself to grieve in my old way for one last day, to give my heart that much before instating my mind to be in charge from now on. Quite frankly, I'm getting pissed myself watching her wear a path in my carpet. Why is she here? What is her problem? After last night, I honestly believed we were in a good place, foolish me. That is never going to be the case with my mother. The storm never ceased in her because she has a hatred she can't surpass with me. I don't know why.

"What the hell are you doing?" She enunciates every single word. She peers at me with venom pouring from that black soul and those dead eyes. She pierces me to the spot I'm in, deeming me unworthy. I turned to shit on her shoe in less than a day's time, and I dare to feel surprised. I dare to believe we were on a path for good, a path for mending. We are in Tornado Alley, and my mother is an F5.

"I was sleeping." I keep my voice as even.

"I told you I wasn't joking around, Miriam. I will take Penelope. I will file. You aren't doing a damn thing I said." Time stands still as she speaks. I can see the spit from her mouth fly forward and fall to the floor. I can see the vein in her forehead pulsate, and every bone in her body fill up with anger. There is no room in those bones for compassion, not even a single sliver for love. I see it all, but I never see a mother. I glance past her to the armoire mirror, and I see myself. The tension in my jaw is set, creating a more masculine feel to my face, and I only see him. I never see her when I look at my reflection. I only ever see the man who helped create me, then left our family. It all becomes clear.

"You're not even listening right now. What an awful mother you are. You only care for yourself. I sacrificed my life to raise you, and you think you would have soaked in some of that when it came to your own parenting. I did everything for you. I gave my life to you." Her words are finally enough. I have had enough. It takes me only seconds, if that, to unbind myself from the sheets on the bed and be directly in front of my mother's face. The slap. The slap upon my mother's face cracks echoes into the room. I hear it all, the flesh slide across her cheek from the inside. I feel it all, the poor elasticity in her cheeks giving way under my hand

and slamming inward. I see it all, the shocked look in her eyes once her neck allows her head to come back to a forward position.

"You will get out of my home. The years I spent neglected and shamed because I look like him and I never guessed it. My father, who left us because he couldn't deal with your shit anymore. I remind you of him. You look at me with disgust because I am his appearance reincarnated. You never loved me as a mother when he left. You tolerated me because you had to. I don't have to tolerate you. You will never have my daughter. You couldn't love her. You are the awful mother." I don't raise my voice. I don't shout. The slap is louder than my words yet they penetrate deeper. The shame etched on my mother's face because her truth is out, the one she kept to herself and prayed didn't show, is all over the room. I can smell the salt from her tears, but I can feel nothing anymore.

"It's time for you to go, Mom." Charlotte's sharp whisper cuts in. I replace everything in my childhood with the truth, and it hurts. Every time I tried to get close to her, now I know the reason she pushed me away. I used to cry for days on end hoping she would love me like she did Charlotte, wondering why she had stopped. I wanted my mother for every second of my childhood after my father left.

My mother cowers in the safety of the door, seeking refuge from her shame. There is no fight in her. The door pops back open for the lack of strength she had behind to close it.

"Did you call her?" I accuse Charlotte.

"No. I swear, Miriam. I didn't know she was here until I heard her shouting, I was sleeping in my room." She testified to the jury, and I found her not guilty. That only leaves one person.

I am dressed and presentable for the afternoon bus drop off. There's no doubt in my mind Penelope will be surprised to see me when she gets off the bus. I ban Charlotte to the house because she is not to be a party to this. She would only mediate or break my will merely by her presence. I need to be firm with my daughter. It is the time she truly understands the situation. She has been treated like the parent the last three years, and it is time I take control of it.

I sip my lemonade as I repeat the speech in my head over and over again. I conjure up all possible ways I can say it to be age appropriate and have it sink in. I listen to it as the parent it is coming from, then I do it again as the child who will hear it. I edit the parts that are too harsh for either side; then I stick them back in. The process continues over and over again until I hear the diesel engine of the bus coming down the road. This is her. I have prided myself on never letting my prejudices against my mother bleed over into my daughter's relationship with her. Today, unfortunately, my hand has been pushed, and this idle dream will blow up in my face. Explode.

The bus stops at the end of the driveway, and I note the achingly slow way Penelope drags her feet down the steps of the bus. When she spotted me from the seat, surely her mind began to race with questions. A closer look at my facial expressions and she knows she is busted. She maintains eye contact until halfway up the driveway when she bows her head in guilty defeat. She remains bent until her toes touch the bottom porch step where she immediately halts and waits for further instruction.

"Sit," I command. I half expect her to plop down on the sidewalk, but she finally moves forward and occupies the seat next to me. The fact that she's staring at her shoes and not at me anymore might make this easier for me to say.

"Mom?" She ventures weakly.

"I need you to listen and not interrupt me. Do you understand?" She nods. "You called Grandma today, and that was not your place." I see the beginning of the mutiny as her body stirs to object, but she keeps her promise and remains silent. "I am your mother. I understand that I have been out of commission for three years and I apologize. That was not fair for you, and I won't make excuses for my behavior, but I also can't keep you in the dark about that night anymore." I take a deep breath. You can do this Miriam. "Your father died in a car accident three years ago. That made Mommy very sad. That night," I stumble, "that night." Come on, Miriam. I look to my daughter at the same time she looks at me. Her eyes hold more strength for me than the clouds did. "I know you've heard Grandma Jones talk about Amelia when you spend the night. I know you remember her. I know everything was confusing after Daddy died and

Mommy had to be in the hospital. Then Grandma Woods changed the rooms around. I know you haven't asked because of that. Amelia was your sister, an she died in the car accident with Daddy."

A tear starts to roll down Penelope's face, mirroring my own. I shut my eyes and take a deep breath. There's so much more to get through.

"She died, and Mommy didn't talk about her. It hurt too much that they took every piece of her from the house. They thought it would be better for you and me, but it wasn't. That's not their fault; it's mine. I thought it was what everyone wanted, for me not to talk about her. Instead of sharing her with you or anyone else, I kept her hidden. It broke my heart to lose your Daddy, but losing her broke my soul. Because you two are my babies, you were inside my belly and grew in me. I can't explain it, and I don't want to make Daddy sound less important. I started to sleep every day; you know that. You also know how these weeks have been. I've been trying and working hard to get back to a good place. When I decided to sleep today, I wasn't going back to being very sad. I told my group about Amelia last night. It's the first time since the hospital that I said it to anyone. It brought a lot of sadness back, but not the same as before. I may not be making sense, but I need you to know that I love you very much. I don't want to go back to being sad Mommy in bed every day. I'll make mistakes, but I am trying to be here for you every day. You can't call Grandma and do that to me because she will take you away from me. She didn't make my childhood a happy experience, and you've already gotten a crap hand dealt to you. I want you to stay with me."

"I want to stay with you." She squeaks out in sobs, and it is an insane relief in my chest.

"Yeah?"

"I was scared this morning."

"I know, baby. That was Mommy's mistake. I just missed your sister." She starts to fiddle with her thumbs. "What is it?"

"I have to tell you something." She looks guilty. Oh no.

"Yes?"

"I saved a shoebox full of Amelia's things."

I'm stunned.

"When they were taking her stuff away I grabbed what I could. I didn't want to lose her stuff. I thought she was coming back."

"May I see the box?" I try to hide my hopeful glee of touching something of Amelia's once again, but I can't.

"Yes." She smiles.

The rest of the night Charlotte, Penelope, and I sit around pouring over the contents of the box and telling stories about Ben and Amelia, and I can finally feel them again.

NINETEEN

"I think Penelope likes Oliver," I whisper to my sister as I lay on her bed. It is early morning, not even time for Penelope to be stirring for school. My sister has been groggy and half-heartedly listening to my rambling since I climbed into her bed twenty minutes ago. Suddenly a sleepy eye lifts to look at me.

"Ah, so you were listening?" I giggle. A grunt is all that produces from the sweet throat of my sister. She closes the sleepy eye to me. I'm apparently not holding her attention that well. I take the chance to study her, the dark circles under her eyes are prominent, and her hair is dramatically thinning that I can't believe I missed seeing she was sick this whole time. I feel ashamed that I invested all our time in my grief instead of looking at those around me. I sigh as I take in the fragile state of my sister's frame. I remember her being so athletic and strong in our youth.

A tear rolls down my cheek, as I think about what it is like being Charlotte. She gives to everyone, no questions asked. She doesn't judge, so people seek her out for advice and she gladly hands it over. They bring all their problems to her and dump them, but she takes it with a smile on her face and an angelic beat in her heart. They never ask about her. I have made this mistake over and over in our lifetime. She fixes someone's problem or listens to their day, but the courtesy is never returned, and she doesn't mind. She never was one to draw the attention to herself, forever standing in the background. I sigh heavily into my pillow and turn to face her again.

"Char, how are you feeling?"

"Tired. That's why I was sleeping." She shoots me a sarcastic eyebrow raise complete with a smirk.

"I mean the . . ." Words lodge in my throat, one more breath and I could shove them out, but they don't come, it is restricted in my lungs.

"Cancer." She finishes for me, a confident tone hanging in her voice that I could never muster for her situation if it were my own.

"Yeah," I mumble, barely above a whisper.

"I'm okay. I've had a good life, and I'll have a good fight." Her eyes are closed tight so that I don't see the pain behind this acceptance, but her lips give her away. She is plastering on her fake grin that I could spot a mile away. Boy, the dying are braver than the living. Oh sure, you could argue that we are all technically dying but I mean those who face it head on with full knowledge their last day is barreling at them. The dead feel no pain. They have no problem with death; it only bothers the living. The dying are braver than the living because they are on the path of acceptance, we have to live our lives without them. We selfishly ask them to put us at ease since they have the secret.

"When's your chemo treatment?"

"Tomorrow."

"Is Mom taking you?"

"No," she laughs, "you scared her, and she doesn't want to set foot near the house now."

I guess my blow out with my mom yesterday put a dent in her relationship with Penelope and Charlotte, just what I wanted to avoid, but push came to shove. I'd give anything to have had a chance to help Amelia deal with death, and my mother is blowing the gift she is being handed. I make plans to call her later, not to make up or apologize but to let her know she can still see Charlotte. She shouldn't waste the time we may not have with her.

"I can take you. I want to."

"I'd like that." She says. "Now, if you insist on talking and not letting me sleep, shut up about cancer. Tell me about the boy." She wouldn't let me make her the center of attention even when I try. Charlotte would much rather listen to another's day than talk about her own.

"Fine." I surrender, not that I was looking to battle since I did come in here to talk about Oliver. "So, Penelope likes him. She told me last night. We were sitting on my bed just talking about everything, and she mentioned him. I could only answer some of her questions about him. I still don't know a lot about him."

"Do you like him?" My sister's eyes are still closed; she must be exhausted.

"Yeah," I admit it. "But what about Ben?"

"I hate to be crude."

"You?" I interrupt. Her eyes pop up for a second, and she winks.

"Ben isn't going to be returning to have a duel with Oliver."

"No," I sigh, "he isn't."

"It is more of a question of are you ready or are you not?"

"I might be." I lay on my back and stare at the ceiling. Why does admitting I like a boy have to be so complicated?

"Then talk that over with Penelope."

"I did."

"What?" Her head pops up from the pillow, and she's sitting up wide-eyed.

"Well, she did." I correct myself.

"Wait. Wait. Start over. I'm confused."

"After she told me she liked him, Penelope said that she wouldn't mind if I dated him or anyone." This is why I came in here to talk to Charlotte. I'm not sure how I feel that my daughter has accepted dating long before I have.

"Interesting." She nods, deep in thought. I think she's about to give me a philosophical approach to life, but she just shrugs and says, "Call him." With that, she shoos me out the door so she can get some sleep.

I turn around when I reach the door. "Char?"

"What?" She is faking irritation with me.

"I love you."

"I love you, too."

I yank the cell phone off the nightstand after Penelope leaves for school. I feel like a teenager again, anxious butterflies swarming in my stomach and my forehead is gathering nervous perspiration. I bite my lip and force my shaking fingers to scroll over and select Oliver's number. Shrieking under my breath, I press the call button. His phone rings. Once. Twice. The third time I just about slam the end button and call it a day, but he picks up.

"Hello, Miriam." His greeting is pleasant and calm. Not fair. I was calling someone so out of my league and cooler than me.

"Hey, you." James Bond smooth, Miriam. I slap my forehead.

"What was that sound?" Shoot he heard it.

"Um. Nothing." Crap.

"So?"

"So?" I respond. This is failing miserably. Crash and burn. Plane into the ground. Kaboom.

"What's up?" His voice is soothing; he could put babies and the elderly at ease with this tone. Unfortunately, it was doing nothing for me today. I want to throw up. I don't say anything. I can't find the damn index card I wrote on for back up in case this happened. Where is it?

"Is something wrong, Miriam? Oh my god, is Charlotte okay? Penelope?" Oh my god, he is just too perfect.

"Everyone's fine. They're good." I answer.

"This has to be the weirdest phone call I have ever gotten." He laughs at the other end, more a relieved laugh that nothing is wrong than a teasing one.

"Shut up. I called to ask you on a date, and it's hard, okay? You could just be a gentleman and patiently wait for me to find the damn index card I wrote my prepared speech on." I spit back into the phone. The nerve of him, laughing at me. I'm having the worst time over here trying to summon up the courage to ask him . . . oh God. I didn't. Crap, I did. "I should just stick to speaking to cans," I mumble once I realize that I just leaked everything out of my mouth that I was supposed to keep in my head.

He is quiet for a minute. Okay, it is more like five seconds. Five Mississippi. That's what it was. I counted. No, I didn't. I shouldn't admit that.

"What day?" His voice has changed subtly. If I weren't concentrating with every ounce of my senses, I would have missed it. Does he not want to date me? Did I read the signs wrong? He sounds all business now. Maybe he is doing it out of pity. He doesn't want to say no to me since I'm a widow and crazy.

"You don't have to. We can just be friends." I try desperately to repair the damage I just caused, Oliver has been a wonderful person in my life, and I can't muck it up.

"Miriam." He is stern. I squeeze my eyes tight and brace for impact.

"Yeah?" I draw out.

"Which one is it?"

"Well, I don't want you to feel like you have to just because I'm crazy. I understand not wanting to date the girl who talks to cans and has verbal diarrhea. I'm probably more of a friend zone person. You're a bit too cool to want to date me anyway."

"I want to." His voice is raspy.

"God, you aren't cool at all." He laughs at me. "Wait, really?" I perk up. One point for dorky Miriam. He asks me when the last time I asked anyone out was, in between his laughter.

"Um, probably tenth grade." I slap my forehead again. He roars with laughter, either because he's identified the noise from earlier or because of what I said.

"Are you going to pick me up?" He's teasing and just like that we slip into our easy banter.

"I'm going to take it back."

"Then I'll just ask you out. I have it on good authority that you want me."

"I wish you nothing but a big giant pimple on your forehead for our date."

"But a pimple won't go with the outfit I have planned." He jokes.

"Will you wear something tight?" Where the heck did that come from? Abort. Abort. Get off this phone before you embarrass yourself even more. Wrap it up. I hear him choke on his laughter. He didn't expect it either, or the porno tone that came out of my mouth when I said it.

"So, how's tonight? I have to take Charlotte to chemo tomorrow, and I'm not sure how sick she will feel after so I don't want to plan anything for the weekend." I spit it out fast, suddenly all professional, I am going to get through the rest of the phone call without another slip.

"Just can't wait any longer, eh?" I feel like he's wagging his eyebrows at me. "Sounds good. 7?

"Yup. Pick me up?"

"You asked me out." He feigns insult.

"I don't know where you live. I haven't taken up on stalking you yet. I probably could ask Charlotte. She tends to delve into the online world of stalking and know everyone's favorite color before shaking their hand."

"I look forward to the day you take up stalking me." Crap, his porno tone. End. This. Call. How am I going to survive a date with this guy, where flirting is expected?

"So?"

"I'll be there at 7."

"Ok. Good. Good. I'll see you at 7." I say.

"Okay, Miriam."

"7."

"Yes." He draws it out. I want to stay on the phone longer, but I need to get off.

"Okay. Uh, I'll see you at 7. Tonight at 7. My house. Okay." Stop. Stop. How did they let you out into society?

"What time again?" He chuckles.

"Oh, shut up." I hang up. I'm so happy and miserable at the same time. Definitely a crush. Crap. I have a date tonight.

TWENTY

Tonight is the night. This was going to be my first date since Ben, and I started dating when I was in high school. I was working as a waitress at an old diner the college crowd used to frequent in our town. One fateful night, there he was. The rest was history, or at least it needed to be tonight. I couldn't be getting ready to go out with another man with the Ben and Miriam saga playing in my mind. No, I needed to do my best to focus on Oliver. Ben isn't coming back, and this is just one more step I have to take to move on and overcome my grief.

I sink my head back down into the water of the tub, just far enough that my ears are covered, but I can still breathe. I'm hoping for the peace and quiet to set my mind, but all I can hear is my heart pounding in my ears. I have heard over and over how drowning would be such a terrible quiet death, falling into the depths of the water and not being able to scream. The thought always frightened me. I would hate to have the last moments of my life pass in horrid silence, unable to hear anything. Not a sound of the world to take with you. I know now that it isn't true. With the water covering my ears, I can hear my heartbeat loud in my head. I wasn't aware of its sound when I was above the water. Drowning would never be a quiet death. You would hear your heart racing to stay alive, the water rushing around your ears, and any movement in the water feels like a siren going off. You would spend your last moments on this earth surrounded by noise. I'm not sure drowning frightens me more thinking it would be silent or knowing now that it would be a string of sounds you can't escape.

I can hear the footsteps approaching down the hallway, that's how well the water amplifies. I wonder how long it will take before someone comes and sees what's taking me so long. I told them I was taking a quick bath before my date. That was an hour ago according to my watch; I watch the time ticking by on it from the spot it occupies on the edge of the tub. I have thirty more minutes to get dressed and done up for my date. The water has gone frigid, and I'm still hesitant to move from it. A knock on the door is pounding in my ears. Water surely isn't a peaceful death.

"Come in," I shout, hearing my voice and breathing deep inside my head. I look up at the door to reveal the identity of my guest, Charlotte.

"Are you getting out soon?" She tenderly asks as if I were a vase on the verge of shattering. She doesn't want the tone or volume of her voice to shake me one way or the other off the balance beam I'm on.

"Yeah, just thinking." I shift my head out of the water and pull the plug.

"About?" Charlotte closes the lid on the toilet and sits.

"Drowning." I figure she'll commit me or give me a chipper date prep talk.

"I think it would be better than cancer." She softly replies, with her demons showing.

"Everyone says it would be quiet, but I bet it would be loud with your heart pounding in your head." I stand and fetch my towel to dry myself. I can tell by the look on Char's face, looking down at her knees, she never thought of it before.

"I wonder if cancer is loud or silent. I imagine the beeping of the hospital machines would drive you crazy. Do you think you can put head-phones on me? I want to go out to my favorite song." This talk was a first from Charlotte, as much as I didn't want my sister talking about dying I didn't want to stop what was important to her.

"Do you have death song, Char?" I try to make light of it, let her feel at ease that she can say it without feeling serious.

"No, I just have a song I want you to listen to when you spread my ashes." She turns her to me with a half-hearted smile to soften the blow, but it annihilates my heart. "Probably not the best time to talk about this when you're running late."

"What's the song?" Forget being late. Charlotte needed to feel important, not brushed off.

"Like a Stone." She says it to the air, not to me, but I soak in every syllable of it. I don't say anything because I don't know if she's done talking or if I can even talk. She shakes her head, clearing her thoughts. Her chemotherapy tomorrow was a shot in the dark the doctor said, she may be too far gone, but we were going to fight like hell. I was hoping for the slim chance he handed us in the statistics. Unfortunately, my sister was thinking about the realm of possibility that the higher statistic was her fate. "You have to get ready for your hot date. Put some makeup on. You look tired."

"Says the cancer patient." I earn a laugh from her. It's the most delightful heartbreaking sound.

"Want me to braid your hair?"

"Yes." When we were growing up, Charlotte was the more girly of us two, and she loved to play with hairstyles and makeup. I was her favorite guinea pig, and I know letting her do this tonight will give her some joy. As I throw on my makeup, Charlotte does her best to tame the wet mop into a beautiful braid design. I end up with five minutes left to throw some clothes on. I wonder if Oliver is an early person, just on time, or late. I know very little about him. Why did I ask him out on a date? He could be a serial killer. What if I am going on a date with a murderer?

"It definitely wouldn't be a peaceful death for you then," Charlotte replies as I retreat to my room to throw on the outfit I chose for the evening. I hadn't realized I spoke out loud. I sound ridiculous.

Oliver is right on time. Seven on the dot. I'm sliding on my jeans when I hear the doorbell. I have made it, all ready to go in less than thirty minutes. Penelope comes into my bedroom to fetch me before Charlotte even gets the front door open.

"Ready, Mommy?" She closes the door behind her. I look in the mirror above the armoire. I'm far from the shell of a human I saw in the reflection the day my mother gave me the list. I'm proud to have my daughter smiling at my appearance this time instead of ducking in shame. This whole time, I was doing it. It is so hard to know when you've hit a goal sometimes, until one day you look up and realize you can see the finish line.

"I guess I am."

"You look beautiful, Mommy." I have never heard a better compliment and looking in her eyes right now, I never felt a better one.

"Thanks, baby." My eyes begin to fill with tears at this miraculous human being before me. She has been given such a crap hand the last three years, and here she was before me, forgiving and selfless. I have barely been raising her, and she was doing great.

"Don't cry. You'll ruin your makeup. I hear that's important on a date." I laugh.

"Who told you that?"

"Kids at school." She shrugs.

"Honey?" I ask. "Are you sure you are okay with Mommy dating?" It was a bit of bad timing, but I have to know before I walk out this bedroom door that she's okay. Penelope looks me dead in the eyes and never breaks contact when she tells me she's more than sure. Here I go.

Oliver brought all of us girls a bouquet of flowers. Penelope's eyes light up when she sees hers. It's bittersweet because I always hoped her dad would be the first to give her flowers. He never got to do that. It's a lovely gesture from Oliver.

He won't tell me where were we are going, only that I'm dressed perfectly for it. I'm not sure what that means and considering the car got stale after the first few minutes of riding, I'm now back to my serial killer theory. I'm on my way to death and start to panic. What's the best way out of this truck? How fast are we going? 45 mph. Can you survive a jump at that speed? I was accessing all the information I had in the back of my mind, conjuring up old physic formulas, but the fact was I can't figure it out. So, it will be a fight then. I begin looking around the cab of the truck for something I can use as a weapon. It's the cleanest truck I've ever been in. Will he clean it again after killing me? Shit. I see a busted CD in the nook of the door that might be sharp enough to slice him. Where can I put my DNA so that people will know Oliver killed me? I tilt my head up to look at the visor. If I stick a stray piece of hair up there will he know to clean it?

"What are you doing?" I jump at the sound of his voice, gripping the door and leaning far away from him.

"Um. Nothing." I try to sound calm even though I have batshit crazy written all over my face.

"What are you over there thinking?"

"Just thinking about. . . . Um. Just thinking about work." A good lie, Miriam. Next time don't stutter.

"Work? I call your bluff." He chuckles. Was it an evil laugh? A laugh at my expense?

"Are you a serial killer?" Miriam! I mentally slam my head into the dashboard for him. The truck swerves just a little before he collects himself. Driving is not his strong suit. A serial killer who needs a chauffeur, interesting.

"What did you just say? Am I a serial killer?" He's shocked. Okay, starting to doubt he's going to kill me now.

"I just . . ." But the words are lost. Did I just ask my date if he was a serial killer? I may die tonight, but it won't be by Oliver's doing, I will die of embarrassment.

He starts laughing so hard I can feel the vibration through my seat. Well, at least he has a good sense of humor.

"Sorry, I haven't been on a date in a long time." I twiddle my fingers in my lap and decide it will be the best place to concentrate my focus for the rest of the night. "You can turn around and take me home if you want." I sigh. I'm a little defeated, the other steps on the list were super hard to do, but this one is making me feel incredibly inadequate.

"I would never." He chuckles some more. "Especially since I'm planning on killing you and all." His words were evil, but his tone is light and sarcastic.

"Sorry." I just repeat my apologies over and over, hoping to do better the rest of the date.

"Don't apologize. It was funny. Besides, you are supposed to ask that before you get in the vehicle. You are out of practice."

My head shoots up. "Someone else asked you this before?"

"Yeah. As I said, I've been on a lot of first dates."

"Where does this one rank?" I was wrought with embarrassment but had to know how severe the damage was.

"This one is the best so far."

"Liar." I smack his arm playfully.

"Just got better." He looks over at me and holds me with those eyes for a second. "You just touched me." Suddenly the cab becomes smaller, and the oxygen level drops. I pray it was water from my damp hair running down my neck and not sweat. I'm in trouble if he keeps looking at me that way tonight.

We pull into a mini-golf course right off an old fifties style diner; this date is already perfect for me. Nothing romantic or fancy, a weight of anxiety lifting from me. I look over at Oliver, and I'm grinning from ear to ear. I'm ecstatic just to go out and be surrounded by people who want to take me to have fun like this. I wonder if Penelope will want to play mini golf on our next mother/daughter date. She would love this. We decide to eat before we play. The diner is decorated with red and white checkered tiles on the floor inside, linoleum tabletops and tons of memorabilia covering the walls.

Before we take our seats, I walk around and take in the framed pictures on the wall. Oliver stands behind me the whole time, never minding that I want to take it all in. He doesn't complain when the other patrons give me curious, odd glances. He is completely comfortable with himself, and he doesn't care what others think. When I find an old Betty Boop decoration, I turn to show him but find him staring at me with a content smile instead. He hasn't been looking at the pictures with me; he's been looking at me. I take him in now, for the first time with a view that I could date him. He is kind-hearted and patient. He doesn't seem like he wants to conform me to get over my grief fast. He is handsome, many ladies in this room have been turning their heads in his direction. I also noticed he didn't turn his. I look at his lips. I remember how good they felt on my forehead in the hallway that night. Would he kiss me good night?

We stare each other down, not a word being said but the heat and tension between us grows to an insurmountable level. The room is about to burst into flames, only saved by the server who comes to ask if we are ready to be seated. We split from our staring contest, but not without one last glance at each other's lips. He was thinking it, too. Good. I like that. Once we are seated, I order a giant chocolate milkshake for my drink, and it makes Oliver chuckle, but he orders the same.

"What?" I lean in over the table once the server has gone to make our shakes. He follows my lead and leans in as well so that we are almost nose to nose.

"Women are supposed to order water and a salad. Don't you know that?" He whispers with a glint of mischief in his eye. He is teasing me again for my lack of date knowledge, but I can tell he enjoys that I'm not turning out to be typical.

"Oh. My apologies. I just figured I'd have dessert before my salad."

"No, you don't get dessert either."

"Wow. Dating sucks. I don't want to do it anymore." I say as I distance myself from him. He makes the oxygen level in the diner decrease as well, and I begin to wonder how he gained that ability.

"You look great." He says.

"So you like the makeup better?"

"Oh no, no you aren't going to catch me with that. My mama raised me better."

"What do you mean?" I'm intrigued.

"My mother always told me never to tell a woman she looks better with or without makeup. It's not for me to decide, she'd say. A woman has the right to have versions of herself, and you have a right to enjoy what she allows you in on. A woman will wear makeup because she wants to dress up for her date with you, she wants to look good and gain your attention showing off a fancy version of herself. When she's without makeup, it means she's comfortable with you seeing that part of herself, the part that society tells her is ugly because she trusts that you don't feel that way."

"Good answer." I play it cool but I'm stunned. I couldn't have said the words better myself, having lived the true narrative on the girl's side.

His mama did raise him right. I feel like I have struck gold and should hide him away before all the wandering female eyes in this diner come and snatch him up. He winks at me and only me tonight.

"So what do we do now?" I ask. "I'm not well-versed in first dates, but I hear you are."

"Well," he says leaning in again, "you have to ask me all kinds of questions, but only give vague responses when I ask you."

"That's manageable enough," I start, but I'm momentarily interrupted by what can only be described as heaven in a glass. The chocolate masterpiece of a milkshake that has just been placed in front of me deserves a second of silence and praise. "Sweet mother of pearl, that looks amazing." I waste no time taking a slurp. I look at our waitress, an older woman, pleasantly smiling at me. "May I place an order for another one, Diana?"

I always look at the name tags of cashiers, servers, retail workers, anyone who is wearing one. It's something I picked up from Ben when we were dating. It intrigued me the first time he did it, I wondered if he had known the lady, but he said he always made it a point to call people by their names if he knew it.

"You sure can, darling. What can I get you to eat?"

"May I please have the cheeseburger combo meal with curly fries?" I ask.

"How do you want that cooked?"

"Medium Well."

"Everything on it?"

"Absolutely." I look over to Oliver to follow suit ordering and catch him with his mouth open. What? Did I break another rule? I forgot the salad. Damn. Well, everything on a burger typically includes a piece of lettuce. That should count. When Diana is done taking his order, she collects the menus and heads off to the kitchen.

"What? Lettuce comes on the burger, that's like a salad."

"I have been on an extensive number of first dates," He says.

I interrupt him. "That doesn't sound good for you."

He ignores me and continues, "No one orders that politely."

"She's a human. You ordered nicely as well."

"I'm just saying."

"Can I ask questions now?"

He sits back and waves his hand in a semi-circle in front of his body as if to say go ahead.

"Um. Do you have siblings?"

"Two brothers, one older and one younger."

"Oh man, you're a middle child. Check, please." I lift my finger in the air jokingly and we both laugh.

"I'm not so sure middle child is a thing when there are all boys. My youngest brother, Aaron, was the one who demanded the most attention. Jack and I were pretty mild mannered growing up." His eyes light up when he talks about his brothers, so I ask several more questions about his family. I find his brothers are both married, Jack and his wife have three kids while Aaron and his wife are expecting their first in two months. He had a happy easy childhood with lots of love it sounds like, or at least he didn't grow up to be a bitter adult holding on to resentment. I envy that.

"What about you, Miriam?" I've forced him to ramble on for most of our meal and haven't been playing my part of answering.

"I'm supposed to be vague." I'm stalling, I don't want to talk about my family because it will dampen the mood of the evening.

"No, I'm being serious now." He nudges my hand with his on the table, reassurance and an excuse for physical contact.

"Um, my father ran off when I was about seven years old. I hear he is an awesome dad to the other two girls he had with his next wife." I quickly shovel fries in my mouth.

"And your mom?" He looks scared to ask.

"She pushed through. We don't have the best relationship but she loves Penelope and of course Charlotte, but who couldn't love those two?"

"Charlotte is your only sibling?" He looks relaxed to have found a safe person to talk about.

"Yeah." I can't lift my voice high even though the sound of her name fills me with warmth and love. I was going to be lonely and destitute if chemotherapy didn't work.

"Your husband?" It wasn't a complete question but it packed a mean wallop, one we would have to get through before there could even be a relationship here.

"Ben." I say and he nods. "He was a good man, my best friend. He died in a car accident, a drunk driver hit him head-on."

"I shouldn't have asked." He says, sorry he dampened the mood himself. But here's my opening, the chance to reveal my whole truth before we get too far and I hurt him.

"No, it's okay. It has taken me a long time to recover and start to openly grieve and talk about that night. I lost Ben, but I also lost my daughter, Amelia, in that accident. She was only six months old. I told Ben to take her for a drive hoping it would help her sleep. I still struggle with the guilt even though there was no way I could have known what I was sending him out to." I chance to look up from the plate. Oliver's eyes are glazed over like he isn't here with me. His eyes are usually sparkling with the flecks of gold in them, now they look hollow and it frightens me. Have I lost him to my confession? Or is there more behind Oliver's story? Suddenly, he's back.

"Do you want to go hit those golf balls now?" His cheeriness is forced.

"Sure."

TWENTY-ONE

"I don't know, Char. Maybe I'm too much for him to handle."

We're two hours into Charlotte's first chemotherapy session, she a veteran and me biting my nails to keep the tension from eating me alive. Both the tension of the date last night and being here watching them drug my sister creates a war inside my mind and body. I have resorted to playing chopsticks on my legs to let off the built-up steam. The bag hangs above us, a dark cloud, dripping the drug that swirls down the tube and pumps into Charlotte's arm. It's our hope and our demise. It's poison. A poison sent to kill the cancer and all we can do is pray it doesn't kill Charlotte as well, or that the cancer will kill the poison. A sadistic treatment when you sit back and think about it.

"What is that supposed to mean?" My sister's wrapped in blankets, looking worn, but she fights to keep the conversation going.

"I told him about Amelia. I don't know. Maybe I should have waited longer." The date last night went sour after my confession. Mini golf was a much quieter game than I remembered and Oliver seemed in a hurry to be done with it. We didn't hang around to chat after we finished our 18 holes he drove me home. No walk to the door. No kiss goodnight.

"Nah, that's your truth. That's your story. He'd have to square with it sooner or later." She shrugs. It's always that simple to Charlotte. Everyone has a story and you need to make your peace with it now or eventually. She doesn't believe in throwing people out of her life, it was evident at our joint birthday party she threw. She was surrounded by the many people from all the stages of her life. No stone unturned, no one left out.

"He looked so pained when I told him. He switched the topic quickly, the rest of the date was rushed through. I couldn't get him to talk, let alone joke again. He dropped me off and didn't get out of the truck. I blew it."

"He blew it." It's girl code to come to your defense, tell you sunshine beams out of your ass and any man that doesn't see it is stupid. It never matters if you slip up, it is the jerk who doesn't deserve you. Charlotte kept to the code.

"I guess so."

"No guessing." She pops her arm that's free of an IV out of the blanket and waves it in a finite way. "Screw him."

"I thought you were Team Oliver?" I laugh.

"I was, but I'm always Team Miriam first." She winks. "What team are you?"

"Team Charlotte Kick Cancer's Ass." I wink back.

"Doing my best, small fry." She nestles her arms back in and tilts her against the chair. I vow to let her sleep now. The magazine basket next to her chair houses a three-year-old home décor magazine. That should work. I grab the magazine and kiss Charlotte on the forehead and she hums pleasantly.

"Hey, Mir?" She asks, eyes closed.

"Yeah?"

"What if Oliver went through something? Don't toss him out yet." I think about her words, I won't doubt I wondered the same thing myself fifty times since last night. Could his actions have been a direct result of his own painful memories surfacing? The past has a funny way of coming up at the worst times, wrecking the future.

"Go to sleep." I whisper. I watch Charlotte's eyebrows raise but her eyes remain closed. The magazine in front of me doesn't distract me. I watch over my sister and continuously pray to God to spare her.

When we get back home, Charlotte goes straight to her room to sleep. I collect Penelope from the end of the driveway, and her eyes light up when she sees me there. I vowed to be a better mother and I wasn't about to slip on that promise anymore. I'm down at the end of the driveway more for myself than her today, the house has been too quiet since we got back. The words of Charlotte keep haunting me as I go through the mundane routine of my everyday life. What if Oliver has a past just as painful as my own? My future doesn't look like it will be void of pain either.

I spent time this afternoon going between which was harder; having a loved one die suddenly with no warning, or having them slowly die in front of you from a disease that you knew they couldn't escape from? On one hand, you could prep for the death of a loved one who knew they were terminal, but don't they always tell you to just rip a Band-Aid off? Does that apply in this situation? Which was going to hurt worse; Amelia and Ben or Charlotte, God forbid? My mind wandered back to that question over and over through the course of the day.

I made dinner tonight, a lot of it. Charlotte isn't hungry at all but my idle hands wouldn't be satisfied with frozen pizza today. I made chicken, homemade rolls, mashed potatoes, green beans, corn, and I even baked a damn apple pie. It is a feast. I bought an audiobook off the internet and walk around with it in my ears, hoping to get into someone else's head for a while, but nothing works. Penelope has homework and can't entertain me so I clean. I scrub the kitchen floor on my hands and knees and wash the baseboards in all the rooms. I reorganize the pantry, throwing out the expired food, making a box to donate to the food bank. I still see Charlotte in everything. I watch her cook breakfast while I scrub the floor, the way she tilts her head back and laughs when she manages to flip an egg without breaking it. I see her singing 'Midnight Train to Georgia' and dancing while I organize the pantry. She's everywhere in this house. Every vision turns to ash and floats away, leaving me shivering. I'm haunted by the living and it is harder to be than by the dead.

Charlotte and Penelope turn in early for the night, most likely to get away from me. I'm becoming an annoyance now that I can't sit still. When there's nothing left to do, I sit on the couch and flip through old scrapbooks, adding pictures of Amelia and Ben for Penelope to see. I'm almost done when I swear I hear a small knocking sound. I check Penelope's room, but she's in a deep sleep. Checking on Charlotte reveals her in the same state. Hmm. I declare it to be nothing and head back to the couch, but the sound comes again. I freeze. The door.

He stands before me, gripping the back of his neck with one hand and three bouquets of flowers in the other. The bags under his eyes are dark and his face is unshaven. He hasn't slept. He's in last night's rumpled clothes.

"I'm an asshole." He states and thrusts the flowers in my direction. I appreciate a man with flowers saying an apology, but I'm not sure the one in front of me needs to do it.

"You're not an . . ."

"I am," he interrupts, "and you didn't deserve that kind of date last night. I just, I got in my head and I couldn't get out." He shoves the flowers even further at me and hits me in the face with the blooms, not an ounce of his usual grace. "Aw shit, Miriam. I'm sorry. I . . . God." He stammers while attempting to doctor my eye. I don't know what he's looking for, but he's determined to find it, he doesn't let up.

"I'm okay." I bat his hands away. "Come in."

"I bought these for you, Charlotte, and Penelope." He states glancing at the flowers, weapons mere seconds ago.

"Thank you, that was thoughtful. They're both sleeping right now, but I'll put them in vases for them to see tomorrow." He follows me into the kitchen like a defeated kicked dog. "Oliver, its fine. Whatever it is, its fine." I truly mean it. I feel no animosity towards him over our date or the floral beating. Charlotte confirmed what my gut had told me last night, Oliver has a story. I just wish I knew it.

"Look. I lost someone." He looks off into space as he recalls the memory. His prepared soliloquy is cut short as he loses the words he practiced before coming here. "I like you."

"I like you, too."

"Good." He looks into my eyes and I see he's on the brink of tears. I rush over to hold him, our physical contact until now has been a bare minimum, yet our first touches aren't traditionally awkward feeling. I wrap around him and hold tight. I hope I hug like Charlotte, with all my love emanating through to the person wrapped in my circle. I hope I strengthen Oliver in my hold.

"I'm sorry." I say it over and over because whatever pain he is in I can relate through my own.

"I had a fiancé," he explained, "and we had a baby." He pulls me tight to him so I can't bend back to see his face. "She was born still. I went to her grave today. When you told me about your daughter, it brought that all back to me."

I knew his pain more closely than I wanted to. How awful. That joyous time being taken from him, and it obviously aided in tearing apart the relationship between his fiancé and him. Not only did he lose a child, he lost a significant other as well.

"I'm going to kiss you," he says after a long time holding each other, "that's how the date was supposed to end."

"Okay."

And he does. Soft and gentle, yet completely encompassing. The passion of his emotions laced behind this kiss sends chills through my entire body, all the way down to my pinky toes. If I had to list this kiss in a category, it would be the most perfect for the Miriam I am now. Broken but whole. It is being saved and saving someone.

TWENTY-TWO

Months have passed by, our days have turned routine. Wake up, send Penelope off to school, chemotherapy or work, therapy, group, mother/daughter nights, and date nights with Oliver. Even with the monotony, things have grown. My relationship with Penelope is stronger. I talk about Ben and Amelia all the time to her, to anyone who will listen, she talks now about her feelings. She doesn't hesitate to share her feelings with me, no longer scared to send me back into my living dead state. We laugh every day; our house is full of jokes and love.

My relationship with Oliver has grown, the kiss in the kitchen sealed our fate to be forever intertwined. Our pain is matched. We might not have been cut by the same knife, but our scars hurt in similar ways, and that is something we can build on. He's opened up about the little girl he lost, Samantha. Sometimes we sit and talk about our girls, it makes us both feel better to share our hurt. He's encouraged my new-found love of photography. I want to take more pictures of the people in my life for fear that they'll fade away. On our dates, we are bantering, having fun or kissing. My feelings for Oliver have progressed.

Something else has progressed as well, Charlotte's cancer. It's been taking over our lives, stealing Charlotte's hair and energy, and draining our hope. The doctor told us that chemotherapy probably wouldn't work. I pressed for a stronger drug, and Charlotte pressed to just go home. I won. I got my way, more poison for my sister's body to take. She isn't pleased, in fact, we haven't spoken in the past three days since the new treatment has started.

I'm sitting on the bench outside the treatment center, they have a small garden out back. It's so breathtaking this time of year, autumn, when the leaves start to change color and descend to the earth. Who knew that death could be so gorgeous? My therapist and I discussed this, he all but came out and said I was a coward for not staying with Charlotte in the room. He told me this is my problem, I need to face death and not revert back to an impossible reality. I generally agree with Dr. Pierce on all his points, but this one we haven't touched in the last couple of weeks.

When chemotherapy first started, I stayed in the room with Charlotte. Those first couple of sessions were fine, we had the same schedule as a few others so we came to know their faces. On the day of her fifth session, one person wasn't there. The sixth, two had stopped going in. The eighth, we no longer saw the beautiful teenage girl with the biggest smile. They all succumbed to their fate, so I stopped staying.

I adjust my camera so I can capture the leaves in the best setting. I hunt for the tree with the most changed leaves and lay underneath it, looking up. It's stunning, so I spend several minutes taking the photos so I can get one just right. I can't wait to show this to Charlotte, this perspective and angle. It's how we greeted fall as children, laying underneath a tree, close to the trunk, looking into the branches, witnessing the scattering of the leaves. We considered it good luck if one landed on you while you were there. We rushed home every day after school, just to try our luck.

I sit up, the memory lodges in my throat. I swallow it with force. I take in the rest of the garden, where a few fall flowers are hanging on with the care of an expert gardener. I settle on a mother and daughter sitting on a bench nearby, and it's obvious the mother is in treatment here, her gown gives her away. She shows her daughter the leaves and talks about the changing of the seasons. They each take bets on which tree will have the next leaf to fall. Before I realize what I'm doing, I lift my camera and put them in focus. Snap. I check the playback, it's perfection, the mother bent with her forehead resting on her daughter's and she is smiling with love. The nagging feeling that this could be their last picture kills me, the last one where they looked happy and not weighed down by cancer.

I can't keep it to myself or erase it.

I hate to interrupt their serene moment but I can't waste time, it's urgent to me. I go to them and tell them about the photo, apologizing for sounding crazy. I show them the playback and ask if I can send the print to them. The mother is elated. The ugly truth is, we aren't in many pictures with our kids. We typically find ourselves behind the lens instead of in front of it. I know this picture would be a treasure, but the sadness behind the mother's eyes as I jot down their address reminds me that her daughter will be the one likely to inherit the photo when she's gone. She wants her daughter to remember her laugh, her fight, her courage. As I walk away, I hear her push forward to regain the moment again with her daughter despite her mortality waving in front of her. I take more photos of them. I can't help myself. I have their address now, I know where to send the memories.

Instead of looking at nature today in the garden, I continue observing the people and discovering their story. I take more photos and I leave with several more addresses. No one asks me to delete the pictures, they all seem grateful. I turn around once I reached the sidewalk that leads me back to the door that houses Charlotte for her latest poison drip. I'll return even after the treatments have stopped. I can't stop doing this now. I need to capture these families' memories that are now so precious and dear to them, as they scramble to make more before they leave this world. Suddenly, I feel it. A leaf on my shoulder.

Charlotte isn't in a speaking mood when I get her in the car to go home, she seems quite pissed. She usually sleeps on the way home, but her anger is winning against her exhaustion. The tension continues once we're home. If I didn't think she was mad before, the screen door slamming on my face is a clear sign. I let her have her anger. I can't place myself in her shoes, cancer and trying another new treatment hoping it would help. I bet she is frustrated with it, and she has every right to be. I decide to ignore it and try to talk about a better topic, showing her the photos I took today. I relay the story about the mother and daughter. Charlotte did not seem impressed. She scoffs at the photo. I admit I'm no professional, but I think it's rather good. Anyway, at least the mother liked it.

Charlotte leaps off the couch and starts pacing in between the living room and kitchen. The new treatment seems to wire her up. I didn't even know that was a possibility.

"Do you want some grapes?" I ask her as I sit in my chair. "Are you hungry?"

"Fuck your grapes." She bellows.

"What?" Was Charlotte mad at me? What had I done? What had the grapes done? It must be the treatment. "Charlotte, the doctor said the new treatment would be a little different, are you feeling alright?"

"I have cancer, Miriam. I'm dying. Don't you dare sit there and ask me if I'm feeling alright when you are the one who won't even let me feel my own death."

"What? What the hell did I do?"

"The treatment. I don't want it. It's not working. The cancer is spreading, the doctor even said this was pointless, but no you have to push. Don't you? You can't look at death and accept it because you're a coward. You'd rather I sit there with a drip of questionable drugs going into my arm and coursing through my body than sit at home with my family before I die."

"I just want . . ."

"You want what, Miriam? What?"

"I don't know. I just thought."

"What do you want?" She badgers, leaning over into my face. Her breath reeks of chemo drugs.

"I want you to live." I scream it at her.

"I'm dying, idiot. You can't ignore it. I won't do this treatment anymore."

"You won't fight?" I sob. I don't understand what I'm hearing. Sure, the treatment is a long shot but shouldn't you try when the alternative is death.

"I have fought. The fight is over, Mir. You can't buy any more fruit, hoping a healthy diet will cure me. You can't bring up articles of alternative cancer treatments at the dinner table as if you just stumbled upon them when really you have been desperately scanning the internet for them. You can't push for any more drugs. I'm done." She lowers her voice, the shouting taking all the energy she has left. "I'm done." She whispers.

"No, we have to keep trying."

"No."

"But, Char." I beg her, I don't want her to give up.

She leans down and strokes my hair, planting a kiss on my forehead. She sits down next to me, gingerly as if her bones would break if she did it any faster, bringing me to eye level. "No. Miriam, I knew I was slipping out of remission back in Ohio. I knew it was coming. Arthur had just watched his brother lose his fight with cancer. I wasn't about to make him watch me go through it again. When Mom called me, I packed up and left that day. I'm not fighting attached to machines anymore. It isn't working, Miriam. You need to understand that. You need to accept it. That picture you took, of the mom and daughter, it could be us. You are busy throwing your efforts to a cure that isn't coming when we could be making memories and saying all the words we want to say before I die."

"Stop." I'm pleading with her to stop. She can't honestly be done fighting. I can't live without Charlotte. I can't imagine my life without her, much less preparing for it to be that way. "Stop, please."

"No, Miriam." She's firm. "I won't baby you anymore. I won't sit here and wait for you to come to it on your own. I don't have the luxury of time. I'm pushing you now, I'm pushing hard. You have to accept that I'm dying. Cancer will take me. Don't waste it sitting here." I turn away from her. It makes her mad. "You can't revert back to the living dead, you are alive, so feel it. Enjoy the people around you. Stop trying to grip me so tight that you'll be under those sheets 24/7 again when I go. Don't let it be a big fucking surprise to you."

She pushes off the chair we're in and moves to the bulletin board I have in the living room, the one I hang all my flowers upside down with pins so they dry out. I chance a look at her. Her back is rising and falling with great effort. She is breathing heavy, trying to reign in her anger. Her hands are fixed on her hips. She's frail, bald, and pale, but damn she is fierce.

"You hang all these flowers up. You pick them when something bad happens or when a day doesn't go your way and you're thrown a curveball.

Why? It makes no sense. All of them." She waves her hand. "None of them make sense. And then what, you'll press them in this book?" She lifts the encyclopedia off the bookshelf next to the bulletin board. "Why? So you can remember only the shitty times? So you can get more depressed? Is it a high for you? To be miserable? I just want to throw all of them away. Rid you of this sickness."

"No." I'm up and blocking her before she can even plot her next move. "Don't you dare touch them, they're mine."

She looks defiantly at me. "You can't hang on to just the bad stuff, Miriam."

"I don't." I place my hands on the encyclopedia in her hands and yank it but she doesn't let go. "Give me them."

"No." She pulls back. We struggle with the encyclopedia, back and forth until I gain the upper ground. But, I lose my grip on it just as I retrieve it from my sister's grasp, and all the contents go flying out onto the floor. "No. Look what you've done. Don't touch them. Don't touch anything."

"Miriam, you need to . . ." Charlotte stops dead in the middle of her sentence. "Miriam?" I glance up at her face and she's pointing down at one of the pressed flowers, I follow the line down to the offender. I know which one it is before I get there. Blood is dried on the white petals and it makes for a gruesome item to spy.

"It was lodged in the car. I picked it out after my hands were cut." My fingers instinctively rub over my palms and the twin scars.

"Mir. I didn't know."

"You don't. You think I keep flowers because they are there in the bad times and I want to remember the ugly moments. You're wrong. Ever since the accident, every time I have a bad day or something bad happens a flower is there. Amelia sends them to me. I don't care what you think of me, it's what I believe and I won't stop thinking it. She's telling me it will be okay." I stare at the flower during my entire speech. It's the one flower I don't look at ever, in between page 45 and 46 where there is an entire section on Amelia Earhart, who Amelia was named after. I don't look back again at Charlotte. I leave the flowers where they lie, except for the blood-stained one. I flip the pages to find Amelia's spot, I can see exactly where it goes. I never dried it before I pressed it, so the blood soaked the page where the flower sat. I kiss the flower and place it back inside. I hold the book close to my chest and let out a deep breath.

"Will you send them to me?" Charlotte asks.

"What?" I tilt my head to her.

"When you spread my ashes, will you put the flowers in with them and send them to me? I want to show Amelia when I get to the other side."

I nod. She sinks down to the floor and covers me with her loving arms. My sister is dying.

TWENTY-THREE

My prized possession, a book of dried flowers, the contents are disbanded on the floor around me. It has been hours. Penelope has come home from school and Charlotte has gone to her room, but I remained just as scattered as the petals of forgotten bouquets, bushes, and plants. October obviously isn't my month, four years is fast approaching and my sister is now dying.

I tighten my grip around the encyclopedia still pressed against my chest as a life preserver, only it can't save me from the type of drowning I need to succumb to. Death of a loved one is staring me in the face again, all while the anniversary of Amelia and Ben's passing is around the corner. I need to go to the cemetery this year, I want to talk to them this time. I've long since avoided the notion of visiting their gravesite on the anniversary, choosing instead to wallow in the deepest despair on the day. How truly selfish I have been. Ben and Amelia cannot come and visit me, yet I let them stay without my presence. I'll have to get Amelia flowers this time, instead of her sending them to me.

"What are you doing?"

Suddenly Oliver is above me, his shadow covering the flowers on the floor except for one white rose. I plucked that one the day I saw the nursery had been changed to a guest room I didn't want, but fortunately have for Charlotte. But for how long, I wonder.

"About to clean up." I sigh. Oliver instinctively bends to help, but I shoo his hands away. "I got it, don't worry." I make haste in replacing the flowers, they have no particular order in the book, only one. It's a quick job that should have been done hours ago. Sometimes it feels comforting to sit in a mess and enjoy the content of your crazy.

"I'm sorry," I say, "I lost track of time, I'll be ready in just a minute. We can leave once the night nurse comes." I hired a nurse to come sit with Charlotte in the evenings I have therapy, group, or a date with Penelope or Oliver. I'm going out tonight with both of them, our first outing with Penelope along. I have been excited all week, planning what would be the best activity, what we could do to ensure fun and nothing awkward. As I head to my room to change, the energy and excitement fails to surface.

"Hey," Oliver grabs my hand as I pass by, "is everything okay?" His eyes are etched with concern. An active listener, he knows all that goes on in my daily struggle and truly cares about helping me through it. I place my opposite hand on top of his arm holding me in place and squeeze gently to reassure him.

"Yes." I simply say. It's neither the truth nor easy. Penelope bounces around the corner, her ears on high alert to Oliver's arrival. She is grinning from ear to ear at the first sight of him. Over the past months, the two have grown rather fond of each other, sharing inside jokes and pranks, mostly at my expense. Oliver comes over at least once a week for a board game night with us. Unfortunately for the girls, we have yet to find a game we can beat him in but we keep trying. Penelope leaps over to him and he drops my arm to pick her up in a giant bear hug, their typical greeting. My icy mood thaws at the sight. I walk away and let them get to catching up, Penelope talking a mile a minute about school and homework, and Oliver's eager ears soak up every word.

I slip into Charlotte's room before I make my way to mine, to find her laying on the bed with earphones nestled into her ear canals. No doubt an audiobook is playing in her head, she loves to escape into another world. Charlotte was never found without a book in our childhood days, but now she has switched to audio. She says it's better when she can close her eyes and be taken to a different world, instead of seeing the same one she wants to escape in the background of the text. I slide into bed next to her and she flinches. I've brought her back to reality and she slides a bud out of her ear.

"Hey. Leaving?" She asks. Her mood is more positive than before. I'm allowing her to take over her treatments. A small token of control for her situation, but nonetheless a satisfying triumph in her eyes.

"Yeah, I was about to go change. I just wanted to say good night." I kiss her on her forehead. She's a touch clammy tonight, I'll have to mention it to the nurse before I leave.

"Okay, Mir. Have a good time. I want to hear all about it over coffee." She winks and plugs her bud back in. Amazing. My sister is laying in her bed, slowly dying from a disease we can't stop, yet she is satisfied to be in a dull routine with me. I'm surprised she isn't hitting a bucket list or something. I poke her gently in her shoulder and she pops an eye open and the bud back out.

"Do you have a bucket list?"

"Had." She answers. I frown. "No, no. Not like that." She corrects my facial expression. "I had a bucket list, but then I checked everything off. The only thing left is to read a few classics and watch my sister find happiness again."

"So if I'm miserable, you'll hang on forever?"

"Mir."

I pop her bud back in and smile at her. I know it's a selfish request, one we can't complete, but wouldn't it be lovely if we could. I kiss her forehead again and head to my room, leaving her blissfully indulging in Jane Eyre's love story.

The night is going splendidly. Oliver and Penelope kept joking and laughing at each other. We ate pizza and played arcade games for dollar store prizes down at the local kid's hangout. When we get back to the house, Penelope darts inside to shown Charlotte her winnings, leaving Oliver and me to linger on the porch for a little while.

"I was thinking of going to visit Ben and Amelia next week for the anniversary." It wasn't often that I brought up the death of my husband and daughter to my boyfriend. After our first date I was gun shy on the topic, but seeing him with Penelope tonight told me I needed to start taking it to the next level. I want to ask him to come with me.

"Oh?" Oliver shifts in his seat on the porch, giving me his full attention.

"Yeah, it will be the first time I visit the graves actually." I sheepishly look down at my shoes and continue, "I was thinking of bringing Amelia some flowers, maybe bring Ben something more metal. He loved metal music, I wonder what I can do with that." I laugh at the memory. "Ben used to always pull his tie from work up to his head like a bandana, every day after he left the office. He would drive all the way home like that, I'm sure the other drivers thought he was a loon." I peer over at Oliver, he's staring off into the distance but I know he's listening. This is when Oliver is listening the most, when his body language says he isn't. It's his guise, his cover, but I figured it out a month ago. "I think you would have liked Ben."

"Sure." Yikes. The tension rolling off Oliver was not at all what I expected to receive when mentioning going to the graves.

"So, anyway, I was thinking . . ." I start working up the nerve to ask him to tag along.

"This isn't going to work for me, Miriam. You're a great girl and all, but I don't think we make a good couple." He's heading to this truck, booking it I should say like he can't escape me any faster.

"Are you kidding me?" I yell. Oliver freezes on the sidewalk but doesn't turn around. That doesn't matter because I'm in front of him, fuming, in seconds.

"What?" He feigns ignorance and finally grants me eye contact.

"You kiss me like we give each other oxygen, and suddenly we aren't a good couple?" I air-quote his words back to him. Before he can say his piece the screen door creaks open.

"Goodnight Oliver." Penelope runs out in her pajamas and grips tight to Oliver's leg, as a tear rolls down his cheek.

"Goodnight Pea." He whispers. She's eight and unaware of his voice cracking. I watch her bound back inside, her brown hair flowing in free childhood innocence. When she's gone, I turn my attention back to Oliver.

"What does it matter Miriam?" He's trying to act like he doesn't care, but he's holding back. The restraint of the contraction in his upper arms says he's forcing himself to say the words, he has no faith behind them.

"It matters to me, Oliver." I reach out to touch his arm but he backs away from my hand like I've burned him. That's it. "Why are you suddenly being a prick? I thought we had fun tonight, I thought we were serious."

"Serious?" He laughs, but it's cold and humorless. "For three months, I have been just your friend while you convince yourself that we are dating. I will never live up to your husband and you constantly throw it in my face. I can't come second."

"You'll always come second . . ."

"That's what I thought." Before he lets me explain, I watch those damn headlights disappear from my life once again.

"You'll always come second because Penelope has to be first." I say it to the night air. Someone should hear me.

TWENTY-FOUR

"He just ended it?" My sister repeats the question for the fifth time this morning, the disbelief still laced in her words.

"Yup." I shove another spoonful of oatmeal into my mouth and watch Charlotte pick at her banana. She never has an appetite the day after a treatment. She has some color on her face today. I resist the urge to believe it was the chemo she got yesterday, I know it's because she got her way and the poison drip is over for her.

"Ass." She grunts. Finally, a new phrase. "Was it because you said you were going to the grave? That doesn't make sense or else he is a real asshole."

"No, he said he can't come second."

"What do you mean? Second to who?"

"Ben." I confess, "I rambled on a bit about Ben when I was working up the nerve to ask Oliver to go to the grave with me."

"I'll go with you." She offers, Oliver forgotten for a second.

"No, I realize I need to visit the first time on my own now." I push my oatmeal around the bowl, it's cold now. The idea of going to the cemetery creates nervous butterflies in my stomach, making eating impossible.

"So, you talked about Ben and Oliver got mad?" Charlotte is back to my relationship woes, or lack thereof since I now do not have a relationship.

"Basically. Then he stormed off saying he won't be second. He feels he's only been my friend the whole time we were dating."

"What did you say to him?"

I gulp. "Well, I said he was second."

"Miriam!"

"See? You didn't let me finish either. That's what I started saying to him last night and he stormed off, poof, down the driveway he went."

"Alright, then finish." My sister sits back, crossing her arms in a challenge. She wants me to prove to her that saying Oliver was second was a good idea.

"He'll always come second, Penelope will always be first. I can't keep pushing her aside. She has to come first." I stand behind my words. I won't be backing down or scooching things around so that what I say pleases everyone.

"Damn." She slams her hands on the table.

"What?"

"He should have listened." She smiles at me. "Come on, let's go for a drive. I want to find a place."

"A place for what?" I'm curious, but a knot in my gut tells me that I'm not going to like the answer.

"A place to release my ashes." With that Charlotte is up and moving toward the door. She isn't taking no for an answer and unlike Oliver, I will listen.

★ ★ ★

Weeks have passed and the day is here. Sitting in the car outside of the cemetery gates, I think about how this year I'm not dreading the day. This time I am looking forward to spending time with Amelia and Ben. This is the first time I'm going to see their tombstones, and it gives me pause. I could have easily come before today, but it felt right to save this until now. It would not be another year before I came again, but making this the first time seems right. My therapist agrees, stating it will be therapeutic for me to acknowledge the day here, not in bed under the covers again.

Therapy has been going quite well for me. I underestimated the good doctor with my previous prejudice, and he turned out to be an excellent fit for me. We have gone through Ben and Amelia over and over in the past month, it seems once I was finally able to open up in the group about Amelia, I couldn't stop. I even booked extra appointments just to bend his ear some more. Recently, I ran out of things involving them that I couldn't solve for myself and I thought for sure therapy was over. That, however, was not the case and I don't think it will ever be. Lately, we have started working through my mother and father issues, mainly my mother.

No matter what I say, I can't shock Dr. Pierce, his trained poker face in place as he takes everything in without so much as an eyebrow raise. This comforts me, kind of has me feeling like I'm not the only person in the world this messed up. When I told him about finally visiting the gravesite, he never changed the expression on his face or judged me for waiting this long. I need to be sitting here, he believed I could get through it and didn't doubt the step. I shouldn't either.

I pull the lever on the car from park to drive and begin edging my way up the hill, memories of the funeral flooding my vision and guiding me to the destination. The fall foliage spreading throughout the cemetery looks the same as it did that day, the road winding just as it did then. I slow when the car crests the hill, this is it. I turn the car off and look to my left, I see the joined stone with hearts on it immediately. The final resting place where father and daughter lay, side by side. I brought some flowers with me, a fall floral arrangement, and an Ozzy Osbourne CD in my old portable CD player to play Ben.

I didn't pause or wait, I dove right out of the car. I'm not going to give myself the chance to back out or drive away. I picked out a tasteful cherub statue to sit behind the grave, an angel to watch over my sweet loves. She's looking down on them now with her arms stretched to touch them both and offer comfort. I look at the headstone, it doesn't feel real. Even seeing it in writing here, carved on this black stone, it doesn't feel real. The date was four years old, but it felt like it just happened. The pain hits me all at once, looking down at these names with the two dates. I have only one date underneath me, it wasn't fair to look at my daughter's name and see two.

Tears flow freely from my eyes as I crash to my knees and land at the foot of the cherub's mercy. I beg for forgiveness; for not coming sooner, for sending him out on that drive, for not taking care of Penelope like I should have, for everything. They waited for me for four years, Penelope had been waiting for me to come around as well. I selfishly neglected the gift of life to live in my grief instead.

Once my tears have calmed, I notice Charlotte visited often because she had left little notes for Amelia and band pins for Ben. I place my bouquet in the vase that was in the middle of them. I laid on my back right in the middle of them.

"Hey, guys." I stutter, tears bursting from my eyes and bouncing in and off my ears. "I'm sorry I haven't been here. I have a lot to tell you." That's what I did until I lost track of time and until I was all talked out. I laid there between them and shared stories of Charlotte, Penelope, and even though we haven't talked in weeks, I shared stories of Oliver. I told Ben he'd always be my first love, Penelope and Amelia's dad. I thanked him for the years of love he gave me, making it a hard task for any man to follow. When I spoke of Oliver, it didn't feel like a betrayal to Ben anymore. I was speaking to my best friend about the feelings I was having, how much Penelope enjoyed his company. I'm a different Miriam than when I was Ben's. So much has happened in my life since that I'm not that girl anymore. I need someone who understood the broken Miriam and loves her all the same. Oliver. I tell Ben that I have to get him back. In the silence, I feel him agree.

When I arrive home, I snuggle with Penelope for hours in silence on the couch while the TV plays. She never complains, only welcomes the touch. I smile into the back of her head, knowing I'm keeping my promise to Ben. She will always be number one. I tell her all about my visit and ask her if I can take her tomorrow. She gladly consents without a single moment of hesitation. I kiss her cheek and leave Charlotte and her in the living room to continue watching the movie while I make dinner. Dinner for my family. I smile at the thought.

It's rare that we eat out anymore, or that I pick up fast food. The fridge is stocked now with snacks and fresh meat and produce. I make breakfast every day now before sending Penelope off to school, then I sit with Charlotte on the front porch sipping our morning coffee. I leave her to do some work, then we drive around taking photos and talking if she feels up to it. At night, Penelope does her schoolwork and I cook dinner listening to her day. Charlotte sits on the back deck, watching the sun go down sometimes. The spark hadn't left her eyes, but her body grows weaker.

I finish cooking just about the time the movie wraps up. Charlotte's quizzing Penelope about the movie because she is thoroughly confused with the storyline; Pea knows it perfectly. After we eat, Charlotte sits in her chair we have put in the kitchen to keep me company while I do the dishes. I'm laughing and throwing bubbles at her, she's doing an internet search on the movie to better understand what she just saw. It's a perfect day.

The doorbell rings. My heart skips. Oliver. I lift my brows at Charlotte and she smiles. I rush to the door without drying my hands, so anxious. When I pull it back, there stands a middle-aged woman with the thickest coke bottle glasses I have ever seen and a clipboard in her hand.

"May I help you?" I wipe my hands on my jeans, disappointed it isn't Oliver.

"My name is Clara Homes. I'm with the Department of Child Protective Services. I'm here due to a recent call we received about the child in your home being mistreated. I just want to come in and ask you a few questions and then I'll be on my way." She went through her prepared speech, rushing because I'm sure her job cannot be easy or well received in this situation.

"I'm sorry, Clara, but you may not come in." I state firmly.

"Ma'am, I need to file a report to make sure the child is not being harmed in the home. If you do not let me in your child could be taken away from you." Straight for the scare tactic eh, Clara? Too bad for her, I had already done my research.

"No. You do not have a search warrant, do you, Clara?"

"Well," she fumbled, "no ma'am, I don't."

"And you can't get one, can you, Clara?"

Silence.

"You don't have enough evidence for one. All you have is an anonymous tip from a person who does not like me, a false accusation from an unreliable source. I don't know you from Adam, Clara, but I'm going to assume you are a good person and you got into this field to do positive things and save children. There are no children who need that in this house, Clara. I have one little girl here who is happy, healthy and loved. You may not come in and look for anything rebutting that without a search warrant."

"I. ." I felt bad for Clara, here to do, no doubt, my mother's bidding. I bet she isn't even a real social worker, just a friend to help Mom out. Emma Woods thought I was going to crumble on this day, and this was her way to check up on me.

"Tell Emma I said hey." Recognition lights up the stranger's face. Yup. Mom put her up to it.

I shut the door behind me and turn to face Charlotte who is fuming with anger.

"She did this?" She spits her words, hardly containing herself. I nod. My heart is not angry, it is heavy thinking of how Charlotte is here with her health failing and my mother is too busy holding on to a grudge instead of spending time with her. It's not fair.

"I have to make a call." I head for my phone. This ends now.

TWENTY-FIVE

When I was pregnant with Amelia, I would spend hours watching Penelope play on the floor with a smile on my face. She would be a great big sister. She would tell me to rest for the baby, or eat a banana since it was healthy, or even correct me to drink more water. She has always possessed a nurturing spirit, looking after the other kids on the playground or her dolls. I never worried about her sister being maltreated by her. She was Charlotte. She was the greatest sister I know, and Penelope has her as an example. She would have flourished in her big sister position.

Sitting next to me, grasping my hand in both of hers, was my rock. My sister. I make the call to my mother with my sister sitting beside me, feeding me strength even when hers was waning. It was her love pushing me on when the line finally picked up.

My mother offers a slightly confused hello through the phone. I know she saw my name, so it isn't confusion at the number that leaps off her tongue. I wonder what my name is in her contact list. Ungrateful child? Demon? Horrible human being I gave birth to? Or did my given name of Miriam cover all the things she saw me as?

"Mother, we need to speak." My voice is firm and steady, the grip on my hand tightens. Here we go.

"Whatever about, Miriam? It is quite late." Her voice is agitated, a tactic my mother hangs on to for intimidation with us, but it won't work. Not this time. Not ever again. This is for Charlotte, who needs her mother.

This is for Penelope, who needs her grandmother. Two people my mother loves dearly but was failing all for her grief against me.

"I got a visit this evening. Thanks for sending your friend to check on me, Mother, but it didn't work. We are fine."

"Is that so?" Intimidation. She doesn't even deny the fact that she set it up, that she's figured out.

"It's over, Mother."

"Well, thanks for the call. I suppose that's all you wanted?" How could someone remain so bitter?

"No. You need to knock it off. I've lost a child, unexpectedly. I didn't get to know that my last kiss to her was my last. You have been given a gift in the darkness, you know the end. Yet you squander your time with this relentless hostility toward me. It's enough." Silence on the line, so I continue. "I won't stop you from coming over to see Charlotte and Penelope. As far as we are concerned, it remains to be seen if the lines are repairable. I know Dad hurt you when he left, and I know my appearance is a constant reminder of him, but you need to let it go. You need to realize that you have a granddaughter that needs you around. Get over your pride, Mom."

I hear the quiver in my mother's lip as her damn pride fails her and tears begin to take over. Disbelief is etched on Charlotte's face, out of the two of us I was never voted most likely to extend the olive branch first.

"Dr. Pierce says he can do a session with both of us, but it's up to you. I won't push you, or beg you to be around. You have to be ready or the change won't work." I add. "I know that."

I sit in silence, listening to my mother's sobbing. This is the first time my mother has shown weakness, she has always been forced to be strong. She had to be to raise two girls while bearing the shame of a husband who had an affair and a new family. She had to shoulder her daughter going crazy after losing her husband and kid, while she had to be strong losing her grandchild. It's not the lack of tears you shed or the things that don't break your poker face that make you strong. It's admitting that you are human and things are tough, but you fight every day to make it. I don't mean that you fight to make it and become harder. You fight through all that shit and you remain a soft feeling human being. Shit, that's strength. For the first time, I can see my mother's.

"Maybe I could come by tomorrow morning? For breakfast?" My mother's voice is meek, timid, ragged from her crying. I wanted to tell her that I understand how humbling it is when your child is more the adult than you, but think better of it. It would do us no good to rub salt in the wounds or open new ones.

"We will see you tomorrow. Good night, Mom."

"Good night, Miriam. I love you." It catches me by surprise. I was certain my mother never loved me, cared for me, or wanted me. A single tear slides down my face in joy. My mother does love me.

"I love you, too." I hang up. Charlotte creeps into my lap and quietly weeps, she's happy she says. I stroke her hair until she falls asleep. I place my fingers gently behind her ear, where I can feel her heartbeat, and try to memorize the rhythm.

I lift her off my lap and tuck her into her bed. The house is peaceful, but my soul won't settle. I have begun the process of healing with my mother, I have opened the door to her for Charlotte and Penelope, and I've begun to accept the position Charlotte has taken on her cancer treatment. There's one last thing I have left unsettled. Oliver. I pick my phone up and begin to compose a new message. I erase it a dozen times, I even write a paragraph only to delete it. Finally, I settle on one line before I'm satisfied and the rush in my mind has quieted. I press send and set the phone on the nightstand. I suddenly feel calm and heavy, it was what I needed all along. I don't even remember my head touching my pillow.

I miss you.

To my surprise, I wake up to an empty inbox on my phone. I open it to make sure it wasn't a dream, but it's there. Delivered. Read. He knows. He's doing nothing about it. Fine. I accept that.

It's a lie. I most definitely do not accept it, it was just something I can't control. I made the step that needed to be made, maybe I had made it too late. There's a time limit on how long you can let things linger without clearing them up, I had let the milk go sour on Oliver thinking he was second to Ben. I ruined it. Now, I have breakfast to make and hope I don't ruin the next relationship I need to mend.

I shuffle out of my bed to the kitchen to begin the coffee and whip up a quiche. I could bake a can of cinnamon rolls as well, I think. Blame my stress eating on the fact that it was a momentous occasion and more people to feed. Sounds like a plan.

I was the first awake in the house, which wasn't abnormal these days with Charlotte being sick. I fill the coffee pot and press brew, then get down to the business of sautéing vegetables for the quiche and beating eggs in the bowl. I fill the premade pie crust, and the meal is ready to bake. Idle hands. I pop it in the oven and decide to take my first cup of coffee on the front porch, the house is too quiet for me and my mind is too full. Watching nature wake up will help that. I need the birds chirping and the cars buzzing past me this morning.

I barely make it through the first cup when my mother arrives in the driveway. Emma Woods is always prompt and early. It was a lesson we were taught as kids; if you were exactly on time for something then you were late. Ten to fifteen minutes before the time was when we needed to be somewhere. Not giving my mother a time last night, I knew she would be early. I want her to be here for Charlotte, not just the meal, so her timing doesn't bother me any.

"Hello, Miriam." She says while walking up the sidewalk. Her voice is laced with hesitation, not sure how she should act. Neither was I. Do we sing songs and tilt our heads back in laughter? Or do we sit in an awkward tension until one of us approaches the elephant in the room? Should that elephant be provoked?

"Hi, Mom." I motion for her to sit next to me. "No one else is up yet. I got the quiche in the oven."

"Quiche sounds delicious." She says it as she sits and begins to watch the squirrel in the front yard running up and down the tree in a hurried fashion. Awkward tension it was.

"Do you want some coffee?" I ask, mainly to sneak into the house and wake Charlotte so she could entertain Mom.

"Coffee sounds lovely. Let's go inside, I'll go wake Charlotte myself. How is she doing?" It takes me a moment to reply, fearful that I spoke out loud about waking my sister.

I settle on, "She's getting weaker." It's all I can say to describe her condition at this point. Mom nods, defeated, as we make our way inside.

My mother removes her coat and shoes then makes the left for Charlotte's room, I make the right for the kitchen. I make my mother a cup and Charlotte one as well. Somethings are trained inside of you, like muscle memory, and the way my mother takes her coffee is one of them. Four sugars and two creams. I fill the mugs with the delicious dark brown brew that molds into a lighter version once met with each woman's condiment choice. I quickly duck in front of the oven to check the quiche. Done. Perfect timing. I take it out and set it on the cooling rack. I don't feel the need for cinnamon rolls anymore, the awkward tension with my mother replacing my insecurities about Oliver, preventing my stomach from stress eating. I turn the oven off and click my phone. Nothing. I sigh. Damn. I pick up the cups and head to Charlotte's room with them.

As I near the room, I don't hear any talking. Perhaps my mother is taking in the sight of Charlotte sleeping. Just sitting and watching her, thanking God for protecting her. I do it myself on mornings that Penelope needs to be woken up for school because she oversleeps. Funny thinking about Penelope oversleeping, she can rely on me now to be there to get her ready for school. I head to the room anyway, coffee burning against my knuckles through the mugs. An uneasy feeling runs through my body as I near the door. It isn't that I can't hear voices, it's that I can't hear Charlotte's. Now that I am closer to the room, I latch on to the small voice of my mother. "Wake up, Charlotte. Charlotte. Charlotte, wake up."

I rush in, the coffee cups slide from my slack grip and break on the floor, burning my feet. My mother has Charlotte by both shoulders shaking her but she won't wake. A scream must have left one of our bodies, whose I couldn't tell you because Penelope appears out of nowhere and is running to the phone to dial 911. I don't know by whose orders she is doing it. I don't remember who called it out. 911 is on the phone, though, trying to walk my mother through the steps to make sure Charlotte is still breathing. She is. Heart still beating. But she's not waking up.

The lady promises someone is on their way, she says it over and over, trying to calm my mother. She prompts what to do as she waits. As we wait. As I wait to take a breath. Penelope is lost with nothing to do, so she starts to clean the floor. What a peculiar thing to do, I think, then I remember the coffee. The coffee I was bringing Charlotte and my mother. Just the way Charlotte likes it. Penelope is worried about my feet. A blister? I don't understand. I'm frozen. Everything is happening around me. I can't move.

The paramedics rush in, I must have gotten the door for them. I don't feel like I'm moving, but I guess I am. It's all a blur. They rush about Charlotte, taking my mother aside. They hook her up to some stuff. I blurt out her medical history, I scream about her cancer. I feel like they don't hear me, they nod though. I'm in automatic mode, muscle memory. I throw on a sweatshirt and shoes, grab my phone and purse that holds all the information. I shuffle my mom into the ambulance. I buckle Penelope into my car. We fly to the hospital. When we get there, Charlotte still hasn't opened her eyes.

It takes ten hours until my sister opens her eyes again. There are tubes everywhere and all around her. I wait. My mother and Penelope wait as well. Suddenly, she just shifts and her eyes open. I release every tear left in my body and Charlotte quietly squeezes my hand, the tubes won't let me hug her. I can't hold her.

"It's okay." She whispers. "I'm still here." I lean my forehead upon her hand and rest it there while Mom presses the call button to alert the nurse that Charlotte has woken up.

We see multiple doctors in the next five hours, the nurses are furiously shooing us out after that. It's the dumbest thing to say that Charlotte needs her rest, she's heading toward the greatest rest of her life. Idiots. I laugh in their faces. Charlotte's small chuckle follows. My mother even joins in the gag. Were they serious? Rest?

The truth of the matter is that her systems are beginning to shut down and her body is done fighting. It won't be long until Charlotte slips into a coma we can't wake her from and silently leaves this world. But, the nurses are determined to give her rest, stating visiting hours would start again in four hours. I look back at my sister one last time, our minds speaking the same thing. *Four hours. I'll be here.* So, home we go.

My mother sleeps on the couch, refusing to leave, and honestly, I don't want her to. I shower the hospital off me and lay in bed. Sleep eludes me even though my body is utterly exhausted. My mind goes through all the things I have to do for Charlotte, what little time we have left. I want to get it right. I creep into Charlotte's room, pushing against the black that threatens to swallow me back to their depths. I have to find her phone. It's still plugged into the charger, where she always places it before bed.

I leave the room before I let the reality hit me and take over. I shut the door to my bedroom so as not to wake anyone. I find the number I need and press send. It's late. Or it's early. God awful early, but these things never come at 10 a.m. The line rings so many times I'm sure I'm going to have to leave a message. The thought of putting it on someone's machine makes me sick. I mentally prep myself for what I should say to the answering box, that I miss the voice on the other end.

"Hello? Charlotte? Are you there?" He says again.

"Arthur?" I ask.

"Yes." His voice is small when he realizes it isn't Charlotte on the other end. My heart breaks for him.

"Arthur, it's Miriam, Charlotte's sister. We need to talk."

TWENTY- SIX

He's sitting on Charlotte's hospital bed, both her hands in his, deep in conversation. They never heard me turn the corner, nothing can break them from this moment. I gaze upon them, the outsider looking in, and all I see is love. I did the right thing, calling him and allowing them to have a better final goodbye than the one that my sister thought would suit. She was hoping to save him the heartache of her disease, but she only looks grateful to have him there. I can't hear their discussion, not that I want to intrude on those final words between lovers. The doctors gave us a horrible prognosis of Charlotte's condition last night, and while I lay in bed thinking about it all morning I still hadn't come to terms with it myself. I don't know what my final words will be. They told us she might not last the week.

When I couldn't choose the words to say to Charlotte, I stayed up running the debate over and over in my mind. Cancer sucks, it robs the body of its potential and possibility. You slowly pass away in pain and anguish. You get the heads up, most of the time, the ability to say goodbye. But is it worse than a sudden car accident, or better? Which one was going to leave me in the worst pain? I selfishly wondered about it all morning while I dressed, if I was going to be able to survive losing Charlotte or if I would crumble back into the state I was in when I lost Ben and Amelia. I still hadn't come up with an answer when I arrived at the hospital today, I'm glad Arthur got here first so I could afford more time to think. More time to come up with all the words my sister needs to hear; all the feelings I want her to be sure of, any misunderstandings cleared up, and any ill will gone.

"Who's that?"

I jump out of my skin when his voice tickles my ear. Thankfully, Arthur and Charlotte haven't taken notice of my surprise. I turn and see Oliver. I whip back around with defiance on my face. My heart may leap for joy at the sight of him but his cold silence rings heavy throughout my mind.

"That's Arthur." I say under my breath, a bite in my tone. From the tension rolling off Oliver's body behind me, it's safe to say that he feels my anger. I'm making him uncomfortable and that's perfectly fine with me. It's kind that he wants to come and say goodbye to Charlotte, they got along so wonderfully when he was in our lives and this shows great character of him. But, I'm not in the mood to pretend to be civil. I need to start preparing to say goodbye to my sister while she's still lucid and awake. The harsh reality of it was tearing away at what was left of my very soul.

"I miss you, too." If every single one of my senses wasn't honed in on Oliver, I would have missed the words. They come so softly, yet hit so hard. Once again, he walks away.

I stand there, still watching the beauty of the relationship that is Arthur and Charlotte before me, frozen to my spot. They touch foreheads as they both close their eyes in a silent gesture that just being together is enough. They've significantly etched themselves into each other's soul, much as Oliver has clawed his way to gain a permanent fixture in mine. I worried half the night that Charlotte never found her Ben, never been loved with a fierce passion. I see now, she didn't just find her Ben, she has an Oliver as well. Someone to love her when she isn't broken, and still feels the same when she falls apart. Damn it all, I won't lose Ben and Oliver.

I take off from the doorway, looking for the person I know will make the heartache on my face turn to content, the way Charlotte's was in that peaceful position. I rush to the elevators just as he's about to get on. I shout his name and watch as his body spins around in eagerness. I know. I know we are made for each other, that in this part of my life he came just when

I needed him most. He is here. He's always been here, patiently waiting for me to decide I want a relationship, never judging when I needed time to get over things, and here for me when my sister is ailing even though he let his demons take over one time. One time. I was going to kick him to the curb for his demons the first time they decided to show up. That's not fair on my part, he saw my demons repeatedly and stayed.

"Miriam, I . . ." I quickly hush him, placing my finger against his lips. I need to speak.

"I shouldn't have given up on you. You didn't give up on me. I'm here. You thought you were coming second to Ben, and I didn't chase you down to explain that you aren't. Ben is gone, I know that. It took me time to admit it. But, that night when I said you would always be second, it wasn't Ben that I was talking about. It's Penelope." Clarity lights up Oliver's face. "I can't let Penelope suffer anymore, I've been a terrible mother in my grief. I hope you are willing to put her first as well, because . . ." He's smiling against my finger before I can stumble out the words. "Dammit, Oliver. You wouldn't have fit with the Miriam I was before the accident, but you fit perfectly with the Miriam I am now."

His eyes well up with tears, he hears my message. I don't know about him, but I can't resist being in just my own skin any longer, I need to be wrapped in his. I pull him close. I can't hug him hard enough or get him close enough. I want to become one with him. The feeling's mutual because he never backs down out of my hold. He only tries to make his that much harder.

"I understand now. Penelope should be first. I think I might love you, Miriam Jones." He whispers the words, and I'm not scared to feel it. It's not a betrayal against Ben, rather a complete circle of my life.

"I love you, too, Oliver." Our foreheads rest together, our eyes close, and although I can't see it, I'm sure contentment is etched upon our faces as we become one.

Oliver says his goodbyes to Charlotte, as I wait in the hall. Arthur left, he couldn't watch the end, stating he wants to remember Charlotte this way. I don't blame him, no one felt ill will towards his decision. If I could go back and never see Ben in that state inside his SUV, I'd do it in a heartbeat. It's a lousy picture to have in your head of someone, and it's something you fight against seeing each time their name comes up. I see happy days now when I think of Ben and Amelia, not the end, but it took a lot to get me there.

Oliver comes out the door, tears in his eyes, Charlotte graces every life she touches no matter how long she put herself there. He winks at me, bends to give me a kiss goodbye. Now, it's my turn. My turn to say goodbye.

"Damn meddling sister." I proclaim as I climb into bed alongside Charlotte.

"Yeah, damn meddling sister." She teases back. She knows I called Arthur, and I found out she was the one to call Oliver. We're famous for having similar thoughts, even near exact outfits miles away, and today we proved it again. We're on the same path of mind and it feels good to know my head is somewhere close to Charlotte's. She's the best person ever, and to have even a sliver of that coursing through my veins will suffice to make me a better person.

I lay my head next to hers and curl my hand in between her fingers. Her hand is tiny and frail wrapped in mine. Her thin frame is cold next to me whereas my body heat rolled off me like a furnace. Her head is bald against my hair and her cheeks sunken in, lips dry and parched. Her skin cracked and is void of moisture, flaking, her body taking all the nutrition possible to the organs inside of her first before attempting to relinquish some to her skin and outer appearance.

I sob, quietly at first, attempting to get the tears under control before they have the chance to upset her. I've been a selfish person most of my life, this moment is not supposed to be about me, but I can't get these damn tears reigned in. The dam breaks free and my body is writhing with the ache of release, soaking the pillow below my head. Charlotte just holds me, taking her other arm and swinging it over my body to ground me. She turns her head ever so slightly so she can kiss my falling tears and tell me it's going to be alright.

Alright. What a horrible word to use in this situation. It's not going to be alright. I'm going to lose my sister to an invisible bully I can't fight.

I can't even manage to stay strong for her and tell her all the ways I love her. The fear rises out of my body and I'm shouting, all the words I want to say. I want her to know I love her.

"Charlotte, I love you. I'm sorry I yelled at you for stealing my sweater. You know? 8th grade. I was stupid. You are great. You are sunshine. There needs to be a better word. I know a better one, soulmate. I can't believe you came to see me. I'm so selfish, Charlotte. You are loved. I love you. I love everything about you. I love it all. You need to know. I'm sorry for yelling at you, fighting with you, making you feel upset. Any time I did it, I'm sorry. That doesn't cover it. Do you want specifics? What can I tell you? What is left unresolved? I want to be like you. I want to grow up to be you, Charlotte. I need you. I don't want you to go. I love you, Charlotte. I fucking hate cancer."

My sister shushes me. I squeak her name out one more time, before succumbing to my tears again. She strokes my hair and shushes me like a baby trying to fall asleep.

"I love you, Miriam. You will miss me, but I'll be fine. I know you love me. I've had a great life, it was filled with love and happiness. I won't be in pain anymore. Don't cry."

Life is horrible, but wonderful at the same time. The dying comfort the living, though it should be the other way around. Those going on to a destination unknown are the ones stroking our hair, holding our hands, and telling us that they are okay and everything will be fine. We look upon them, lying on their death bed, and we need to hear them say that they're alright with it. It is the most natural thing to die, it is the one common bond we all share; we are all going to die one day. Yet, it is still the most unnatural thing to witness and cope with. We don't know what is next, quite frankly those dying should be horrified of the possibility before them, but they aren't. I didn't want Charlotte to die, and suddenly she had made peace with her fate. Why wasn't she kicking and screaming about how unfair it is?

She'll never raise children. She'll never see Arthur again. Charlotte won't watch Penelope graduate high school or college. She won't ever marry. She won't be able to see the Grand Canyon or any other place she still wants to travel to. She'll never do mundane things like sleep in her bed again, or pick out clothes from the closet. She won't cook again, dancing in the kitchen while doing it. She won't put on jewelry for a night out. She has so much to be mad about, but she is holding on to comfort me right now.

I spend the rest of the afternoon trying my best to comfort her, failing miserably because she doesn't need it. She is at peace. It terrifies me.

TWENTY-SEVEN

Charlotte slipped into a coma the next day that we couldn't wake her from. She died three days later. I feel numb, but I don't crack. I promised Charlotte I wouldn't fall apart and resort back to hiding under covers to escape the pain. I walk with it now, my forever companion. Death follows some people, maybe it had an attachment to me, or I was dealt a lousy card in my life. I want to do better for Charlotte and her memory. She hoped to save me from the grief I was drowning in when she came. It would be a shame if she failed.

There were no significant speeches made on the day my sister died. No parade. No news coverage. No candlelight vigil held. She slipped quietly away and just ceased to breathe. The world will never know about her passing, it won't be covered by the stations. She was not famous, so only the few who knew her would care. The world is shattered, but everyone around is oblivious. They don't know. If it weren't for the anguished screams coming from the room, I'm sure those visiting and staying at the county hospital that day wouldn't have known either.

I needed sedation from the medical staff. I woke up after to bear the news again, but my voice was so hoarse it didn't have the sound left to let the world know that I had lost my best friend. My mother had to leave, the pain of one daughter losing her life while the other lost her mind was too much to handle. I didn't blame her. I had been there before. The ache is still felt in the arms of a mother after the child has left the embrace forever. Oliver never left me, when I woke I found his head in my hand. In the corner of the room was Arthur. They later told me that my screams only added to his pain. I wanted to throw things at them, tell them how stupid they were for thinking that. One doesn't just lose a soulmate easily; my screams were drowned out by those inside his heart. They discharged me a few hours later, charged with a simple panic attack.

I make all the necessary calls for the memorial, cremation, and viewing. All the things Charlotte asked of me, I did. I wear her black dress, I'll be damned if I buy another funeral outfit. Today is the day. The day we sit in the pews and discuss her life, her spirit, and grieve over her passing. The urn is to come home with me, Charlotte will come back home. She didn't want to be buried, but she wanted a headstone placed next to Ben and Amelia to show she lived. My mother didn't fight me on any part of it, except for once when I told her Charlotte wanted to be cremated. It was more upsetting for her to realize that she didn't even know what her daughter wanted after death.

There isn't a large crowd at the memorial, not in the thousands like a celebrity's funeral. Not what it should be for a life as great as Charlotte's was. There's no camera to take in the sight of her peers and loved ones coming to say goodbye. It hurts me most to know that there's never going to be that for Charlotte. The dawning fact that there are millions in this world that never got to know her love and light.

Oliver sits next to me holding my hand, Penelope flanking my other side. The preacher gives his sermon about life and death, what God promises for those who have passed on. He leads us in a prayer, asking God to give us strength in this difficult time and praying for a time with no disease, death, or sadness. I close my eyes hard during the prayer, trying to feel every word, hoping someone up high would bring me some kind of peace. After all, faith is something you can't see but feel. I conjure up that place the preacher talks about, with no sickness or death, and all I can see is Charlotte. Sitting on a bench, her arms spread out on the back, her head tilted back feeling the sun on her face. She's healthy once again, the color back in her non-sunken cheeks as she smiles brilliantly. Wherever she is, she's blessing a new kind of crowd with her personality. They are a lucky bunch.

It's time for me to deliver the eulogy I wrote for my sister, a foreign task I took to with much confusion and hatred. What does one write to say in front of all the people who loved and cared for Charlotte? Do I speak about my own stories of her, sharing her through my eyes? Or should I recite poetry that would touch and bring imagery to their minds about a time they were with her? In the end, it was a bit of everything. I reach the pulpit, stopping at her urn to say hello. Hello and goodbye. Flowers are strewn on the table holding the black and gold urn, I twirl one of them in my fingers. *One more to send you.*

"Charlotte once wrote me a note after the passing of my husband and daughter. It said, 'Love doesn't die.' That's it. Those were her words of wisdom. I used to hate them, wanting to crumble that paper every single day I saw it. I never did because I grew to understand them. The love we all have for Charlotte will never die. We are forever changed from having spent even a minute with her. You all know that. I don't have to elaborate because you've all met Charlotte. She was a true force, working her way into your soul instantly. The way she selflessly thought about everyone else around her instead of focusing within. Love doesn't die. Although today we say goodbye to Charlotte, her love for all of us will never die. Her love will always live on. I am a better person for knowing her, loving her, but I will forever be better because she loved me. I was loved by an amazing woman, whom I got to call my sister, a soulmate, my best friend. You were all loved by her, too. She gave you all something to take with you forever. We are a bunch of lucky bastards to have known her. When you feel blue, please remember that you knew Charlotte, I guarantee you'll be smiling in seconds." I direct my next words to Charlotte, "I'll miss you forever. I won't let you fade out. I love you."

There is a typical dining experience after the memorial, but I can't eat. I sit back looking upon everyone my sister had touched in her life. There isn't a thousand, but there is enough to show how amazing she was. They were laughing over their meals, telling stories of Charlotte and reminiscing. I hear some familiar tales and some new ones going around the tables. I watch Arthur wander around from table to table, listening to the tales of Charlotte, soaking in every ounce he could gather of her. My heart broke for him, he is as lost as I had felt when Ben passed. The loss of a great love. My mother wears the other look of heartbreak I know so well, the loss of a child.

Arthur makes his way over to me, unlike my mother who is keeping her distance. I don't know what the future holds for us, but I know I'll always look like my father and that will always hurt her. Possibly therapy will help us, I'm hopeful. If it doesn't, we can never say we didn't try. I just long for her to be in Penelope's life, to aid in shaping my daughter as a person. My mother loves Penelope deeply, that's evident, and it's all I want.

Arthur sits beside me, heavy on the chair, and without hesitation, I immediately take his hand in mine and we gaze about the room at all of Charlotte's people. Oliver's coloring with Penelope at a corner table. She's taking the death of my sister hard as well, her little mind can hardly wrap around the conclusion. She immediately asked for a shirt of Charlotte's to hang in her closet. I acquiesced instantly, considering I already have a sweater in my drawer along with Ben's polo and a onesie of Amelia's that Penelope gave me. Our joined fear that someone would come in to change the room around on us may have been silly in hindsight, but we changed the locks after we got home from the hospital. Just in case.

"I miss her." Arthur finally breaks our silence with his admission.

"I do, too." I squeeze his hand so that my comradery is felt and not just heard. He smiles slightly at the gesture and squeezes back, then he stands to leave.

"If you find anything of hers, that no one wants . . ." Arthur sheepishly looks at the ground, terrified of looking desperate. Why would someone hand off possessions to someone who wasn't family? That's the look his face held. I don't agree with it, so I interrupt him to say I'll send it his way immediately.

TWENTY-EIGHT

It's a windy day, one of the stipulations Charlotte gave me for this task. *The day must be windy enough to carry me.* I could hear her voice in my head and I smile at the comfort it affords me, reminding me of all the things she wanted for this moment. The car stereo is blaring her song, the lyrics soothing the ache in my soul. I let the sound cover the hilltop, competing with the wind as it whips against my ears. Wind? Check. Song? Check. I open my eyes to the view below, up here on the hilltop I can see the entire small town below. When I look straight ahead, I'm next to the heavens. It creates the nauseating feeling that I'm up too high and about to fall or fly.

We had driven past one day, on one of our many trips to talk and take pictures, and Charlotte yelled for me to stop. She hadn't noticed the slide of the car on the road or the trembling of my hands when I finally corrected the car, she only noticed the sky. When I could reign in my temper that was bubbling behind the tongue I was so desperately biting, it was all I could notice as well. I recall it all, I gently navigated the car into a spot, taking note of what road we were on. This was a popular spot for hikers to park and go on the trails, but also for spectators to take in the view. We stepped out, Charlotte in linen pants that enveloped her entire body and a large knit sweater that swallowed her whole. A faded floral silk scarf covered her shaven head, a decision we had made the night before because of the immense loss of hair she was experiencing. She was a heavenly sight basking in the glow of the sun. I took her photo immediately as the wind began to whip her scarf tie backward and her clothes to the back of her body. She was barefoot, choosing to leave her flip flops in the car and enjoy the earth beneath her feet. She told me it grounded her to be barefoot, she felt the power of the earth shoot up her entire form when she did it. Her eyes are closed in the picture, the sun lighting her face and her angelic beige outfit.

"Miriam, this is the place." "The place for what?" "The place you have to come and spread my ashes. I'm so close to heaven here." I couldn't argue with her, even though the entire conversation was morbid and unwelcome in my mind. She had the right to speak of her fears, her planning, her death, and how she would go after. It was her right and I would be the worst person ever not to grant her that, so I didn't argue but I never did reply. I just silently kept taking photos of this place, knowing I could never look at them later. Charlotte stayed in the same position for the longest time; sun on her face, wind blowing her clothing behind her, arms open wide like a bird, and a serene smile dazzling her face. I never shut my eyes. I only stared at her, intermittently taking my pictures, until I began to wonder when we would be leaving. The place was beautiful, but the thought of what it meant to Charlotte was unnerving me. *"You can't be sad when you come here, Mir. You have to be at peace, I don't mind sitting on the shelf until you are at that place." "You want me to come to a giant cliff after you die and expect me not to jump?" "You won't. You will be at peace."*

Well, it took me a whole month after Charlotte's passing, but I was here, at peace, on this cliff. I've driven past many times since the crematory gave me her ashes. Each time the thought of jumping came to mind, so I kept driving. Today, I woke with the peace she spoke of. It is not something you can acquire just from wishful thinking, it takes time. Everything takes time. Isn't that the age-old saying, "Time heals all wounds"? It must be true because I'm here, eyes shut and arms wide enjoying the wind as I stand in peace. I feel my sister's spirit whirling all around me, she's delighted with my progress. I feel it. She's going to be released today, to her that's an exciting new journey but to me, it's scary to let go. Wind? Check. Song? Check. Spot? Check. Peace? Check.

"You have to come early, sunrise. Let me go with the sun, begin your day

releasing me. Please, Miriam. I want to dance with a new day." Sunrise? Check. I pull the urn and the small box next to it from the front seat of the car. Okay, Charlotte. Here we go. "*Do you need me to say any words?*" "*No, play my song loud and let me go into the wind.*" As the song begins to sing about wandering on, I do it. I open the box, all my pressed flowers inside of it, and pile them into my hand, covering the scar deeply set in my palm. All except for one. I pour the ashes into my hand over top of the flowers, some spilling and catching the breeze prematurely. So damn impatient Charlotte, hold on. I lift the last flower out of the box. It's the flower from the night of the accident. It's time to send the flowers Amelia had sent to me to Charlotte. I kiss the dried petals and place it on top of the ashes in my hand. I rise clenching tightly to my sister with both hands now, her ashes spilling over my other matching scar.

I bend deep with my knees and in the last instance before I pitch her out into the wind, I doubt the probability that this will work, but it does. It's like a movie. The ashes swirl in a small tornado, dancing with the flowers, some of Charlotte falls in my hair. I don't bother to shake it out, holding on to that last kiss on the top of my head before letting the next hard wind blow her away again. She's dancing in the sunrise light, along the line you can see into the heavens and she looks happy. I close my eyes and see her standing there in that beige outfit. I wonder where she will land. I allow myself to hope she'll continue on with the breeze until she falls upon a cloud. It's wishful thinking; logic tells me otherwise but I don't allow it. She's in a cloud. As the song ends, I make my way to sit on the cold ground. December was an awful time of the year to go barefoot, but I can't help myself as I pull at my boots and socks.

Standing back up, I imagine what Charlotte told me over and over since we were teenagers. "*The ground just vibrates up my body when I'm barefoot. I feel so grounded and at peace. You have to try it, Miriam, you're too uptight.*" As I watch the sun come up in the sky, I feel the vibration. I feel peace.

At home, Oliver and Penelope are still asleep snuggled up on the big king size bed in my bedroom. I look upon them, quietly snapping a photo with my phone. He took her in without question, it was never an issue.

I'm blessed. In all this pain and heartache, I am still filled with things to be thankful for. The road will be rocky ahead, as I grieve three people. Therapy is helping, tonight is my first session with my mother joining in. Dr. Pierce warned me that it isn't just as easy as acknowledging the sadness. I am working through the steps that allow me to live day to day in a healthier way. I'd love to say I'm already healed, it would be nice to have an exact achievement on such a life event that stated when it's over. There isn't because this is life. It is messy, unforgiving, and painful. But, this morning as I snuggle into bed with two people who hold my heart, I have never wanted to be more alive.

EPILOGUE

"Penelope! Come on. We have to go." Oliver shouts impatiently. I don't know why because my husband doesn't even have his shoes on so we aren't going anywhere soon.

"Relax." I grab his shoulders and make him face me. "Breathe. People have babies all the time, it's going to be okay." I could see the deep-set fear in the back of his mind, he won't relax until he knows this kid is screaming and alive.

"I'm just nervous." He states. I point to his feet, only then that he realizes he isn't wearing any shoes and quickly rectifies the situation.

"You're not the one doing the pushing." I scoff. Just then a contraction hits me. I try my best to take it with ease and not worry Oliver, but my face gives it away.

"Penelope!" He screams.

"I'm right here, Dad." He nearly jumps out of his skin as our ten-year-old shouts behind him. She's standing by the door. Oliver adopted her the day we married, but I'll always smile when I hear her call him dad.

"Alright. Let's go. We have to drop you off at Grandma's house on the way." By the time he finishes his sentence, he's already in the car.

"Do you think he'll leave without us?" Penelope asks me, taking my hand and helping me over the front steps.

"I sure hope not. He's so nervous, I wish you were the one going with me right now." She laughs.

After we are buckled in, Oliver speeds to Mom's house to drop

Penelope off. I'm glad my mom knows Oliver well enough now that she is waiting in the driveway, betting on his impatience to take over today. I roll down my window to chat just to have some fun with him. Why not? I'm the one in labor here.

"Hey, Mom. How's it going?" I talk in a singsong voice as if it is Sunday and we have come over for our normal weekly dinner.

"Miriam, really?" Oliver chastises me. Party pooper. My mother shakes her head at both of us and leans her head in the window to kiss my cheek.

"Good luck, dear. Call me the second you want me to bring Penelope in."

"I will, Mom. I love you."

"I love you, too." She strokes my hair and pins the right side behind my ear before ducking out of the way of the car. Our relationship has become much more loving with the help of therapy, I feel like we are making up for lost time.

"Let's go, dear. I'm going to give birth." I tap Oliver's leg and he shifts into reverse. The rest of the ride is a blur as the contractions grow stronger and I try to concentrate on relaxing.

We make it just in the nick of time, so I guess Oliver's rushing is justified. I'm not in the hospital door fifteen minutes and our daughter is born. She's chubby, adorable, and healthy. I finally see Oliver relax as he takes in her tiny little features in his arms. There's nothing more heartwarming than a man becoming a father. He's been a father to Penelope, no doubt, but watching him get to experience this moment without any complications of birth or anything sad, is truly a happy feeling.

"Well hello." He says to her, the tears swallowing his words as they slide down his cheeks. "Do you want to see your mommy?" He walks her over to me, I know I don't have long before he will want to take her back.

I envelop her in my arms, she's swaddled in her hospital blanket so all I can see is her chubby little face. She has a tiny nose like me, small ears like her father, and something in her manner that reminds me of my sister. I know we have chosen the right name for her.

"Hello, Charlotte."

ACKNOWLEDGMENTS

I want to first start by thanking my sister, Christa, for all her dedication to me throughout this entire project. You've been a constant support, and I could never have done this without you. Thank you for reading every chapter about a million times, and for always believing in me.

Shout out to my husband, Brian, for telling me to go after this dream and giving me the time to do it. You're my best friend and partner in this life. I don't know where I would be without you and the kids. I love you more every day.

Special thanks to my kids, who have taught me the art of multitasking, if they hadn't this would have never been done. Thanks for challenging me and inspiring me, tiny humans. Mommy loves you to the moon and back.

To my parents, for always being those two pillars of strength in my life and for raising Christa and I thinking that we could do whatever we set our minds on. I love you both beyond words.

To Danielle (Gurk), thank you for your unconditional friendship and love. Shaff and Gurk still going strong.

Monica, Danielle, Daesha, thank you for the coffee and playdates that turned into a kick-ass girl squad.

My sister-in-law, Melissa, thank you for beta reading and your input.

To everyone along the way who has cheered me on, thank you from the depth of my soul. We should all be so lucky to be surrounded by people who enjoy building each other up, as I am.

To my editor, Ami Waters. Thank you for all your hard work and advice. You helped me shape Miriam's story into something I'm even more proud of than the day I sent it to you.

To my cover designer, Teddi Black, I can't thank you enough for bringing the cover to life. It's better than I could have imagined.

To Christine from Type A Formatting, thank you for helping the inside of this book look just as amazing as the outside.

Lastly, to whoever finds themselves reading this, thank you. This book has been a constant dream of mine. Chase yours.

Made in the USA
Middletown, DE
25 May 2019